Praise for How
Buffalo ~~~

"Canadian author Howard Shrier's first novel, *Buffalo Jump*, is a winner." —*National Post*

"Well-written, smart, keenly observed, often funny and utterly suspenseful." —*Canadian Jewish News*

"Blunt action, realistically and graphically described and paced with just enough time to catch your breath before the next sudden eruption. Add the right feel for dialogue, a plot and writing that's just the ideal temperature for a mystery-thriller and you have *Buffalo Jump*. . . . A debut novel with a well-juggled storyline brimming with dry humour, a cast of oddball characters and graphic scenes that come alive with action."
—*The Hamilton Spectator*

"A great debut novel . . . in what is certainly going to be a fine series. The plot is tight, the characters engaging and this one even has a believable—and sympathetic—bad guy."
—*The Globe and Mail*

"Contemporary Canadian crime writers are not exactly plentiful in number, and . . . Howard Shrier is a welcome addition to their ranks. *Buffalo Jump* . . . introduces a strong, clear voice with a wry sense of humour. . . . Continues the tradition of Robert B. Parker and Robert Crais with a hearty and promising Maple Leaf Twist." —*Quill & Quire*

"This first book by Shrier is top-notch, a page-turner to rate with the best of them and with some memorable characters. It also contains just the right dose of cynicism and dark humour, both of which mark the best of the private-eye novels."

—*The Guelph Mercury*

"*Buffalo Jump* jumps right off the page. It's a barreling freight train of a mystery, and I can't wait for Jonah Geller's next case."

—Linwood Barclay, *Toronto Star* columnist
and author of several critically acclaimed novels,
including *Stone Rain* and *Lone Wolf*

"*Buffalo Jump* is a fine debut novel." —*The Record*

"Delivers a fast plot with the requisite brutalities and, not least, a sharp look at what happens to people—Americans—who lack anything like sensible health coverage."

—Joan Barfoot, *London Free Press*

"A cast of compelling oddballs; a complex, funny and always surprising hero; and a plot as fresh and twisty as today's headlines—Shrier juggles them all deftly and nails his first crime novel with the aplomb and impact of a seasoned pro."

—René Balcer, Emmy-winning executive
producer/head writer of *Law & Order*, creator of
Law & Order Criminal Intent, winner of the Peabody Award and of four
Edgar Awards from the Mystery Writers of America

"A crime story that is both thrilling and thoughtful."

—Kelley Armstrong, bestselling author of
the Women of the Otherworld series

MYS

HIGH
CHICAGO

HOWARD SHRIER

VINTAGE CANADA

Vintage Canada Edition, 2009
Copyright © 2009 Howard Shrier

www.randomhouse.ca

Grateful acknowledgment is made for permission to quote on p. vii from
"Fall on Me." Words and Music by Mike Mills, William Berry, Peter Buck
and Michael Stipe, © 1986 Night Garden Music. All Rights Administered
by Warner-Tamerlane Publishing Corp. All Rights Reserved. Used by
permission from Alfred Publishing Co., Inc.

Library and Archives Canada Cataloguing in Publication

Shrier, Howard
    High Chicago / Howard Shrier.

ISBN 978-0-307-35608-6

I. Title.

PS8637.H74H53 2009   C813'.6   C2008-906574-3

Cover and text design: Jennifer Lum

Printed and bound in the United States of America

10 9 8 7 6 5 4 3 2 1

To Harriet and the boys, for their love and support.
And to Dennis Richard Murphy (1943–2008). A fine writer and a
better friend, taken far too soon.

HIGH CHICAGO

PART ONE

There's a problem, feathers iron
Bargain buildings, weights and pullies
Feathers hit the ground before the weight can leave the air
Buy the sky and sell the sky and tell the sky and tell the sky
Don't fall on me
Fall on me
Fall on me

R.E.M., "Fall on Me"

PROLOGUE

Tell anyone you're flying into Chicago and they advise you to avoid O'Hare. Too big, too busy, too far from town. One of the worst records in America for delays in and out. Fly into Midway, they say. What they don't tell you is that it's virtually impossible to go direct from Toronto to Midway on less than a day's notice, and that's all the time I had. O'Hare it was.

It was the last week of October, still pitch black when I left my place in the east end of the city at five-thirty in the morning. The cab driver made it to Pearson in under half an hour, perhaps mistaking the 401 for the Autobahn. I then spent an hour crawling through security and U.S. Customs at the airport and another hour at the gate. Nearly two hours in the air. A half-hour sitting on the tarmac in Chicago and another half-hour to make my way to the baggage claim area and find my suitcase. It was ten-fifteen Chicago time by the time I reached arrivals.

Anxious faces were looking my way. Families looking for family members. Friends looking for friends. Drivers holding cards with the names of business-class passengers. And one mountain of a man with thick dirty-blond hair and a neatly trimmed beard who bellowed my name and lifted me off my feet in a bear hug that left my ribs little room to do the breathing thing.

His name was Avi Sternberg and we hadn't seen each other in over ten years. "Jonah Geller," he grinned. "Jonah goddamn Geller. Look at you, man. You look fantastic." He gripped my biceps in his big hands. "Buff too. Check out the arms."

His teeth were whiter and straighter than they'd been when I'd last seen him and he wasn't wearing thick glasses anymore. His eyes behind contact lenses were the pale blue of a winter sky.

"You look good too," I said.

"Liar. I've put on like fifty pounds."

He'd been a beanpole then, six-three and maybe 170 pounds. But his new-found bulk was nicely encased in an expensive grey wool suit, the kind a lawyer might wear in Chicago on an Indian summer day. And since he was a lawyer now, and there were a dozen reasons why I might need one, I didn't hold the suit against him.

"Flight okay?" he asked.

"Pretty painless," I said.

"The security as tight up there in Canada as it is here? Make you dump all your liquids and everything?"

"Even the bottled water."

"All right. Let's get you out of here. That all your stuff?"

"Yup." I'd packed everything I thought I'd need into one big suitcase on wheels. The less you took on board with you, the easier it was to clear security. "I really appreciate you coming out to get me, Avi. You look like a busy man."

"I'm paid to look this way. And don't thank me. No one should have to make their way out of this hellhole alone."

He looked around, got his bearings and told me to follow him. Like a fullback clearing the way for a runner, he aimed his bulk forward and made people clear a path. A man with too many suitcases on his cart had to stop short to avoid hitting Avi and the bags went tipping over. The man cursed but Avi just kept going; didn't hear the man or didn't care.

When we got out of the terminal, I moved past the knot of smokers you see outside every public building nowadays and stopped to take a few deep breaths. Unclouded by jet fuel, tobacco or body odour, the fall air was crisp and fresh. Warmer than it had been in Toronto. I wondered how many people come to Chicago from a colder place.

"Listen," Avi said, "why don't you wait here. I'll get the car and come around."

"You sure? My bag's on wheels."

"Trust me," he said. "It's a schlep. Anyway, I have to check in with the office and I might have to make a call that's privileged. I'll be back in ten minutes. Watch for a silver Navigator."

I pretended to be shocked. "Avi Sternberg driving an SUV? You used to say they were invented by Arabs to keep us begging for oil."

"I'm a big guy, Jonah. I need room to move." He turned away, pulling a cellphone out of his pocket. Then he turned back and said, "By the way? It's Stern now. I dropped the 'berg' when I came back to the States."

"You're kidding."

He just looked at me. It took a little getting used to, seeing his eyes undistorted by glasses.

It took Avi twenty minutes to get back. Twenty minutes I spent thinking about our time together on a kibbutz in northern Israel, two outsiders trying hard to be accepted by the sabras—native-born Israelis—who tended to view us as softies who weren't in it for the long haul. I thought about Dalia Schaeffer, my lover who had been killed by a rocket fired from southern Lebanon. Avi had been her close friend, and had been almost as devastated by her death as I was.

When he pulled up in his hulking silver beast, I heaved my bag in through the back hatch and climbed into the most comfortable car seat ever to favour my backside. He touched a button on the steering wheel and a song began playing, one I knew from the first riff: "Begin the Begin," the first track on R.E.M.'s *Life's Rich Pageant*. "Remember this?" he said. "We wore this record out on kibbutz."

"We didn't have that many to choose from."

"The days before iPods. Whatever did we do?"

We drove all of a hundred yards before the traffic ahead forced us to a stop. "What's the population of Chicago?" I asked.

"About four million."

"They all out here today?"

"Once we get out of the airport, it won't be too bad."

And it wasn't. After we cleared all the construction zones around the airport, Avi took the Dan Ryan Expressway south, driving his Navigator too fast, too close to other cars. A serial lane-changer, moving to the far right lane as if exiting the expressway, then bulling his way back into traffic at the last minute. I gripped the handle above the door as he squeezed in between two trucks, focusing on the city skyline that loomed in the far-off haze like Emerald City down the yellow brick road. A distant Oz where wisdom could be received, hearts restored, courage found.

"So you're an investigator now," he said.

"Uh-huh."

"Hardly what I expected."

"What did you expect?"

"Geez, I don't know. A social worker, maybe. An activist of some sort. Just not a PI. I mean, our firm uses PIs all the time and you just don't fit the mould."

"The ex-cop mould?"

"Yeah."

"Truth is, I kind of backed into it. Mostly I met the right man at the right time. He thought I had what it took."

"And what exactly are you investigating? You were very tight-lipped on the phone." He checked his side mirror and gunned the Navigator into the passing lane, overtaking a delivery van that was trailing a cloud of burning oil.

"Three murders."

"Three—Jesus H." He glanced over at me, then back at the road ahead. "I thought it was some sort of fraud thing."

"There's a fraud at the heart of it. But it's murder now."

"This happened in Toronto?"

"Yes."

"So what brings you to Chicago?"

"The killings were ordered here."

"The Outfit?"

"I almost wish it were."

"You're being very cryptic."

"Because the man who ordered them is going to be a lot harder to nail than a mobster."

"Why?"

"Because he's Simon Birk."

Avi's head whipped around. He gaped at me. "*The* Simon Birk?"

"Watch it!" I planted my right foot against the floor as if my side had a brake. He looked back at the road and slammed the brake hard, stopping inches from a beat-up old Mazda with three bodies crammed in the back seat. Nearly three more deaths to add to the tally.

"You're telling me that Simon Birk—*the* Simon Birk—had three people killed in Toronto?"

"Yes."

"Then why aren't the police handling it? Or are they?"

"Not so far."

"Why not?"

"They're not buying my theory."

"You have proof?"

"Not enough. Not yet."

"So you're down here on your own."

"Yes."

"Going after Simon Birk."

"Yes."

"*The* Simon Birk."

"Yes."

"Jonah goddamn Geller," he said. "You're even crazier than I remembered."

"That," I said, "may be the only advantage I have."

"Did you call me because I'm a lawyer?"

"I called because you're a friend. The only person I know in Chicago. I didn't even know you were a lawyer till your mother told me."

"How long did it take her to tell you?"

"First or second sentence."

"That's my mom."

"You might be able to help," I said. "If that's something that interests you."

"Help you investigate Simon Birk."

"Maybe shed a little light on his business practices."

"That I could probably do. What else?"

"I don't know. Get me out of jail if need be."

"Jail—what would you end up in jail for?"

"How should I know?" I said. "I just got here."

"But I don't practise criminal law."

"This could be your chance."

Avi used his thumb to lower the volume and R.E.M. faded away. "I think you'd better tell me everything," he said. "What the hell happened in Toronto and why you think Birk is involved."

"I know he is, Avi. He ordered those people killed because they were in his way."

"Then convince me," he said. "Because if your only friend in Chicago doesn't believe you, who else will?"

CHAPTER 1

O f all the hard lessons I learned last June, fighting for my life in the Don River Valley, chief among them was this: the justice system can't always protect those who need it most. I had taken a man's life because I knew if I let him live, he would order my death, and others, from prison. It might have taken days, weeks or months—or more likely hours—and that would have been that. If the system couldn't protect me, with the resources I had, I knew there were other, more vulnerable people out there who needed a different brand of justice, and someone to mete it out on their behalf.

And so I left Beacon Security, the only place I'd ever worked as an investigator. Left the employ of Graham McClintock, who had trained me, believed in me, mentored me like a seasoned horse breaker. I *had* to leave after the lies I told him, the actions I took, the absences I couldn't explain. I made the most graceful exit I could manage and my friend Jenn Raudsepp opted to join me. I never asked her to: she had a good thing going at Beacon and my departure might even have opened up new opportunities for her. I knew my new agency, as it was forming in my mind, might prove a low-income, high-risk enterprise. But she volunteered to come aboard and I welcomed her. When she told me her parents had offered her $20,000 against the eventual sale of their farm, and she was willing to invest it, I was all over her.

She put up twenty per cent of the start-up costs and I put up eighty from the sale of a house I had owned with my ex-girlfriend. Which meant I got to name the company.

You could say we argued about my choice a little.

"No one will know what we do," Jenn protested.

"That could prove useful. Help us stay under the radar."

"Why would we want to?"

"Because of the kinds of cases we'll be taking."

"We'll get all kinds of bogus calls."

"We won't answer them."

"How will we know they're bogus?"

"We're investigators, Jenn. Trained by the best. We'll separate the clients from the chaff."

"What do you know about chaff, city boy? And why should we make it hard for clients to find a new business no one knows about?"

"If they need our kind of help, they'll find us."

I held fast and World Repairs is the name of our agency. Clients—especially well-paying ones—have proved somewhat elusive so far, so maybe Jenn had a point. She had suggested T.O. Investigations, T.O. being shorthand for both Toronto and *tikkun olam*, the Jewish concept of repairing the world, making it a better place wherever you can.

I'm a cultural Jew, not a religious one, even though I was raised in an Orthodox home. As much as I love the comfort and rituals of the Jewish community, I haven't felt God's presence since I was fourteen. Might have been the onset of reason, might have been my father's sudden death at forty-four that same year, but to this day I believe in God like I believe the Maple Leafs will win the Stanley Cup before my gums cave in.

But I do cling to the notion of *tikkun olam* and that's more or less what Jenn and I practise, though she is descended from by-the-book Lutherans.

World Repairs: We do what we can do and fix what we can fix. Sometimes we're messengers, sometimes mediators, and sometimes we forget to mind our manners.

Our office was on the third floor of a renovated factory on Broadview Avenue: the same street I lived on, though at the extreme southern end, close to both Lake Ontario and the foul mouth of the Don River. Our neighbours included two ad shops, a photographer's studio and a web design firm and, next to us, the PR phenomenon known as Eddie Solomon. I knocked on his door around nine-thirty that morning and he called out "En-tuh!" doing his best Walter Matthau, circa *The Sunshine Boys*.

Eddie could have been fifty, could have been seventy. I pegged him as early sixties, but if even half his stories about celebrities he's represented, befriended, bedded and brought to the brink of stardom were true, he'd have to be a hundred and six. He is taller than five feet, but not much, and weighs about two hundred pounds. His head is shaved and his face surprisingly smooth for someone who has spent so many late nights paving the way for the stars. With his ready smile and his twinkling eyes, he emits light like a candle: warm, bright, steady.

"Hail the conquering hero," he cried when I entered his office. "My Jason! My Argonaut! Come here, you lumbering hunk, let me shake your hand for a job well done."

"I haven't even told you what happened."

"You're here, you're smiling—that is a smile, right? It's not gas or something?"

"It's a smile, Eddie."

"So tell me, bubeleh. Can I call Chelsea? Tell her it's over?"

Chelsea Madison was an American TV star filming a movie-of-the-week in Toronto. Best known for playing the squeaky-clean mom of a group of wisecracking teenagers on the sitcom *Den Mother*, she had complained to Eddie that a photographer named Stan Lester had been stalking her sixteen-year-old daughter, Desiree, trying to get photos of her going in and out of a rehab centre that had accepted her into a day program while she accompanied her mother to Toronto.

"It's done," I told Eddie. "Lester won't bother Desi again."

"You sure? Some of these guys, they just won't stop. Forget Desi, you should see them follow Chelsea around. She's got another seven, eight weeks to film in Toronto and she's got the mongrel hordes all over her."

"I think it's Mongol hordes," I said.

"Not when you speak of paparazzi."

"Well, Stan Lester is sidelined indefinitely," I said. "Out for the season."

"Do I want to know how?"

"No."

"Come on," he said. "Spill. Vicarious thrills are the only kind I get at my age."

"That's not how we work, Eddie. You only get to know the results."

In truth, there wasn't that much to tell. Lester had been in his car this morning outside the rehab centre, waiting for Desi. I was parked three spaces behind watching him. As soon as she exited the building, he levelled a camera with a long lens at her. I stepped between him and his target and all he got was shots of my jacket. A frank and candid discussion then ensued about his right to take her picture versus her right not to have her picture taken by him. In the end, he saw things my way. But not right away. Not before I grabbed his lens and drove the camera body into his face, opening a cut on the bridge of his nose, then banged the heel of my hand against his head behind the ear, hard enough to set his bells ringing. Then I told him if he came within a mile of Desiree Madison again,

I'd give him a colonoscopy with the widest fish-eye lens I could find in his bag.

"Well," Eddie said. "As long as I can tell Chelsea it's over, and she can get back to blowing lines."

"You can."

"Well done, Prince Valiant. Well done." He gripped my hand in a firm handshake and looked up at me with a grin. "To be your age, Jonah," he sighed. "To be tall and strong like you. Christ, to have your hair! I'd have girls falling over me."

"That's nice of you to say, Eddie. But I'd rather have my fee."

"Don't worry, kid. I'm seeing Chelsea tonight at her hotel. I'll bring it by tomorrow."

"In cash, right?"

"Not a problem. You want a coffee, mighty one?"

"Can't," I said. "We have a ten o'clock client."

"So go meet your client and send Jenn."

"Don't start, Eddie."

"What? Start what? What did I say?"

"I can read it on your forehead like it's a drive-in screen."

"Can I help it if she's gorgeous?"

"Not to mention gay."

"The blonde hair, the blue eyes, the sweet face. And the body, my God, the body. The gayness just fades away."

"Just don't give yourself a heart attack before you get my money," I said.

"And those legs." He was panting, hamming it up now, dabbing his forehead with his tie. "She's so tall, I'd have to go up on her!"

"Eddie," I said. "What am I going to do with you?"

"Nothing," he said, and laughed. "I'm too old to change and I'm too young to stuff and mount. Anyway, you know I'm kidding. Even if she was straight, I wouldn't stand a chance. I've got daughters her age. I'm like a dog chasing a car, Jonah. What would I do if I caught one?"

"Just don't let her catching you talk like that," I said.

"Come on. She'd know I was kidding. Wouldn't she?"

"She'd stuff and mount you," I said. "Unfortunately for you, in that order."

Eddie was right. Jenn Raudsepp exudes a wholesome sexiness that's hard to ignore, whatever her sexual orientation. Men and women alike take note when she dashes across a street or emerges legs first from her car or smiles or tosses back her blonde silk hair. Men stammer when they approach her. They mumble into their drinks. They become stupider than they were before the drinks.

I'll never know her sexual side. That belongs to her long-time lover, Sierra Lyons, who's a terrific match for Jenn and a good friend to me. Not to mention an ace nurse practitioner who can stitch wounds without commenting on how you look in your underwear. As an investigator, though, Jenn brings it all. She's smart, she's fun, she's good with clients and she works as hard as I do. And as placid as she can seem when she wants, a whole other side emerges when she gets riled.

One night, we were leaving the office late and came across a guy beating a Native woman in the laneway where Jenn had parked her Golf. He was stocky and built but clearly drunk, and when I told him to get away from the woman, he sneered at me, "You wanna do something about it?"

"No," Jenn said, stepping forward. "I do."

And she did. Unfolded those lovely long legs of hers and dropped him with a spin kick, then broke most of his ribs with a roundhouse. From there, she did everything but make him eat his car keys. I could have done it quicker but no better, and it seemed important to her that this particular world repair be done by a woman.

The Estonian wonder girl did indeed have a pot of coffee brewing, a continental dark, and once I had a cup in hand I told her how things had gone with Stan Lester, giving her the details I had spared Eddie Solomon.

"Eddie pay you?"

"Tomorrow," I said. "A thousand in cash."

"Today would have been better. Scary Mary called from the bank."

I shuddered. Scary Mary is the assistant manager at our branch and a devout Christian with a phone manner so artificially nice, so honeyed with false promise that each of us usually tries to pawn her off on the other. I said, "So sorry I wasn't here to take the call."

"You should be. She likes you better, you know." Then Jenn, a gifted mimic who'd once been a member of a comedy troupe, nailed Scary Mary's breathless menace: "'This is Mary McMurphy from Toronto-Do-*min*-ion calling. Is that Jonah? What a nice name. Isn't that a *Bib*-lical name?'"

"Brrr. You do her better than she does."

"Why, *thank* you."

"If she calls back, tell her to relax," I said. "We'll have Chelsea's thousand and a retainer from Marilyn Cantor."

"How retentive a retainer?"

"My brother referred her," I said. "If she knows him, she's bound to have money."

"She called, by the way."

"When?"

"Ten minutes ago."

"Please say she didn't cancel."

"Just confirming her appointment."

"Phew."

"You have two other messages," she said, a wicked grin starting to form as she slid two scraps of paper across her desk.

"What?"

"Nothing."

"Like hell."

I looked at the two slips she'd filled out. The first was from my mother. The second was from the Homicide Squad of the Toronto Police Service.

I looked at Jenn, at the sunbeam of a smile lighting her face.

"What?" I asked.

"Oh, you know. Homicide. Your mother," she said. "Just wondering who you call first."

CHAPTER 2

I met Katherine Hollinger last summer while I was still at Beacon Security. Her investigation into the murder of a Toronto pharmacist overlapped with the case I was working on: another pharmacist whose family had been targeted for extinction. Hollinger was about thirty-six and already a detective sergeant. Five-seven with a lithe build, glossy black hair and eyes whose colour was somewhere between honey and caramel. My feelings for a woman almost always start with the eyes; I liked her from the first look and felt it was mutual. Of course, I'd been stabbed the night before by a badass mobster and was sailing along on Percocet, so my judgment could have been skewed.

The next day one of my co-workers was shot to death and Hollinger, in addition to her many other charms, was the first to pick up on the heartwarming fact that the hit had been meant for me. She even turned up at my door late one night, supposedly to ask me about the shooting victim but really, I think, to check up on me.

After everything crashed to a head those last hot days of June, with more than half a dozen killings in two countries to account for, Hollinger and her mouth-breathing partner, Gregg McDonough, had more than a few questions for me. The sessions were long and tense. We sat in a small interview room with four bare walls, a small table, three hard chairs and a video camera that stood above us all on a tripod, recording every question they threw at me and every poor excuse for an answer I gave back. I bobbed and weaved my way through it, telling no outright lies but providing nothing near the truth. None of the killings could be attributed to me, though I had seen and done enough that I still wake up shuddering, chasing away images of faces under water, of bullet-riddled bodies in hot closed rooms.

Hollinger and I hadn't spoken since. I had thought about calling her half a dozen times, asking her out for coffee. Then I'd stop and wonder what exactly we could talk about.

How about those corpses in the Don River, Katherine? All that sorted out?

Well, not quite, Jonah. Don't suppose you could clear that up for me. And pass the skim milk.

Like Hamlet and Gertrude sitting across a table from each other, plates piled high with funeral baked meats.

Now she had called first, so I called back from the reception area—away from Jenn's rolling eyes.

When she answered, I said, "Hey, Sarge."

"Hey, yourself, Geller. How are you?"

I liked her voice almost as much as her eyes. An alto with just a slight husk. "I'm good," I said. "How about you?"

"No complaints. Except people keep murdering each other."

"The mayor just put out a press release saying what a safe city we have."

"The mayor doesn't work my crime scenes. So," she said, "how's the new agency?"

"We're doing all right. Finished one case this morning. About to start another."

"Good," she said. "Okay. So . . . listen, Jonah. I have some news I thought would interest you."

"What's that?"

"I had a meeting with Gruber this morning." That would be Les Gruber, the new head of the Homicide Squad. "We're closing the Di Pietra cases. All of them."

"With what smoke and which mirror?"

"I wouldn't question it if I were you. As far as we're concerned, Ricky Messina and Stefano di Pietra were responsible for all six murders."

"They did keep busy."

"We also believe Ricky and Stefano both died as a result of injuries sustained during their fight in the river."

"Who came up with that? You or Gruber?"

"It does wonders for our clearance rate."

"Gruber, then."

"He's got his black marker out as we speak. And I'm not going to second-guess him on it. We have too many red cases as it is."

"So no more questions for me?"

"Just one. How late do you work?"

"I set my own hours."

"Yeah? 'Cause I was wondering if you maybe wanted to have dinner."

"Dinner?"

"Tonight, if you're free."

I said, "Tonight?" Smooth, Geller. Smooth as shrapnel.

"It opened up just now. I took it as a sign. If you don't want to . . ."

"No," I said. "I mean yes. I do."

"You sure?"

"Very sure."

"You like Italian?"

"Of course I do," I said. "Scratch a Jew, find an Italian. Except on Sunday evenings, when we all convert to Chinese."

"A friend of mine recommended a place that has real southern Italian cooking and decent prices."

"Won't leave us much to complain about."

"It's Toronto," she said. "There's always weather and real estate."

Call number two.

"So you're seeing Marilyn Cantor today?"

"Any minute, Ma."

"Such a tragedy," she said. "I went to the shiva and she was a broken woman."

"I didn't know you knew her that well."

"I don't really," my mother said. "She was on the board of volunteer services at Baycrest when I chaired it a few years ago." My mother makes her living—and a good one—as a real estate broker, but she's also one of those dynamos who manage to sit on half a dozen boards of arts, culture and community service organizations. How anyone in Toronto gets along without her is beyond me. "But a situation like this," she said, "you pay your respects. If you were more connected to the Jewish community, you'd understand."

And there it is, ladies and gentlemen. The first shot across my bow.

"I don't know that much about her situation, Ma."

"Daniel didn't tell you?"

"I didn't speak to him."

"But he referred her to you."

"Not directly. His assistant set it up."

"And you didn't call to thank him?"

Shot number two.

"I was going to, Ma. Right after I meet Marilyn."

"Jonah," she said. "Honey."

Oh, God. Not the "honey."

"You have one brother."

"So does he."

"Which means?"

"Which means he could have called me himself, instead of having Sandra do it."

"So take the high road. Call and thank him. It's not as if your business is booming."

"Ma—"

"Is it?"

"I wouldn't say booming but we're doing all right."

"Are you, dear? Really?"

"Yes, Ma." Stretching the definition of all right, perhaps, but this was my mother. Telling her how close to the bone we were would only send her to that place we've been too many times before: unwanted career advice, which ranked right up there with matchmaking.

"I wish I knew what it was with you two."

What it was—what it had always been—was that Daniel was more successful. A lawyer, and a highly esteemed one at that, senior partner in the firm of Geller, Winston, Lacroix. Married with two adorable boys. A shul-goer, on the board of Young Israel congregation, and a contributor to charity. All the things a mother hopes for or, in the case of a Jewish mother, demands. All the things I wasn't and felt I'd never be.

"I'll call him the minute Marilyn leaves," I said. "Before the door swings shut."

"Just be good to her," she said. "Do right by her. Her youngest child killing herself . . . she's had such a terrible time."

"Her husband hasn't?"

"Her ex-husband," my mother said. "And him, you never know what he's feeling. Half the time I was there, he was taking phone calls. During shiva!"

"Listen, Ma, I think that's her at the door," I said. And no lightning bolt struck me down.

"At least it's just a family matter," she said. "This business you're in, I worry so much about what could happen to you."

"I know, Ma."

"No, dear. If you knew—if you *really* knew—you'd get into something safer."

"That's definitely her at the door," I said.

"You'll call Daniel?"

"Yes."

"And you'll be careful?"

"Like you said, Ma, it's a family matter. How dangerous could it get?"

CHAPTER 3

Marilyn Cantor's knock, when it came, was barely audible. Two soft taps, a pause, then a third tap. I wouldn't have heard it had I not been in the front reception area.

I opened the door and saw a woman of about fifty, dressed casually, comfortably and expensively in jeans and a maroon suede jacket. Five-four, slim, with auburn hair and blue eyes. Deep indigo smudges under her eyes, as dark as if she had recently broken her nose. But I knew from what my mother had told me that she'd endured far worse.

I introduced myself and Jenn and got Marilyn seated in one of our guest chairs. She declined coffee but when Jenn offered to make tea, she gratefully accepted. "Something decaffeinated or herbal, if you've got it," she said. "I'm having trouble sleeping."

As if the dark pouches under her eyes hadn't told us that.

"I almost didn't make it," she said. "Here, I mean." She was having trouble making eye contact. Looking around the office, out the window, at the mismatched file cabinets and desks we'd bought at a school board auction. "I spent all morning wondering why I made the appointment. What I hope to accomplish by it. Whether there's anything to be gained."

"Is that why you called to confirm?" I asked. "Most people don't bother."

"Yes," she said. "I think you're right. I needed to push myself out the door. I needed someone to be expecting me."

The kettle came to a boil and Jenn placed a mug in front of her, a bag of decaf English breakfast bobbing on the surface.

"Tell us about your daughter," I said. "And what you think we can do to help."

It didn't take any more than that to make her eyes well up. I pushed a box of tissues toward her from my side of the desk. The tears she could wipe away; the dark pouches seemed there to stay.

"Her name was Maya," she began. "She was the youngest of two. Our baby. She would have been twenty-two next month. She was studying theatre arts at York—she'd wanted to be an actress since she was a little girl. And she was beautiful and sweet . . . our gift from God." Her arms went around her body, hugging herself, trying to provide comfort where none was to be had.

"Do either of you have children?" she asked.

I said no. Jenn shook her head.

"I'm not sure you can understand how this hurts," she said. "Not just that she's gone. But how she died. Why she did what she did. Why I—oh, God—why I didn't know. If she was hurting so badly, if she was so depressed, why didn't I sense it? Why didn't she tell me? Reach out to me? We were close. We'd always been close. More so than Andrew—that's our oldest. He keeps everything inside. If it had been Andrew, God forbid, I think I might have understood. But Maya . . . I keep asking myself, was I so wrapped up in my own life? Was I not approachable in some way? Divorce affects the entire family, we all know that, and it certainly laid me pretty low the first year. Especially when Rob took up with his girlfriend. But Maya is—was outgoing. Upbeat. She seemed to enjoy her life, her friends, her courses. She was cast in two productions last year and even directed a one-act that was—I'm sorry, I'm rambling here."

"You're doing fine," Jenn said.

"The hardest part was shiva," she said.

Jenn glanced at me. "A week of mourning," I explained.

"It's supposed to be a time of consolation," Marilyn said softly. "A time when friends and family hold you up until you can get back on your feet. To me, it felt more like an inquisition. I felt everybody's eyes on me, as if they were asking themselves what I had done wrong. As if I had failed my daughter and everyone in the room knew it. Every day, until it was over, I thanked God that we cover mirrors during shiva because I couldn't stand to look at myself," she said. "I live alone now, and except for the one in my bathroom, they're all still draped in black cloth."

She used another tissue to wipe her eyes. The office was silent, except for the hum of computers and the buzzing of an overhead light.

"Actually," she said. "I was wrong. Shiva wasn't the hardest part." She pinched the bridge of her nose as if she could cut off the supply of tears to her eyes.

"Take your time," I said.

She swallowed hard a few times then willed herself to go on. "It was the day after she died," she whispered. "When the arrangements had to be made."

I knew where she was going with this, but Jenn wouldn't, so I said nothing.

"We're not really Orthodox Jews," she said. "But Young Israel is an Orthodox shul. A synagogue," she said to Jenn.

"That much I know," Jenn smiled.

"Did you know that Orthodox Jews who commit suicide can't be buried inside the walls of their cemetery?" Marilyn said bitterly.

Jenn's smile vanished. "No."

"I had to plead with the rabbi. Go around and around with him, asking for special dispensation. All this with my daughter in the morgue, and time running out. We're supposed to bury our dead quickly, right? He agreed in the end, but you know why?"

Jenn couldn't answer that one; I could, but didn't want to.

"He said if she had taken her own life, then it could be said that she hadn't been in her right mind, and therefore couldn't be held responsible for what she did. Do you understand how that felt? Him saying my daughter was out of her mind? If she was, goddammit, then someone *was* responsible. For knowing it. Seeing it. And that person was me."

"What is it you need from us?" I asked.

"I need to know why," she said. "I need someone to tell me why Maya would take her own life. Maybe there are friends she talked to. Or classmates or teachers. People she trusted more than—more than me. I can't bring myself to ask them. Maybe there are things she wrote down in a journal or underlined in a play, but I can't go through her things. I need someone else to do it for me. I need you, if you'll do it. Money is no problem," she added. "My hus—my ex-husband paid me dearly for the right to sleep with a woman half his age."

"Was Maya seeing anyone?" Jenn asked.

"I don't think so," Marilyn said. "Not that she told me. But now of course I wonder if she would have."

"Can you provide a list of her friends?" Jenn asked.

"I already did." Marilyn produced a folded sheet from her purse. Half a dozen names were typed on it, along with phone numbers, cell numbers and email addresses. "These are the girls she's known the longest," she said. "The ones who grew up on our street, went to the same high school, the same summer camp. I'm not sure about her friends from theatre school but I've brought some programs from plays she was in, which will have most of the names. And her teacher is Theo Harris. Maybe he knows what was going on with her. She spoke well of him. She spoke well of everybody . . . that's the kind of person she was. Not an enemy in the world."

"Marilyn," I said gently. "If it's not too painful, can you tell us anything about the night she died?"

She took a deep breath, as if trying to expel a toxic cloud

that had formed inside her lungs. "It was two weeks ago. She had dinner at her father's house that night. Her and Andrew. I know something happened there between Maya and Rob. Neither of them told me what it was about, but I know from Andrew there was a bit of a row and Maya left early. Probably something to do with Nina. The new wife."

"Why do you say that?" I asked.

"Because she's a bitch to everyone. Anyway, a few hours later—around midnight, the police said—she jumped off . . . oh God . . . I'm sorry . . . she jumped off her balcony. From twelve storeys up."

"They're sure she jumped?" I asked. "Could she have somehow slipped?"

"There's a waist-high concrete wall around the balcony," Marilyn said. "If she had simply fallen over, they said, she would have landed differently. Closer to the building or something. They were pretty sure she climbed up onto the wall and then jumped."

"Marilyn," I said, "do you know if Maya was into drugs at all? Maybe if she was upset after this dinner, she—"

"No! She wasn't a drug user, or even much of a drinker. She didn't even like being around people who were. She liked herself. Liked *being* herself. That's what makes it so damn hard to understand." Her slim body started to heave and huge racking sobs followed. Jenn went and sat next to her and put a hand on her shoulder. A few minutes passed before she could speak again. "Please, Mr. Geller—"

"Jonah."

"Please, Jonah. Jenn. Find out what happened to my baby. Find out what went wrong. Where I went wrong. I can handle that. I can handle anything but this wondering. This not knowing."

"Why take it all on yourself?" Jenn asked. "You weren't the only parent she had."

"Please," she said, giving us the closest thing she had to a smile. "Rob is the most self-absorbed little pri—the most self-absorbed man on this planet. If Maya literally had been crying out for help, he wouldn't have heard it. Or he would have told her to wait till he got off the phone. He was that way when we were together and he's been even worse since we split. Between his new bimbo and his big new project—he's quite the mover and shaker now. No, I'm the one who was supposed to be there for her. And for Andrew too, even if he never seems to need anything from anyone. It was up to me to help the kids get over the divorce and get on with their lives and I failed. Or at least I failed Maya. Completely."

I looked at Jenn and she nodded at me.

"We'll do what we can," I said.

I asked if Maya had left a note of any kind.

Marilyn shook her head.

"Do you have a recent photo?"

Marilyn reached into her purse and withdrew what had been a five-by-seven once. It was now five-by-four with a ragged edge on the left. The photo showed a beaming young woman with sea-green eyes and chestnut hair that fell to her shoulders. She had her arm around her mother, who stood on her right.

"I'm sorry," Marilyn said with a half-smile. "When Rob told me he was leaving me for the trophy girl, I cut him out of most of the photos."

"What about her apartment?" Jenn asked. "Have her things been moved?"

"Not yet," Marilyn said. "I haven't been able to deal with it. I paid the rent until the end of next month. Maybe by then I'll be able to sort through it and see what I want to keep."

"With your permission," Jenn said, "we should have a look. Her phone records and credit card bills might tell us something."

Marilyn nodded.

"Did she keep a journal?" I asked.

"I'm not sure. She told me once that she had to keep a journal of a character she was playing—it was Helena, one of the lovers in *Midsummer Night's Dream*—God, she was so funny in that, so goofy—but whether she kept one of her own? I don't know."

"If she did," I said, "maybe we'll find it at her place."

"I'll get you a set of keys," she said. "Or maybe I should go with you. I might be able to tell you what's important and what's not."

"That's a courageous offer," Jenn said. "Do you think you could manage it?"

"Now that I'm here—now that I've met you—yes, I think I could." She put her hand over Jenn's and squeezed it.

"Why don't you guys go ahead," I said. "I'd like to talk to her dad."

Marilyn recited Rob's office, cell and home numbers. "But good luck getting hold of him. Ever since he got involved with Simon Birk, he thinks he's more important than God."

"*The* Simon Birk?" I asked.

"The man himself," she said.

Everyone knew Simon Birk. Even me, who paid little or no attention to matters of big business and real estate. Birk was one of the highest-profile developers in the world, Chicago's answer to Donald Trump, only with hair that could be explained by science. He and Trump were known to be bitter rivals. When ground was broken on Trump's International Hotel and Tower at Bay and Adelaide, the Donald arrived in a stretch limo and used a golden shovel. Several months later, at his own groundbreaking ceremony, Simon Birk made his entrance by helicopter, the rotors scattering hats and ruffling the hair of dignitaries and journalists. He scoffed at the shovel he'd been offered and commandeered a backhoe to crack the dry earth and scoop out the first bucketful of soil.

"So the big project of Rob's that you mentioned," I asked, "is the Birkshire Harbourview?" It was a massive new complex on a long-neglected part of Toronto's port lands.

"Yes."

"How did he manage that?"

"Birk wanted to build in Toronto and Rob had the one thing they don't make any more."

"The land."

"Acres of it, all south of the Keating Channel."

"How did he swing that?" Jenn asked.

"Depends who you ask," Marilyn said.

CHAPTER 4

The plaza outside the Cadillac Fairview tower was bathed in sunshine, and full of people basking in it. Smoking, chatting, munching hot dogs from street vendors, or just leaning back and letting the light shine down on them. *Enjoy it while you can*, I thought. Despite the unseasonable warmth of the past few days, the long Canadian winter was coming. As the days grew shorter, faces would get longer, brows more furrowed, shoulders more hunched. Moods would get blacker, hopes would dim.

My own mood hadn't been great since Stefano di Pietra had died at my hands, the would-be Don lying motionless under the waters of the river of the same name. Sleep had been restless, sometimes elusive altogether. My dreams had been the kind you strive to forget when you awake. Sometimes I'd be lost: in a tunnel, a hotel, a subway station, in my own apartment. I'd be fighting with assailants, firing guns without bullets, swinging my fists uselessly, getting no power behind the punches. I'd be surrounded by flames with no way to douse them. I'd be on trial for crimes I couldn't remember committing.

In winter it would only get worse.

I walked through the sunlit lobby, a two-storey atrium with full-length windows on three sides. The floor and walls were pink marble, the railings highly polished brass. Two fountains at the base of a marble stairway created a rushing sound like a bountiful stream in nature. It was the only natural thing about the place.

I took an elevator to the fourteenth floor and walked into the glassed-in reception area of Cantor Development, where a woman sat behind a workstation made of dark wood in two shades, cherry and mahogany.

"Good morning," said the receptionist.

"Good morn—"

"I'm sorry, he's away from his desk right now," she said, and I realized she was speaking not to me but into a headset. I waited next to a rack of publications that included *Condo Life*, *Canadian Builder*, *Greener House and Home*. The cover of *Canadian Builder*, placed at eye level, showed two men: according to the caption, the one on the left was Rob Cantor; on the right was Simon Birk. Cantor was tall and fit, with thick dark hair. Birk was easily half a foot shorter, squat but powerfully built, grey hair cropped close to his skull, his head thrusting out of his suit as if trying to burst free of constraints.

"Yes?" the receptionist said.

He reminded me of someone . . . Norman Mailer or Rod Steiger . . . a pugnacious attitude that suggested he was ready to rip off his pinstriped suit and scrap in the street. You might beat him, the look in his eye said, but you'd know you'd been in a fight.

"Sir?"

I turned. The woman was looking at me now.

"Sorry," I said. "Are you talking to me or the headset?"

"To you, dear," she said.

"I'm here to see Rob Cantor," I said.

"Is he expecting you?"

"He is." I gave her my name.

"Oh, yes. Let me call Florence for you."

I flipped open *Canadian Builder* to the article on Birk and Cantor's partnership. The Birkshire Harbourview complex, it said, was being built at a cost of more than $500 million. No expense was being spared: it would feature only the finest marble; the rarest hardwood; the highest-end kitchen appliances; the most expansive and state-of-the-art workout facilities and spa.

I was wondering when the writer would run out of superlatives when a tall, dark-haired woman emerged from behind glass doors and introduced herself as Florence Strickland, Rob Cantor's executive assistant. She was holding a BlackBerry in one hand. Her handshake was firm, as was her voice when she told me Mr. Cantor would not be able to see me after all.

"He knows what it's about?" I asked.

"I told him, yes."

"And he can't spare a few minutes?"

"Something came up."

"I don't mind waiting."

"That won't do any good," she said. "He had to leave the office."

I remembered what my mother had said about Rob spending time on the phone during his daughter's shiva.

She glanced at the BlackBerry. "He does have a 2:30 slot free tomorrow," she said.

"Unless something comes up."

"He's a busy man, Mr. Geller. Shall I reserve that time for you or would you prefer to rebook at your convenience?"

I could tell I wasn't going to get any further with her. Not without ice tongs. "All right," I said. "I'll take the 2:30 tomorrow."

"We'll see you then," she said, and her fingernails skittled over the BlackBerry keyboard. "From 2:30 to 2:45. Will that do?"

"I guess it'll have to."

She smiled and thanked me—for what, I couldn't guess—and turned back toward the inner sanctum, just as a young man came out. He wore a dark suit too serious for his age and carried a long cardboard tube under one arm.

"Where's my dad?" he asked Florence Strickland. His dad. This, then, would be Andrew Cantor. He was twenty-five, his mother had said. His hair was dark but his complexion was pale. His neck was mottled with old acne scars.

"He had to go down to the job site," Florence said.

"Why didn't he tell me? He has to sign off on these drawings."

"Something came up," she said. "Would you like me to try his cell?"

"No. I'll take them over. They'll need them down there anyway. If he calls before I get there, ask him to wait there for me. Or to try my cell."

"I'll tell him."

She went back through the glass doors and Andrew walked past me as if I were invisible. He told the receptionist he would have his cell on.

"Of course you will, dear," she said. "Should I call you a cab?"

"Please."

I followed Andrew into the hallway. He punched the down button on the elevator and stared at his reflection in the stainless steel doors. A warped reflection that made him seem shorter and wider than he was.

"I'm heading down to the site too," I said. Why not use the time to hear what the closed-up son had to say about his vibrant, stage-struck sister. "I can give you a ride if you like."

He said, "Are you a supplier?" With the frosty welcome he'd give if that's what I were.

"No," I said. "Jonah Geller. I'm a friend of your mother's."

"So why are you going to the job site?"

"To talk to your dad."

"About what?"

"Your sister."

He looked back at his reflection. "If it's all the same to you," he said, "I think I'll take the cab."

CHAPTER 5

The cranes had returned to Toronto. As I drove east along Lake Shore Boulevard, they stood out against the sky, raising girders and great buckets of cement up to the tops of buildings that grew taller by the day. During past recessions and lulls in the market, tower cranes had all but disappeared from the landscape, as landlords couldn't give away office space or condos. Now the town was booming again, buildings going up everywhere you looked, even on a narrow verge of land right next to the elevated Gardiner Expressway, built so close to it that occupants could lean over their balcony railings and high-five drivers going by.

I took Cherry Street south across the Keating Channel, a man-made canal that allowed freighters to get close enough to factories and industries for derricks to unload their goods. The port lands between the channel and the lake had long been home to heavy industry, everything from oil refineries to tire manufacturers. Any new project being built there had to reclaim the abused land. Brownlands, they were called. Turning them green was hugely expensive, which was why they'd been neglected so long. Tracts had been bought by retailers intending to build superstores, then abandoned when they realized how polluted the land really was, and how expensive it would be to treat or replace the soil.

But some developers were clearly able to absorb the costs. Either they'd been lucky enough to find land that had been used for lighter industry, or they'd conceived projects whose profit margins made remediation worthwhile. And with the blighted Gardiner supposedly coming down, the door had never been more open to reuniting the city and its waterfront.

I turned east on Unwin Avenue, the last road north of the lake. On the south side was the tree-lined shore of Cherry Beach and its marina, closed for the season now with empty slips and boats in dry dock, but a hive of colour and activity in the summer. There were trees and grass and gorse bushes turned a vibrant autumn red.

But on the north side, it was all barbed-wire fences and tired-looking buildings. At the far end of Unwin, looming like a poor cousin of the Washington Monument, was the 700-foot smokestack of the Richard L. Hearn Generating Station, decommissioned and mostly abandoned now; the new Portlands Energy Centre was being built alongside it, over considerable opposition from area residents. I drove past great piles of salt and sand used for the city's roads; hills made of gravel and aggregate; twin peaks of broken stone to be taken to landfill sites; rusted transmission towers standing like sentinels with their arms akimbo.

According to *Canadian Builder*, the Birkshire Harbourview was being built on a thirty-hectare tract of land between Lake Ontario and the Keating Channel. I don't know a hectare from Hector, Prince of Troy, but it seemed like a huge parcel to me. I had to pull close to the edge of the road to let a dump truck rumble past me, coming out of the site with a ghostly cloud of dust billowing out from under a tied-down tarp. I left my car parked outside the site and got a hard hat from my trunk. I keep a number of hats, jackets, shoes and other items there: surveillance work often calls for a quick change of appearance, and hats are an easy way to fool someone into thinking you're not the same guy they just saw in their rear-view mirror, or behind them on a crowded sidewalk. I also took out a clipboard and a pen, and began a slow circuit around the hoarding that surrounded the site. Each panel had been papered over with images of model suites with sweeping views of the harbour and the Toronto Islands behind them or of the glittering city skyline to the north.

Informational panels showed how the building would conform to the highest LEED standards for green living. Another showed the price range: starting at $1.5 million for a 1,500-square-foot one-bedroom and topping out at $12 million for a two-storey penthouse unit. And to think I was making do with a thousand square feet at a thousand a month. Then again, my view was every bit as good, even if it showed the city rising out of a dark ravine, and not smiling at its glittering waterfront reflection like Narcissus.

I walked around the south side to where the park would be. An artist's rendering on the rear hoarding showed a lush wooded parkland; all I saw was bare, fragile new saplings where said forest would be and fenced-off areas that had been reseeded with grass. The parkland as drawn would connect to Tommy Thompson Park and the Leslie Street Spit, a man-made five-kilometre peninsula jutting out into Lake Ontario, built with landfill as a breakwater and now a favourite spot for weekend walkers, birders, joggers and cyclists. It would host a variety of wildlife—foxes, coyotes, rabbit and groundhogs, cormorants, night herons and of course ring-billed gulls. Their colony just west of the spit is one of the world's largest: the squawking from their breeding grounds in mating season sounds like a million nails being dragged down a blackboard; the spit itself looks like it's been paved with dung and feathers.

Coming back around the north side, I found a gap in the hoarding and got my first good look at the hole itself. The size of a full city block and five or six storeys deep, a quarry whose inner walls had been lined with wooden planks, shored up at intervals by massive timbers. A steep dirt road led down into the hole, its surface showing the herringbone pattern of heavy tires. Dozens of workmen swarmed the bottom, all wearing bright yellow hard hats. Some were on scaffolding, shoring up braces in the corners. Parked down at the centre was a crane, but at its end was a massive auger boring a hole ten feet wide. Near it were holes already finished, into which great steel caissons were being lowered, each as wide around as a fuselage. One dump truck was straining up the road to ground level; another prepared to descend and gather up the earth being dug out of the foundation. The air rang with the whine of machinery, the cries of gulls and the shouts of men trying to be heard above them.

As I came to the main entrance, a truck with a flatbed loaded with caissons was entering. The driver had his window open, elbow out, cigarette dangling at the end of his fingers.

"How far down do those things go?" I asked.

"The caissons? Till you hit bedrock. A hundred and ten feet in this case, maybe one-twenty. Ask the engineer. I just drive 'em in and dump 'em."

I stepped away from the truck as the driver shifted into first, and almost turned my ankle in a tire rut. Diesel fumes soured the air around me. Maybe it would smell like a park one day but not today, not with dump trucks and transit mixers coming, going and idling as drivers shot the shit with each other.

I adjusted my hard hat, hefted my clipboard and entered the site. A sign said all visitors had to report to the office, a double-wide trailer standing on four cement posts. I was walking toward it when the door banged open and a red-faced man stormed down the three steps to the ground and stalked out toward the road. He had blond hair and a moustache and wire-rimmed glasses. Another man appeared in the doorway and called after the blond, "Martin. Martin! Don't do this. Come back here and talk to me."

Neither man had seen me. I eased behind a fenced-in electrical supply unit that had been installed to provide power to the site. From there I got my first look at Rob Cantor, looking every bit as tall, dark and handsome as he had on the cover of *Canadian Builder* next to Simon Birk, just a touch of grey at the temples and a grey suit with a subtle green weave that gave it a luminous shine.

"Dammit, Martin!" he called.

Martin kept going.

"What about Eric?" Rob yelled. "Have you thought about him?"

This time Martin turned to face him. His eyes looked like they were tearing up. He unclenched his jaw and said, "I *am* thinking about him."

"Not if you're walking away."

"What would you know about—"

"I *know* you should come back and sort this out with me. Thoughtfully, Martin. Carefully."

But Martin turned away and didn't stop walking when Rob called his name again. Rob looked like he was fishing for something else to say, then gave it up and went back inside. I waited half a minute and then knocked and entered.

Rob said, "I knew you'd come—" then frowned when he saw I wasn't Martin. He had a set of working drawings spread out on a counter in front of him, his cellphone holding down one side, a hard hat the other. "You from Superior Electric?"

"No."

"Swifty didn't send you?

"No."

"Then who the hell are you? Swifty was supposed to have his guy here like ten minutes ago." His cellphone trilled and he held up his hand in a stop sign. One side of the drawing rolled when he picked up the phone and he smoothed it back across the table with his other hand. He said, "Yeah?" and then it took all of two seconds for his face to crease into a frown. "What are you talking, six hundred a ton. I can get rolled steel for that price. Charlie, don't mess around with this, you're flirting with the big time and you're blowing it. Excuse me? No, Mr. Birk does not deal directly with suppliers, Charlie. You have to go through me and at that price, I'm telling you, don't bother. Get back to me with a price I can live with or don't get back at all." He hung up the phone and looked at me. "If you're not from Swifty—"

"Jonah Geller."

"Who?"

"Geller. We had an appointment today."

"You're the guy Marilyn hired? Daniel's brother?"

"The same."

"I don't believe this. I told Florence to cancel you."

"And she told me. But I was passing by so I thought I'd stop in."

"What do you mean, passing by? No one passes by here." His cellphone trilled and he looked at the caller ID; picked it up and pressed answer before the second ring. The plan started to roll up again and he slapped it flat sharply, then shifted a coffee mug onto it.

"Douglas?" he said. "Have you looked at the brochure? Yes, it's beautiful. Have you looked closely though? Really carefully? No, I didn't think so, because then you would have noticed that on page three—you have it in front of you? No? Get it . . ."

He rolled his eyes and stared at the ceiling, his body stiff with tension.

On top of a file cabinet behind him was a three-dimensional scale model of the final site: two point towers joined by a five-storey podium that mixed retail and professional offices. At fifty-four and fifty-five storeys, they would be the tallest buildings in the port lands—for now. The model featured a lush-looking park at the south end; small plastic children were posed as if playing on swings and a jungle gym.

"You got it?" Cantor said. "Yes? So look at page three. See what it says? 'Only the finest Carrara marble will grace the lobby floor'? Look again, Douglas. You spelled it c-a-r-a-double r-a. No, that's not how it's spelled. It's c-a-double r-a-r-a. Yes, it's a big difference. It's a *huge* difference. What are we trying to sell people here? What does Mr. Birk stress at every meeting? Quality at every point of contact. We're telling them this is Carrara marble from the same quarries Michelangelo used. Why bother saying it—hell, why bother getting it—if we can't spell it right. Rip 'em up, Doug. You heard me. Rip them the fuck up and start over. And it's coming out of your fee because you're supposed to proof this shit. I don't care who signed off on it here. You're my last line of defence, are you not? Well, you will if you want to get paid!"

He snapped the phone closed. "Moron," he said. Then to me: "Why are you still here?"

"Mr. Cantor, your wife hired me to look into your—"

"First of all," he said, "she's my ex-wife, thank God. Second of all, I've got no time for this. I have a giant hole in the ground where two towers are supposed to be."

"I'm sorry about your daughter," I said. "I'm sure it must be difficult to talk about. But your ex-wife just needs to know—"

"She needs. She *needs*. Well, her needs are not my problem anymore."

"She's in a lot of pain."

"You think I'm not? You think this doesn't affect me?" He was running his hand through his hair as he spoke, finger-combing it back.

"I'm sure it does."

"I just handle things differently than Marilyn. I'm not the wallowing type. I stay busy. I stay focused. It's taken me twenty-five years to land a deal like this and I'm not taking my eye off the ball."

"Can't you just give me a few minutes?"

"To do what?" Still combing his hair back. If he kept it up, he'd have a reverse Mohawk soon.

"Talk to me about Maya. Tell me why she might have done what she did."

"You think I know?"

Everything about the man—the darting of his eyes, the hand running through the hair, the stiffness in his body— suggested he might indeed have a clue.

"Maya was the last person you'd expect to take her own life," he finally said. "She was never one to mope around or feel sorry for herself. She's—she was—like me. When she was down about something she worked through it, like I'm trying to do now. So if you'll excuse me—"

"What did you fight about the night she died?"

He glared at me. "What? Who said we fought about anything?"

"Marilyn."

"She wasn't even there so what does she know? God- dammit, I wish that woman would just get on with her life and let me get on with mine."

"But there was a fight?"

"Whether there was or wasn't is none of your business. I only agreed to see you because I know your brother."

"But you didn't keep the appointment. You skipped out."

"Skip—I didn't *skip* out. Who the hell do you think you are? My construction director called in sick and I had a problem here I had to deal with. Every minute of every day generates problems on a project like this. I have electricians, architects, engineers, bureaucrats, all with questions that need answers."

"Which one of those is Martin?" I asked.

He stiffened like he'd been kicked in the kidneys. "What do you know about Martin?"

"You didn't seem too pleased with him just now."

"Join the club," he said. "Now get off my site. If you're still here in thirty seconds, I'll have you thrown out."

I held my hands up. "It's all right," I said, backing away. "I'm going."

Maybe I should have felt sorry for the man, for his unthinkable loss, but he hadn't made it easy to do.

Andrew Cantor's taxi pulled up as I was walking to my car. He paid the driver, and walked toward me with the long cardboard cylinder under one arm.

I said casually, "I could have saved you the cab fare."

"The company pays," he said.

"So spare me one minute."

"About Maya? Why? What business is it of yours?"

"Your mother is trying to figure out why she killed herself. She asked me to help."

"What are you, some kind of therapist?"

I had to laugh at that. When it came to therapy, I probably needed it more than anyone I could counsel. "I'm an investigator," I said.

"My mom hired an investigator? About Maya?"

"She needs help."

"You're telling me." He looked down at the rutted earth around him and scratched absently at his neck, where the old acne scars were. "Look, I have to show my dad these drawings."

"Your dad said Maya wasn't the type to mope about things."

"He spoke to you?"

"Sure," I said. "Just now. So help me out here. Help your mom. Two minutes, Andrew. Come on."

"You said one minute before. And there isn't much I can tell you," he said. "We weren't that close lately. We used to be when we were little. When we were going to the same schools and summer camps. When we were living in the same house. But we grew apart once I got into the business."

"When was that?"

"After university. I worked summers for my dad while I did my business degree—straight construction jobs, nothing fancy, so I could learn everything from the ground up. Like he did. But Maya never had the slightest interest in business. Not Dad's, or any kind."

"She wanted to be an actress?"

"Always. And she was good. I always went to see her plays. But she was into other things lately that seemed to get between us."

"Like what?"

"I don't know. All this environmental stuff, I guess. She used to look up to me when we were younger. The older brother, right? Now all of a sudden I couldn't do anything right. She'd bug me if I was having coffee in a Styrofoam cup instead of a mug. Or because I drive instead of cycling—like I could do that in a suit—or that I don't take public transit, which I can't do with all the places I have to be every day. I mean, I don't care what other people do. I don't bug them about it. But she was getting obsessive about it lately—like she wanted to impose a carbon tax on everyone."

"The night she died, Andrew."

His face darkened and his shoulders stiffened inside his coat. "I have to—"

"Just tell me what she and your dad were arguing about."

"I don't think so. Dad says what happens in the family, stays in the family."

"And look where it got Maya."

"That's not fair. You make it sound like it was Dad's fault she killed herself, and it wasn't. It's not like they had a big screaming match."

"But they did argue."

"Everyone argued. A little."

"What about?"

"I don't even know you. And you're prying into things . . ."

"That hurt?"

"That are none of your business."

"Doesn't your mom have a right to know?"

He glared at me for playing the mom card then sighed deeply. "Maya was just being Maya. Getting on Dad's case about this project."

"Why?"

"I don't know exactly. It started in the den. First she got into it with Nina. Don't ask me what about. Then with Dad. I didn't hear everything. Maya was afraid this project would have a big impact on the environment. Maybe a few ducks would lose their habitat or something. Which is bullshit."

He pointed to the southern expanse of the job site, where a lone Canada goose was drinking from a small stream that had formed in ruts left by giant tires. "All that is going to be parkland," he said. "Twelve per cent of the land. And we were only required to allocate ten. There will be grass and trees and ponds." He swallowed hard a couple of times. "It's all going to be beautiful. The park, the marina, the residences, the shops. All of it. And we're the ones building it."

A tear rolled down his cheek and he wiped it with the back of his hand. "I just wish my sister was here to see it," he said.

slipped through a curtain into a room that had been painted entirely black. Walls, ceiling, floor, stage, all the same flat black. A square the size of a small bedroom had been taped off on the stage. The tape glowed lightly as if radioactive.

About twenty people were watching a young man who was sitting at a desk, reading a thick blue book, pencilling notes in its margins. A pretty blonde with dishevelled hair stood behind a line of tape and knocked on an invisible door, stamping her foot twice to provide the sound. The man looked up from his book, his face darkening, as though he'd been expecting—dreading—this visitor. He closed the book and walked to where the woman stood. He mimed opening the door and stepped aside as the woman entered. Before either of them could say anything, an older man sitting in the front row called, "Stop."

He was in his forties, muscular, bald with a wispy hairline of implants combed back from his crown. Theo Harris, who had been Maya Cantor's drama teacher.

The actor looked at him with a petulant frown. "Why'd you stop us so soon? I didn't think we got far enough to screw up."

"Don't jump to conclusions, James," Harris said. "I just want to try something here."

He climbed up onto the stage and took the actress aside. He whispered briefly in her ear, then went into the darkened wings and returned with something held behind his back. He slipped the object into the pocket of her coat and then climbed down and took his seat. "Once more, please."

James sat down at the desk and resumed reading. I moved quietly to the back row of chairs and eased into one.

The actress stamped her foot again. James closed the book as he had before and went to the door with the same dark look on his face. He opened the invisible door but before he could look away, the actress pulled a small black revolver from her pocket and jammed it against his chest.

James jumped back with a startled look. "What are you doing? That's not in the scene."

Harris stood again. "*You* weren't in the scene, James. You knew before the knock who was going to be there and why she was there. Didn't you?"

James stared sullenly at the black floor.

"Joe Clay doesn't know who's there, does he?" Harris asked.

"No."

"If he did, would he open the door? Think of what Kirsten represents to him now. To you. You've finally achieved sobriety. You're finally on the road back to your self. And she is dangerous to you, isn't she?"

James's jaw was set so tightly, the word "Yes" barely escaped.

"I pulled that little stunt with Alicia because I wanted to see surprise on your face. I wanted to see the look of a man who can lose everything he has in a split second if he isn't careful. That's where Joe is right now, isn't he? That's where you are if you are Joe."

"I guess."

"Don't guess, James. Know. Know that you are on a tight-rope with no net. All you have is the little bit of strength you've discovered since you started going to AA. So if it takes a gun to find it in yourself, next time she knocks on the door I want you to see that gun whether it's in her hand or not."

"We were devastated when we heard about Maya. Devastated. This sort of thing happens so often with actors—they're hardly the most stable beings on the planet—but Maya Cantor? No one saw it coming."

We were sitting in Theo Harris's office one flight up from the theatre, drinking coffee. He was also wolfing down an egg salad sandwich, for which he apologized. "If I don't eat before my next class, I'll be tripping from hypoglycemia."

"What sort of student was she?" I asked.

He mulled it over for a moment before answering. "Capable, I would say. She certainly had talent. I wouldn't say she was gifted, not in the sense that Alicia Hastings is. If you'd seen more of Alicia's work in that scene today, you'd know what I mean. I never should have paired her up with James. He is so mannered, so constipated emotionally. She blows him away without even speaking."

"And Maya?"

"An attractive girl. An attractive person. Open to her emotions and her instrument. Some students come by it naturally and others have to work at it. Maya was more in the second category and she did work at it—more last year than this, I have to say."

"Why do you think that was?"

"My impression? Something else had captured her imagination. Maybe a boy. Maybe another career idea. A lot of kids come in here thinking they're going to be the next Seth Rogen, the next Ellen Page, but they realize pretty quickly how tough it is out there. Competition for parts in our productions is fierce and to be honest, the U of T program isn't considered among the elite. The really talented kids go to New York or to Yale or skip school entirely and get right to work."

"You think Maya had come to that realization?"

"It's possible. She auditioned well enough and acquitted herself honourably in the parts she did get, but like I said, that hardly paves the way for a career in the theatre."

"Did she ever seem depressed to you? Despondent about her prospects?"

"Let me tell you something, Mr. Geller. I have seen some pretty high-maintenance people in my time. Not just as a teacher, but as a director, which I was for many years in the outside world." He pointed at the wall behind him, where posters of his professional productions of *The Threepenny Opera*, *Twelfth Night*, *Fifth of July* and others had been framed. "I've seen actors threaten to kill themselves when they weren't cast at Stratford or the Shaw Festival. I've had students who've dropped out—not just out of school but their very lives—when they didn't get parts they wanted. I've had the drunken midnight phone calls, the sob sessions right in this office, even threats . . . all the histrionics they couldn't deliver in their work. But Maya Cantor conducted herself quite professionally in everything she did. Last year, she directed *Trojan Women*, and she handled the cast beautifully, which was no easy task. She had a boatload of drama queens in that one and never lost her cool."

"What about the last month or two?"

"She wasn't as focused on her work. A few weeks before she died, we held auditions for a production of *Women in Transit* and she didn't sign up."

"Was that unusual?"

"Let me put it this way: Very few plays have as many good female roles. Every actress in the program auditioned for it."

"Did she say why she didn't audition?"

"No. Not to me, anyway. I heard she was involved in an outside project—a guerrilla theatre sort of thing where actors confront politicians or business types about one issue or another—but that shouldn't have prevented her from trying for a part."

"You weren't concerned?"

"Not really. In retrospect, maybe I should have been. But she didn't seem down at all. Quite energized in fact. It's just that her energy was being applied elsewhere."

"Was she seeing anyone that you know of? Anyone from her class?"

He thought about it, then shook his head. "A lot of mingling goes on in a theatre program. People work intensely together. They fall desperately in and out of love. They're trying on new personalities, in a way. Behaving outrageously, passionately, even foolishly, as if it's expected of them as artists. Again, Maya didn't seem to go for that. She knew who she was." Harris looked down at the papers piled on his desk, snippets of drama written over the centuries, words to be spoken by students vying for their moment in the spotlight.

"At least I thought she did."

CHAPTER 7

When I got back to the office, Jenn was slumped in her chair looking utterly downcast. If the cloud over her head had been any blacker, the room would have been filling with the smell of ozone.

"How bad?" I asked.

"Bad enough to go through the apartment of a girl who killed herself," she said. "But to do it with her mother . . . I can't tell you how many times she cried. My shoulders must be soaking wet."

"Sorry you had to do it."

"You are not. You're just relieved it wasn't you."

"I won't argue. So what was her place like?"

Jenn sipped from a cup of tea. "Neat for a student. Well organized. Nice enough furniture but nothing too fancy. A step above the usual garage sale look. Lots of film posters and theatre books. Lots of music."

"Anything stand out?"

"One thing," she said. "The kind that makes you go, 'What's wrong with this picture?' Her bed was made. I stood in her bedroom, wondering who makes their bed in the morning and kills themselves at night?"

"Maybe someone tidied up after."

"Nope. Marilyn said no one has touched anything since she died. Everything's exactly as it was when they found her."

"What else?"

"She had a laptop but Marilyn didn't know the log-on or email passwords."

"We can get around those."

"I told her that. She let me take it, as long as we share everything with her once we get in."

"You bring it to Karl?" Karl Thomson owned a shop called Hard Driver, and had helped us set up our computers when we opened our agency. He could crack passwords the way other men crack wise.

"I dropped it off on the way here. He said he'll call later today or first thing tomorrow."

"What about her phones?"

"A land line and a cell. Luckily they both stored recent calls, incoming and outgoing." She passed a handwritten list across the desk, with one number circled. "She got nearly a dozen calls on both phones from this one the week before she died. Called it a lot too."

"*Cherchez l'homme?*" I asked.

"Let's call and find out."

I dialled the number and turned on the speaker. After three rings, a male answered.

"Hi," I said. "Who's this?"

"You called me, you should know," he said. "This a sales call?"

"No. It's about a girl named Maya Cantor."

"Aw, geez. She's the one who, um . . ."

"Yes. Someone at this number called her a lot."

"Not me, man. My roommate."

"What's his name?"

"I don't know if I should give that out. Who are you?"

"My name is Jonah Geller. I'm working for her family.

Trying to find out a little more about why she killed herself. Was your roommate seeing Maya?"

"Seeing like in dating? No, man, I don't think they had that going on. Look, tell you what. Leave your number and I'll give it to Will. He wants to call you back, it's up to him."

I wrote "Will" on the paper next to the number.

"Tell me something. Is he a theatre student too?"

"Will? Get out. He's in enviro studies. Aw shit, I shouldn't be telling you any of this. Ask him yourself if he calls you back." And he hung up.

Jenn used the phone in the front room, working through her list of Maya's friends. I searched a media database for news accounts of the Harbourview project and found one critic repeatedly quoted: a developer named Gordon Avrith, president of a company called SkyHigh Development, which was building a sixty-storey tower at Bay and King.

When I told his secretary I was calling about the Birkshire Harbourview, she put me right through.

"What's your interest in the project?" he asked.

"Not quite sure yet," I said.

"But you're an investigator, so you must be investigating something."

"Must be."

"You could start with how he got that piece of land. I bid on that too, but somehow he walked away with all the marbles. Then there's all the variances they got from city council. Zoning, density, land use. How the OMB rubber-stamped everything despite concerns about the environmental impact."

The OMB is the Ontario Municipal Board, the body that resolves land use and community planning issues when the parties involved can't come to an agreement.

"How'd he get his variances?" I asked.

"If I knew that," Avrith said, "I'd be doing the same damn thing. This business," he sighed. "Sometimes I think I'd be better off cleaning toilets with a toothbrush."

"How well do you know Rob Cantor?"

"I've known him since he worked for his old man. You know his father, Morton?"

"No."

"Christ, I've known *him* since he went by Mendy. It's a family business, right? Like a lot of these companies. Rob's grandfather, Abie, was a plumber, worked for a landlord that had buildings up and down Spadina. He saved up enough to buy his own building and when Mendy—sorry, *Morton*—was old enough to work for him, they bought more buildings. Never built any, just bought. Set up a property management company, and that's where Rob started out. Cleaning apartments. Painting when tenants moved out. Schlepping out the crap they left behind."

"How did he get into development?"

"He's a smart kid, I'll give him that."

"Kid?"

"Hey, to me he's a kid. I'm his father's vintage. Older even. I won't say how old, except to say too goddamn old for the way things are these days. Anyway, he went to school, got a degree in architecture. When his father retired, he took the company in a new direction. Sold off the old buildings and started putting up new ones. Cantor Property Management became Cantor Development. And now he's hooked up with Simon Birk and thinks the sun shines out of his ass. But I will tell you this. Something is going on with that project. I don't know what it is—and I got too many of my own problems to hire you if that's what you're looking for—but there is no way in hell he got that piece of land without paying someone off. In my humble opinion. Could have been a new addition on someone's house, a new deck at the cottage. Hell, I once got a councillor's vote by guaranteeing him a parking spot in his mistress's building. But proving it?" Avrith chuckled. "That's another story. They never leave proof, these *gonifs*, they leave slime trails. Anyway, you're the investigator, so go find something. And when you do, I'll buy the party hats."

"You have something against Rob Cantor?"

"He's competition, isn't he?"

I surfed the Ontario Municipal Board website until I had grasped enough of the lingo regarding regulations, legislation and appeal process to call the office of the chairman, Mel Coren. I told his assistant I wanted information about the Birkshire Harbourview project.

"Are you one of the parties involved?" she asked.

"Not exactly."

"Either you are or you are not."

"Okay, not. I'd just like to ask Mr. Coren—"

"Mr. Coren cannot comment on hearings or decisions of the board," she said. "The legislation expressly forbids it."

"Couldn't I—"

"No, you could not. Copies of all decisions are posted on our website. We recommend searching by case number. Do you have one?"

"No. I don't suppose you could—"

"No, I cannot."

"Is there anyone else I can ask about the decision?"

"No, there is not."

Boy, who saw that coming.

"The Board operates like the court system," she said. "Allowing staff members to paraphrase or interpret decisions creates a risk of distorting or confusing the original decision. Letting the written decisions speak for themselves prevents ambiguity and confusion. Are you familiar with the phrase *res ipsa loquitur?*"

"No, I am not," I said.

"It means 'the thing speaks for itself.'"

"You certainly do," I said.

Jenn had reached one more of Maya's friends while I'd been getting frosted by the OMB.

"Her name's Stacy Manning," she said, "and she's known Maya since grade school."

"And?"

"More of the same. Maya was the last person she thought would ever do it. She even said, and I quote, 'I'm more the type to kill myself, or at least threaten it.'"

"For someone in drama school, Maya wasn't very dramatic. Did Stacy know anything about Will?"

"Never heard the name. Speaking of which . . ."

"Yes?"

"Where's his number?"

I passed it to her and she dialled it. "Watch how the big girls do it."

"Hello?" she said breathily. "Is that Will? Oh . . . are you his roommate? Oh, hi there. He told me about you. What's your name again? Evan, that's right. Evan," she said dreamily, "when will he be in? Oh. Well, I wonder if you could do me a favour."

Evan couldn't see how beautiful Jenn was, but her voice alone would have made me jump through flaming hoops. I half expected her to break into a chorus of "Happy Birthday, Mr. President."

"I met Will at a party the other night and he *really* wanted my phone number but I usually don't give it out to guys I don't know. You know how it is . . . So he wrote down his number and his name—oh, geez, I can't even read his last name. Sterling? That's funny, it looks like Steeling here. So will he be in later, you think? Oh. Okay. No, I'll try him again. Thanks, Evan. What? Oh, that's sweet. I hope to meet you too."

My eyes had pretty much rolled to the back of my head by the time she hung up.

"Guys," she said. "They are so defenceless."

"Let's hope Will is too," I said.

Now that we had his full name, I called the U of T's Environmental Studies Program.

"I'm trying to get in touch with a student named Will Sterling," I told the man who answered.

"I'm sorry," he said. "We can't give out a student's number."

Okay. At least he'd confirmed Will was a student there. "I'm supposed to meet him before his class tomorrow morning," I said. "Could you tell me what time it starts?"

I heard the rustling of paper . . . "Enviro 1410," he said. "Starts at 9:30. You know where the Earth Sciences Building is?"

"Do tell," I said.

Jenn was looking at the list of phone calls Maya had made during the last week of her life. "Between calls to her mom, her dad, her girlfriends and Will Sterling, I think we've accounted for all of them," she said. "Except this one."

It was a 312 area code—not a local call. I dialled it, listened for a moment and hung up without saying a word.

"What?" Jenn asked.

"That," I said, "was the office of Simon Birk."

What are we doing wrong?" Jenn sighed.

We were scrolling through floor plans of the penthouse units of the Birkshire Harbourview website, logged in as prospective buyers. As if.

"Those twelve-foot ceilings . . . those windows . . . those views. And that kitchen, my God, it's bigger than my whole top floor!"

"We're not doing anything wrong," I said. "We just don't aspire to that lifestyle."

She flashed me a look that was both contemptuous and somehow compassionate. "How little you know me," she said.

"Never mind, Ivana. Go to the part where the man himself speaks."

She clicked on a feed of a video Simon Birk had recorded the previous spring, when his partnership with Rob Cantor had first been announced. He stood at the top of a skeletal iron tower in Chicago, many storeys above the city, wind ruffling the hem of his overcoat.

"My name is Simon Birk," he told the camera. "And some of you may have heard of me." A grin at his own joke, his capped teeth white as virgin snow. "You've seen my name on some of the greatest buildings on the continent. You've stayed in my hotels, played in my casinos, eaten in my restaurants and danced the night away in my clubs. You may think of me as a man who builds towers like this one, Chicago's own Birkshire Millennium Skyline, scheduled to open next spring. But what I really build, my friends, are dreams."

The camera moved in closer. Birk was not a handsome man in any conventional sense. He had a bulbous nose, fleshy lips, bushy eyebrows, and a thick bony ridge hooding his pale blue eyes. Yet it was a face that commanded your attention.

"What are your dreams? That somewhere in your great city of Toronto, a city I love almost as much as my native Chicago, is a residence that reflects your desires, your aspirations, your success? Built by a man who spares nothing, cuts no corners, to bring you the very best in luxury living?"

"Think he's impressed by himself?" I said.

"I choose my projects carefully," Birk was saying. "And my partners even more so. So I'm delighted to be working with Toronto's finest developer, a man who shares my drive for perfection in every detail, Rob Cantor of Cantor Development. Together, we are creating an unforgettable domain where you'll be surrounded by the best of everything: Indonesian hardwood, granite countertops, travertine marble and stainless steel appliances. You'll know from the moment you visit this website—or even better, our model suite—that this is where you want to live."

"My kingdom for a Dramamine patch," I moaned.

"Shut up," Jenn said. "My aspirations are climbing by the minute."

"To meet your expectations," Birk said, "we have sought out only the finest craftsmen, the finest goods, to bring you the new crown jewel of the Toronto port lands, the Birkshire Harbourview. For a virtual tour of the complex, just click on the link below. Better yet, click on the green link to join our exclusive mailing list."

"How exclusive can it be if anyone can join?" Jenn muttered.

"These magnificent residences will sell out fast," Birk said. "We anticipate every unit to be pre-sold before completion, so—"

Jenn had finally had enough too. She clicked off the web feed and left Simon Birk in mid-sentence. Something, I guessed, not too many people did.

"Hey," she said, looking at her watch. "Don't you have a date to get ready for?"

"Won't take me long."

"You're not going out dressed like that, are you?"

"You been talking to my mother?"

"Seriously. Why don't you knock off?"

"What about you?"

"I'll hang here awhile," she said. "Karl said he might swing by with Maya's computer after he closes up."

"He cracked her password?"

"Like an egg, he said."

"That's our boy. It'll be interesting to see what's on there," I said. "Because no one so far has a clue about why Maya did it. Her mother, brother, father, even her theatre prof: can they all be in denial?"

"It's the same with her girlfriends," Jenn said. "They were just as sure—insistent, even."

"She was a doer, Jenn. She wasn't withdrawing from the world, giving her things away, dropping hints, crying out for help. She'd never attempted suicide before, and how many people succeed on the first try? She was energetic, involved, engaged in things. And by all accounts, she wasn't faking it."

She looked at me across the desk. "Her mother said it couldn't have been an accident, not with that high wall around the balcony."

"You check it out?"

She nodded. "It's more than waist high on me, and I'm six feet. Marilyn said Maya was five-seven."

We sat for a moment in silence, broken only by the hum of machinery, traffic on Broadview, the sound of our breathing, the beating of still-living hearts.

"Why did she call Simon Birk?" I asked.

"Maya?"

"Yeah."

"He's her father's partner."

"What could he tell her that Rob couldn't?"

"Or wouldn't."

"We know she had a fight with Rob the night she died."

"And she had a bug up her ass when it came to the environment."

"We know a lot of the port lands are polluted."

"Except they'd have had to clean the site before they started building. Wouldn't they?"

"Yes. You can't break ground without an environmental assessment. The soil and water have to be analyzed and cleaned first."

I sat back down at my desk and went back to the Birkshire Harbourview's web page, then clicked onto a link that listed all the partner firms involved: the engineers, architects, banks and construction company.

The engineering firm that conducted the water and soil testing on the site was called EcoSys.

"Check this out," I said to Jenn.

The founder and chief executive officer of EcoSys was one Martin Glenn.

CHAPTER 9

I did indeed change my clothes for my date with Katherine Hollinger. I showered and shaved and put on clean black jeans and a black shirt that I smoothed on my dresser with my hands—one day I'd buy an iron—and over that a black cashmere blazer, the one jacket in my closet that didn't look like it had been fished out of a donation chute.

Hollinger lived in a condo on Bay near St. Joseph. I took the Bloor Street Viaduct across the Don River Valley, watching the last light of the setting sun through the Luminous Veil, two walls of metal rods built on either side of the bridge to keep people from jumping. The viaduct had been the city's main suicide magnet for years, the combination of the fall and oncoming Parkway traffic a guarantee of success. I doubted the Veil had cut the number of suicides, just shifted them elsewhere: another bridge, a subway, a razor or pills. Dorothy Parker had once written a poem about the many ways to do yourself in, but each had drawbacks, she wrote, so you might as well live. Maybe they should have etched those words in the stone of the viaduct, instead of spending $5 million installing the Veil's nine thousand rods.

I parked in front of Hollinger's building and entered the lobby. She was waiting there for me, her black hair tied back in a simple ponytail, leaving more of that face to savour.

"I figured I'd save you the trouble of parking," she said. "You leave your car here for a second and they ticket you."

All I could think of to say was hello.

"Hello yourself," she said and leaned in and kissed my cheek. Whatever scent she wore was lightly floral; just a trace of it to cloud my thoughts. When she stood back, I took a long, slow look at her. I could see murder suspects confessing just to keep her eyes on them, just to win a smile.

"Jonah?"

"Yes?"

"Shall we go?"

"Go?"

"They don't serve food in my lobby."

We drove to the entertainment district, where old warehouses on Richmond, Adelaide and surrounding streets had been turned into massive nightclubs that turned drunken patrons out into the streets by the thousands at closing time. Spewing, pissing, weaving around in search of their cars, getting into fist fights over nothing. Occasional gunshots ringing out, usually directed at bouncers who had turfed out punks whose manhood was measured by the length of a gun barrel.

At this time of night, though, it was peaceful, the coloured lights of restaurant signs sharp and clear in the brisk autumn air. The temperature had dropped. Hollinger had drawn her coat closer around her as we walked up John Street. I wanted to put my arm around her, warm her the way her eyes warmed me, but it seemed a little soon for that. Maybe on the way out, with a good meal and a glass of wine or two inside me.

A black belt in karate, an expert in Krav Maga, a guy who could dismantle most opponents before they knew they were in a fight, and I felt like a hapless schoolboy around this woman.

Man, it felt good.

Then I saw the name of the restaurant we had stopped in

front of, and my stomach dropped like an elevator whose cables had snapped.

It was called Giulio's.

She had said it was a place that served real southern Italian cooking. I should have asked the name. Because there was no way in hell I was going in there, not with Hollinger. One look at the owner, one hint that he and I had a relationship, and I'd be lucky if all she did was slap my face and walk out. Lucky if I didn't wind up cuffed.

Giulio's was now owned by none other than Dante Ryan, once a notorious hit man for the crew run by Marco di Pietra. He had told me this weeks ago on the phone, thanking me for my help in getting him out of the contract killing line and into something he could live with, telling me I'd never have to pay a bill in the place. That I could put my name on a stool at the bar. He'd told me how the man who had run it for forty years, Giulio himself, seventy pounds overweight and proud of it, had finally been ready to retire just when Ryan was looking to buy a place. He said he was keeping the name, the staff and most of the menu, adding just a few dishes from his mother's own collection of Calabrian recipes.

He said he was there every night, menus in hand, greeting guests the way Giulio did, even putting on a few pounds for the cause.

So how exactly was I going to explain to Hollinger—a cop who'd spent the last four months pondering the deaths of the Di Pietra brothers and their associates—that Dante Ryan was a personal friend of mine.

"Uh, listen," I said.

"Yes?"

"Let's go somewhere else."

"Why? I thought you liked Italian."

"I, um . . ."

"What?"

"I had Italian for lunch."

"Jonah. We agreed on Italian before lunch. Why would you—"

"I forgot."

"You forgot?"

"My client took me out. She insisted on Italian."

"I can't believe—"

"Plus this place got a shitty review."

"Where?"

Grab that shovel, Geller. Dig yourself a deeper hole.

"One of the papers."

"Which one?"

"Come on, Kate. This street is full of restaurants."

"All of which require a reservation, which we happen to have at Giulio's."

"You don't feel like a good steak or something?"

"If I did, I would have made reservations at a steak house. Jonah, what's going on?"

"I just don't feel like Italian."

She crossed her arms over her chest, tightening up, widening the space between us. Pretty soon I wouldn't be able to see across it. "This is not starting well," she said.

"Greek?" I asked.

"Fuck Greek and fuck steak. There's something you're not telling me and I don't like it. I get lied to all damn day, Jonah. I get lied to by suspects, by snitches, by reporters—Christ, half the time by my partner. I do not need it from you."

"Kate . . ."

"What!"

I put my hands on her shoulders. They didn't relax one bit. "I can't."

"Tell me why. Right now and no bullshit. I have a very keen detector for it and I'm this close to calling it a night."

"Walk with me for a minute," I said.

—

I don't claim to know how many people Dante Ryan killed during his time in the Mob. I do know he was in it some twenty
years, and he hadn't spent his time stuffing envelopes. Then he
was given a contract that required him to kill a five-year-old
child, a boy the same age as his own son, Carlo, and he hadn't
been able to do it. He sought me out and demanded my help in
finding out who had ordered the hit, determined that the boy
not be part of the price the father had to pay for trying to get
free of a Mob enterprise.

We did it, too. Saved the lives of the boy and his parents.
Saved each other too. And somehow became friends. Ryan had
decided by then he had to get out of his old life in order to save
his marriage, his soul, and I had helped. He had helped me too,
in his own way. If it wasn't for our misadventures, I'd still be at
Beacon Security, working other people's cases instead of my
own. And there was a spark to him you don't find in everyone, a
warmth you wouldn't expect in a man who had done all that he
had done in his life. An old-fashioned devotion to his family.
Generosity and loyalty to anyone he considered a friend.

I could explain it to myself, rationalize it a dozen different
ways. But what could I say to Hollinger, who was searching my
eyes with hers, hoping for some truth.

We found a table at a small café a few doors down from
Giulio's. The hostess told us they'd had a last-minute cancella-
tion and took our drink orders: Black Bush for me and a vodka
martini for Hollinger. It gave me a few more minutes to look
for a starting point to my story. I was still looking for it when
the drinks arrived.

"This isn't going to be easy," I said.

"Great opening, Geller. I'm brimming with confidence."

"Do you know who owns Giulio's?"

"No," she said. "Should I?"

"No. But you would have if we'd gone in there."

"Why?"

I sighed like a shot-out tire. "Does the name Dante Ryan ring a bell?"

There was a candle in an amber glass on our table. Its flames were dancing in her eyes, until they narrowed and the reflecting flames grew smaller. She said, "Alarm bells. Big loud ones."

"He's the owner."

"Okay," she said. "I get it. You were trying to protect me, is that it? You thought I'd be uncomfortable, vulnerable somehow, eating in a place owned by a mobster?"

She had given me the perfect out. But taking it wouldn't have been right. If Hollinger and I were going to go anywhere, she needed to know the truth—at least about this.

"There's more to it," I said.

"How much more?"

"For one thing, he's not a mobster anymore. He's out of the life now."

"No one gets out of that life."

"He did."

"Even if that's true, I'd like to know how you know it."

The look she was giving me made me feel like we were back in the interview room at police headquarters. "He's a friend," I said.

"Dante Ryan is a friend of yours? The same Dante Ryan we've looked at for, I don't know, half a dozen killings?"

If all they'd looked at was half a dozen, it had to be because of jurisdictional issues. The other killings must have taken place in Hamilton, Peel Region, or areas covered by the Ontario Provincial Police.

"Yes."

She sat back in her chair, arms across her chest again. "And he's a friend of yours."

"Yes."

"Not just a passing acquaintance."

"No."

She said, "Well. This is surprising, to say the least."

"You understand why I didn't want to—"

"Oh, yeah."

"I never expected it would come up. Not tonight."

"That makes two of us. So was he out of the life when you became pals?"

Cue the sound of a toilet flushing. Any chance I had of a relationship with her was swirling down the tank and into Lake Ontario. "No. He was still in his previous occupation."

"Hired killer."

"He worked for Marco di Pietra. I'll leave it to your imagination what he did."

"Do yourself a favour. Don't."

The waitress picked that moment to lay two menus on our table. Then she pointed to a blackboard where the evening's specials were written in coloured chalk. Pink for the meat dish, yellow for the fish, white for the pasta.

Blue for the mood.

"Please give us a minute," Hollinger said to the waitress.

"No worries," she replied.

When she was gone I said, "I never hired Ryan, if that helps."

"Be serious, damn it. Jonah," she said, trying to rein in her anger, keeping maybe half of it in check. "I'm not like you, I didn't just fall into being a detective. From the day I started in the Niagara Regional Police, I wanted to be a detective, and from the day I made detective, I wanted to be Homicide. There are thirty-two of us, not counting support staff. We're the elite. We do the best work, get the highest job satisfaction ratings on internal surveys. Wear the best suits. Life satisfaction isn't always the highest—way too many of us are divorced—yeah, me too." The first small grin. "Another cop in Niagara, a hometown boy. I left him behind when I was offered the Toronto job. The point is, they call us the Snappy Suits for a reason. It's all men, except me. There was another woman, Carol Wisnewski."

"I know the Noose."

"She's on mat leave now. So it's me and the guys. If I treat the men under me well, they think I'm soft and try to get away with everything they can. If I'm hard on them, I'm a bitch. Half the meetings I go to, I could be chairing, everyone's saying, 'Guys . . . get out there, guys . . . ' You know how hard it is to make Homicide sergeant before the age of forty? Not easy for a man and ten times harder for a woman. I can't afford to get blind-sided, Jonah. Not by anyone. So tell me how on earth a man like you—or the man I thought you were—becomes friends with a contract killer?"

I was liking her better by the minute, even as she slipped farther away. "Our paths just crossed a while back," I said lamely. "By accident. He needed help with a personal matter, and I helped him."

"Aren't you neighbourly."

"Kate, I know it looks bad—"

"Looks bad? It fucking stinks, Jonah. He kills people for money. Where are your boundaries?"

"He has nothing to do with the way I live."

"Judgment, then."

"Who am I to judge anyone?"

"Well, I have to judge you," she said. "I have to be dead careful about who I let into my personal life, because the second I do let someone in, he shows up on my work screen. And you're already up there." She reached into her purse and withdrew a twenty from a zippered pocket. "That should cover the drinks."

"So that's it? Guilt by association?"

"Not just *any* association. Don't you get it? Dante Ryan is the kind of man I live to put away. Day in, day out, I work this job of mine. I see kids being shot by other kids because they gave them the wrong look. Husbands who kill their wives because the pork chops burned. And men found in the trunks of their cars because they got involved in organized crime. Dante Ryan kills people—not in passion or anger or on the spur of the moment—but for money, plain and simple, and if I had anything to say about it, he'd be doing life in Millhaven, not running a restaurant that I almost took you to."

"If you knew the truth . . ." And then I had to cut myself off, because there was no way I could tell her the truth about Ryan and me without including the nasty ending in the Don River Valley.

I'm not sure what would have happened next—would she have walked out on me?—because her cellphone rang. She unclipped it from her belt, drawing a dirty look from people at the table next to us, and answered with a terse "Yes?" Pause. "Hey, Gregg."

McDonough, her throwback partner. I was glad he couldn't see us. He would have had a hoot if he knew who was sharing her table.

"Where?" she said. "How far away are you? No, I'm closer. I can be there in fifteen minutes. All right. See you there."

She snapped the phone closed. "I have to go."

"You were leaving anyway."

"I'm sorry, Jonah. Can you at least understand why I have to be careful?"

"We all have to be careful when we meet someone we like," I said. "You were the first door I opened in a long time. I didn't expect everything to be easy between us. But I was willing to try."

"I still have to go."

"Where?"

"Church and Wellesley," she said. "A man was beaten to death."

The heart of the gay village. "A bashing?" It wouldn't be the city's first but doing it in the heart of the village was beyond audacious.

"I'll see what the scene has to say when I get there."

"Let me drive you."

"I don't think so."

"Please. It's ten more minutes out of your life. What if there was something I could tell you that would help us get over this hump?"

"I can't imagine what that would be."

I took Adelaide across the lower part of the city, through the deserted financial district, tension filling the car like second-hand smoke.

"There's a lot I can't tell you about Ryan," I finally said, "for your sake as well as his, but I can say this: we came together because he was trying to make good on something and he needed my help to do it. He was trying, believe it or not, to save a life. Not to take one, Kate. To save one. He was trying to prevent something truly horrible from happening. Whatever you might think about him, he was trying to do something good, and he did. And I helped him. I paid a price for that. A high one. And I've been paying for it ever since. But I'm not sorry he came to me, and I'm not sorry about what we had to do. The only thing I am goddamn sorry about is that it came between us tonight."

We were heading north on Jarvis, which had more lanes and less traffic than Church. When we got to the corner of Maitland, Hollinger said, "Drop me here, please."

"You sure?"

"I have a crime scene to work and I need to arrive there on my own. I don't want to be teased or distracted by anyone or anything."

I pulled over and shifted into park. She snapped her seat belt open and put her hand on the door handle. Then she paused. She kept her gaze fixed straight ahead, but her voice seemed to warm a bit when she spoke. "I'm sorry if I seem paranoid about this. I was so ready for a nice evening with you, Jonah. I really was. I thought because the Di Pietra cases were all closed, the time was right, but hearing about Ryan—knowing his association with that crew—it threw me."

"No kidding."

She turned to me and surprised me with a smile. Nothing that lit up the night, but a smile. "Give me some time to process this. Maybe after I've slept on it, it won't seem so bad. If it doesn't, then maybe I'll give you a call."

Two maybes. Hardly ironclad.

She got out of the car and walked toward the alley that ran south off Maitland, where a man's life had ended. I drove one block farther south and parked. I didn't want to crowd Hollinger, but I was curious to see her work a crime scene. I put on a ball cap from my trunk, slipped an old raincoat over my blazer and walked back to the alley.

It was brightly lit—unnaturally so—by halogen lights mounted on stands. Crime scene investigators on TV might walk around with dinky penlights, but in real life they tend to flood scenes with light so as not to miss anything. A crowd had gathered outside the tape that crossed the mouth of the alley. I stood at the back where Hollinger couldn't see me. She was squatting beside the body of a blond male in a grey overcoat, talking to a uniformed officer, probably the first on the scene. After noting how the body had been found, she snapped on a pair of latex gloves and reached carefully into the dead man's pockets. From the breast pocket of his jacket she withdrew a wallet, examined the contents, made a few notes in a spiral notebook, and put the wallet back. A medical examiner came over and lifted the man's head and showed her something at the back. She frowned and touched the area gingerly. The tip of her gloved finger was bloody when she removed it.

She sighed and got to her feet and nodded to two men waiting with a body bag and a gurney. They laid the bag on the ground and unzipped it. One knelt by the victim's head, the other by his feet. When they lifted him over the bag, his head flopped forward and I got a clear look at his face. I gasped loud enough to make people around me turn.

Good thing I was standing near the back.

The dead man was Martin Glenn.

CHAPTER 10

World Repairs pays handsomely to subscribe to a variety of databases, one of which is called BizServe. I logged on remotely to the office server from home and read everything it had on EcoSys then moved on to the company's own website. Between the two of them, I got a pretty good picture of the work that Glenn had done.

He was an engineer by training and had worked for more than a decade for the Ministry of the Environment, helping it define and develop its site assessment policies. At the height of his career, he did what many civil servants do: resigned so he could offer the same services back to the private sector at a consultant's rate, instead of as a modestly paid government drone.

Glenn and his associates helped clients assess the level of groundwater or soil contamination of their property and whether it was worth the cost of reclamation. If so, they would create a remediation plan. Restore soil to levels that matched samples taken from non-polluted sites. Build underground barriers to prevent toxins from seeping into or out of the site. Treat groundwater so polluted you wouldn't use it to put out a fire. Guide clients through the maze of government ministries that might be involved in a large project: the Ministry of the Environment, of course, but also Natural Resources, if a project posed an ecological risk to wetlands and other sensitive areas; and Finance if there were potential tax breaks to be had.

EcoSys would take clients through every step they needed to get a clean Record of Site Condition that met all criteria under ministry guidelines and the federal Environmental Protection Act.

Most of the time, according to the website, the ministry would review the RSC and audit the process to ensure all requirements had been met. "But when a trusted partner like EcoSys has done the work," the site boasted, "with all the necessary skills and judgment, clients can rest easy that the RSC process will be approved in a timely manner."

Martin Glenn had been qualified. As a former employee of the ministry, he would certainly have been trusted. An RSC submitted by him would in all likelihood have been rubber-stamped.

He had left the Harbourview job site in a fury earlier this afternoon and was now on the way to the morgue. I wondered what the hell he had gotten himself into. I also wondered who Eric was. Rob Cantor had told Glenn to think about Eric, and Glenn had been so angry he'd barely been able to respond.

It was ten o'clock when I was done. I was tired and I was also ravenous. I looked in the fridge and found little of interest. So I got into my car and drove back to the entertainment district.

The interior of Giulio's was warm and inviting: the walls a deep vermilion, the tables and chairs glossy black. A fire burned in a stone fireplace along one wall; along the opposite wall was a long bar, where sparkling glasses hung upside down from wooden slats. Dante Ryan was standing at a podium with a reservations book open. When he saw me, his eyebrows raised and he broke into a smile. He set down the red leather-bound menus he'd been holding, came up to me and offered me his hand. We shook, then he pulled me into an embrace, clapping my back twice. "Took you long enough to show your face," he said.

"The place looks fantastic," I said. "*Mazel tov.*"

"You hungry? You here to eat?"

"Yes and yes."

"Have a seat at the bar. I'll have a table for you in five minutes. Gino," he said to the barman. "Whatever this man wants, it's on the house." Then he walked to the back of the room to speak to one of the waitresses.

Gino was a slight, balding man with thin strands of dark hair pasted across his dome. I ordered Black Bush on the rocks. He poured a standard shot then topped it up with another ounce or so.

A loud roar went up at a table behind us where four men in business dress were hoisting drinks and toasting one another. By the look of it, they'd been dining on steak and pasta, with plenty of wine to wash it down. One of them—big, beefy and red-faced—was crowing over a deal that had apparently been consummated that day. "We took no fucking prisoners," he bellowed. "We took fucking scalps."

The patrons at the table next to them glared for a while then went back to their meals. I nursed my drink, wondering what Hollinger was doing now. Still at the crime scene, probably, combing the alley for evidence. Maybe directing a canvass of the neighbourhood. Almost certainly not thinking of me or what the evening could have been.

"Hey!" came a shout from the noisy table. The big man had an empty wine bottle in his hand. "You, behind the bar. Angelo, or whatever your name is. Bring us another bottle of red."

The bartender looked like he wanted to send the bottle airmail. Then Ryan appeared from the back of the restaurant, walking briskly toward the table.

"Sir," he said to the big man. "If you want a bottle of wine, we're happy to serve it to you. But show a little respect for our staff and the other diners. All right?"

The man broke out laughing, egging on his compatriots until they laughed with him. "Oh, sure!" he gasped. "We'll respect the little fucker, won't we?"

Ryan shook his head. I eased off my stool. There were four of them, all drunk enough to mess with Ryan, something no sober man would do. If things got ugly, I'd have his back.

Ryan leaned down, his hand on the table next to the man's dinner plate, and spoke very quietly into his ear. He had once boasted to me about his powers of persuasion, and whatever he said now prompted the man to settle right down, reach into his wallet and pull out a credit card.

Ryan waved down a waitress. "Monica, these gentlemen have to leave," he said. "Bring their bill right away, please. And add a nice tip—twenty per cent okay with you?" he asked the big man, still leaning over him like they were pals. The man nodded quickly.

Only then did I notice the man's steak knife was no longer next to his plate.

The food was outstanding. Ryan wouldn't let me see a menu, just kept sending out dishes for me to sample. First what he called poor man's caviar—herring roe in oil flavoured with hot peppers. Then chilled eggplant seasoned with garlic and oregano. Tuna marinated in a lemon and black olive sauce. And finally lamb chops, Calabrian style, carefully arranged on a plate with grilled red peppers, artichokes and mushrooms.

"I spared you the octopus salad," he grinned. "It's an acquired taste for most people—and for a Jewish guy? I figured it might be over the top."

Each course came with a glass of well-matched wine. The best was the Montepulciano he brought to go with the lamb. "Life's too short to drink cheap wine," he said.

This from a guy who used to shorten lives professionally. Hollinger probably would have broken the bottle over his head.

When dessert came—a tart that was both sweet and fiery—he brought two espressos and sat with me at the table.

"That's made with orange marmalade and a chili jam," he said. "We call it Devil's Tart."

"After the owner's heart," I grinned.

"How was everything?" he asked, his dark eyes fixing on mine. "Honestly."

I said, "Mmph," as I had just stuffed a forkful of tart into my mouth. When I could speak, I said, "You've outdone yourself."

"Thanks. So how come you showed up out of the blue like this? No phone call, nothing."

"It's a long story."

"You and your long stories. I've sat through a few before."

I inhaled the last bite of Devil's Tart and pushed the plate to the side. "Remember the Homicide sergeant who dropped in on me that night?" He'd remember which night: the two of us eating pizza, drinking wine and planning to murder his boss.

"Sure," he said. "Kate? Katie?"

"That's right. Katherine Hollinger."

"Wait a sec. Hollinger. We had a no-show tonight. Seven o'clock for two."

"And you're looking at one of them."

"What happened?"

"She didn't tell me which restaurant she picked. And I didn't ask. Once we got here, it was too late. I had to tell her about us."

"About us what?"

"Being friends."

"And she had a prob—oh, yeah. I guess she would, being Homicide."

"Yup."

"Sorry, guy."

"It's not your fault."

"I can still be sorry. So listen," he said, leaning in. "There's no grief coming my way, is there? About what happened last summer?"

"She told me they've closed the books," I said.

"Because there's no going back for me."

"I think you're clear. I think we both are."

"All right."

"How's Carlo?" I asked.

"He's terrific, thanks. Cara too."

"I'm happy for you," I said.

"Thanks, Geller. And how's your new business, this repair shop of yours?"

"We've got a case."

"I hope it works out better than ours did."

"We did all right."

"Let me rephrase it then: I hope so many bodies don't pile up."

CHAPTER 11

'm walking up a trail in a northern forest, a steep, narrow path lined with club pine and Labrador tea and the brilliant yellow petals of Arctic cinquefoil, opened wide to catch beads of morning dew. I walk carefully over moss-covered rocks that can turn an ankle, past trees scarred by bear claws, birches rubbed free of bark by moose antlers. Step around a nasty clump of wolf shit full of coarse white fur, probably from a meal of rabbit. I come to a fast-running stream and start across a path of stepping stones. I'm almost at the other side when the second-to-last stone gives way under my foot. I look down and it's not a stone at all but the submerged face of a man dressed in a suit. "Watch where you're going!" he snarls and my foot slips off his face and I tip over into the freezing water. Fish bump against me. Something long and slick slides over me. I put my hand down to brace myself and it sinks into the mud and I can't pull it out. The harder I try, the deeper I sink. "You ruined my goddamn suit," says the underwater man. "I'm never going to get these stains out." And the water rises higher around me until I too am beneath the surface.

I woke up with my stomach in a knot, my breath shallow. Seven in the morning and nowhere to go but into the shower, where I tried to wash away the memories of Stefano di Pietra and his miserable end in the Don River. Maybe seeing Ryan last night had brought them back.

I made coffee and took a cup out onto my balcony to look out at the city, as I did every morning. Indian summer was finally ending. The sky was overcast, the morning light weak. A wind was blowing down out of the north through the valley, leaving poplars trembling, stripping them of their remaining leaves.

I wolfed down a bagel and cheese, then grabbed my gym bag and drove a few blocks east to Carlaw Avenue and parked in back of a two-storey building with a sign that said Gym: By Appointment Only.

I had been studying and teaching *shotokan* karate for years. That's how I met Graham McClintock, the man who first recruited me as an investigator. But before karate, while serving in the Bar Kochba Infantry unit of the Israel Defense Forces, I had learned Krav Maga with my sergeant, Roni Galil. Krav Maga is a system of self-defence created by an Israeli army man. It is more elemental than karate, teaching you how to use your own strengths and instincts to fight off attackers. I had only recently gone back to it: it seemed more right for me now than the formal, scripted *katas* of *shotokan*. Krav Maga assumes that every situation is life-and-death, that your attacker has to be put down with maximum efficiency. It is not a sport; it will never be featured in the Olympics. The name itself means close combat: the only rule is there are no rules. Whether fighting one attacker or more, whether they are armed or not, you use everything you can, including objects at hand. You always run if you have the chance. If not, you counterattack at the earliest opening. You bite, gouge eyes, butt heads, rip testicles. You do as much damage as humanly—or inhumanly—possible.

This anonymous gym on Carlaw was run by a man named Eidan Feingold, a former Israeli and world judo champion who'd embraced Krav Maga during his own army stint. I had seen him disarm a volunteer assailant with a knife while the assailant was still thinking about where to stab him. I had seen him slap away a gun pointed at his face before the trigger could be pulled, then take the gun away and pretend to pistol-whip the attacker. He had demonstrated defences against shotguns, garrottes, machetes, anything short of a rocket-propelled grenade, and somehow I think he could deal with that too.

"Yoni," he greeted me. "You're too early for class. Nothing starts before nine."

"I know. I was hoping for a little one-on-one."

He looked at his watch and shrugged. "Sure," he said. "I can give you half an hour." He led me into a small locker room, where I changed into a T-shirt and sweatpants. I put on a helmet, mouth guard, protective cup and arm and shin pads. Eidan did the same. Then he strapped my left arm tight to my body with a belt. The last time I'd been in, we'd been working on a scenario where one arm had been wounded and I had to fight him off with the other.

"Ready?" Eidan asked.

"Ready."

Then he smiled and proceeded to try to kick the living shit out of me. He aimed kicks at my weak left side, punches at my head, keeping me on defence as long as he could. He tried to choke me from the front, which I broke up with a knee to the abdomen. He tried to choke me from behind: I stomped his foot, the way Brazilian jiu-jitsu teaches, then delivered a hammer strike to his head. With only my right arm free, I had to deal with my own mounting frustration as well as his relentless attacks. I finally dropped to one knee, as if exhausted. He moved in with a kick aimed at my head, and my opening came. I planted my right hand and used my legs to sweep his out from under him. As he fell onto his back, I dove on top of him, got my forearm across his neck and head-butted him across the bridge of his nose. Then I rolled away from him and looked for a weapon to use. There was a phone on the wall: in a real-life situation

I'd have ripped it out of its base and either thrown it at him, hammered him with it or wrapped its cord around his neck. I sprinted to it and put my hand on it.

"Stop!" Eidan yelled. "Rip it out and I charge you sixty bucks."

"I wasn't going to. I just wanted you to know I'd found a weapon."

"Like hell," Eidan laughed. He got up off the mat and freed my strapped-in arm and patted my shoulder. I was glad to see I'd made him raise a sweat—a light one, but still a sweat.

"You did all right," he said.

"For a one-armed man."

"You put me down and you found a weapon. That's good."

"But?"

"But you should have run, Yoni. A phone might be okay if there is no way out. But to hit me with it or strangle me—that's what you were thinking?"

"Yes."

"Then you have to get close again. But maybe I'm faking, yes? Maybe I'm waiting for you to get close only to attack you again. And if I do, then maybe I end up with the phone and I am hitting *you* with it or strangling you. You see? We're supposed to be tough guys, yes? But if Krav Maga teaches you anything, it's that you run if the odds are against you. There is no shame in that, Yoni. There is only shame in getting killed when you can save yourself. We like to say Krav Maga is about life and death, yes? But first and most, it's about life."

I was in the office by eight-forty, drinking coffee and wondering if it was too early to call Hollinger, when Eddie Solomon rapped on the door and stuck his head in.

"I heard you come in," he said. "You want to try a fabulous coffee I got? Comes from Indonesia. They only pick the beans after they've been eaten and shit out by some kind of monkey."

"That's some recommendation, Eddie. I think I'll stick with what I have."

"Why the downcast look, my white knight? No dragons to slay?"

"There's no shortage of dragons, Eddie. I'm just not sure I can slay them. You have our fee?"

"Chelsea stood me up last night, but I'm meeting her for lunch so I'll have it this afternoon. One thousand in cash for your labour."

"That's great."

"Beats cleaning out stables, mighty Hercules."

I had to smile. You can't not smile around Eddie Solomon.

"That's better," he said. "I'll drop by after lunch. Your lovely partner will be here, I trust?"

"She'll be here, Eddie. For all the good it'll do you."

"You chase your cars," he said, "and I'll chase mine."

Jenn came in at nine on the dot. "I wanted to call you last night," she said, "but I didn't want to rain on your parade."

"Someone beat you to it," I said, and filled her in first on the disaster that was my date with Hollinger, then on the death of Martin Glenn.

"Jesus," she said. "Between that and Maya's email, there can't be any doubt she was murdered too."

"What email?"

"Karl Thomson came by just after you left." Jenn opened a Mac notebook computer, waited for it to come off standby, then tapped in a password. "This is Maya's sent log," she said. "A lot of the usual things you'd expect from a student: gossip, chit-chat, notes on class projects, scheduling meetings. And then there were a whole bunch to someone calling himself EcoMan."

"Will Sterling?"

"None other. Look at this one, Jonah. Sent the morning of the day she died."

Will, having dinner with dad 2nite . . . will try to find what u need . . . try my cell after 12 . . . M.

"After 12," I said. "Could have meant that night or the next day. Either way, that clinches it. This was not someone who was planning to kill herself."

"She knew something about Harbourview."

"The land. The way it was cleaned."

"Or not."

I needed to get going if I was going to catch Will Sterling before his 9:30 class. "See if you can find out who approved the Record of Site Condition at the Ministry of the Environment," I suggested.

"Why do I get the bureaucrats?" she groaned. "And don't give me any majority owner crap."

"Will flattery work?"

"You can always try."

"You're far more adept at getting people to open up."

"Bureaucrats are not people," she said. "They're like the last mussel on your plate, the one you keep avoiding because there's no place to stick your fork in."

If only I could send in Dante Ryan, maybe with a steak knife in his hand. "Martin Glenn was one of theirs," I said. "Used to be, anyway. When they hear what happened to him, they'll talk to you."

"I still don't feel like I've been flattered much."

"Then consider the majority owner crap pulled."

CHAPTER 12

A handful of young people stood outside the entrance of the University of Toronto's Earth Sciences Building on Willcocks Street, engaging in the distinctly non-environmental practise of smoking.

"Any of you guys know Will Sterling?" I asked.

"Sure," said one of them, an Indo-Canadian girl with blonde streaks in her jet-black hair. "We're in the same chem lab."

"He's probably inside," another said. "He's usually in early."

I had my hand on the door when the girl said, "Wait a sec. That's him coming up behind you."

I turned to see a tall, lanky fellow in black cargo pants and a long black coat kicking his way through fallen leaves, head bobbing to music playing through an iPod. He wore a watch cap over long sandy hair and beat-up black Converse high-tops. The bottoms of his pant legs were stained white with what looked like paint or plaster.

I walked down to meet him before he could get to the door. "Will?"

He didn't hear me and started to move around me. I put my hand on his arm. He flinched, a startled look in his eyes. I could see the question form in his mind—*Do I know you?*—as he pulled out his earbuds.

"I need to talk to you a sec."

"What about?" He had a prominent Roman nose and a slight growth of beard on his chin.

"About Maya Cantor."

He stepped back from me and folded his arms across his chest. "What about her, man?"

"How she died."

"Who are you?"

I told him.

"An investigator?" he said. "For who, her father? I've got nothing to say to you."

He tried to brush past me but I planted myself in his way. "I'm not working for her father, Will."

"No? Then who?"

"For her mother. Marilyn Cantor."

"What for?"

"She wants to know why Maya killed herself. But to be honest, Will, I don't think she did."

"No?"

"No. And I doubt you do either."

"Why?"

"You got her email that night."

"So?"

"I think someone killed her."

"Like who?"

"I don't know yet. Why'd you ask if I was working for her father?"

"Because of who he is and what he does."

"Which is what?"

"Fucking lie, for one thing. Screw up the environment and lie about it."

"How do you know?"

"It's what I do, man. Soil testing and analysis. Environmental policy. Land use. Everything we study here, that man contravenes. Taking land that could all be parks, marinas, wet-lands and building fucking condos for the rich and famous."

"She said in her email to you that she was going to try to find something out at her dad's the night she died. Do you know what?"

"You know anything about PCBs?" he asked.

"Will?" a voice behind me said.

He looked past me and said, "Oh, hi, Professor Jenks."

A trim man in his fifties was standing at the entrance to the building. "I'm late for my own class," he said. "And if you're behind me, what does that make you?"

"Even later," Will said. "Look, man," he said to me. "I gotta run."

"Can we talk later?"

"Got a pen?"

I took out a notebook and pen and he dictated his phone number, which we already had, and an address on Markham Street. "I have some lab work to do, but I should be home by four, five at the latest, and then I'll be in all night. You come by, and I'll give you a lesson in environmental degradation."

He followed his professor into the building. The last of the smokers followed them in.

CHAPTER 13

Forest Hill is one of the wealthiest neighbourhoods in Toronto. The homes are large, the lots huge, the trees dominating, and yet most lawns had nary a leaf on them. They had all been raked, blown, swept and gathered into biodegradable paper bags lined up at the curb for pickup. The larger the lawn, the more bags there were, like rows of tackling dummies bracing for impact.

Rob Cantor's home wasn't the biggest on his block of Dunvegan Road, but it still was in the $2-million to $3-million range. A grey stone château on a fifty-foot lot, with a Japanese maple still hanging onto scarlet leaves, its trunk circled by wilted hostas that had given it up for the year. A massive Infiniti SUV was parked in the driveway, handy in case the new Mrs. Cantor had to transport a cord of firewood or seed for the south forty.

Nina Cantor was the only person left to talk to about the night Maya died, about the fight she'd had with her father. I walked up the flagstone path and used a wrought-iron knocker set in the mouth of a stone lion's head.

No one answered.

I put my ear to the door and heard the loud thump of a bass track that seemed to be coming from the rear of the house.

I walked around the back, where the lawn sloped at least a hundred feet to a cedar gazebo. The house was built on a grade: below ground level at the rear was a set of French doors that led to a finished basement. I knocked on the door. Nothing. The music was louder here, the repetitive techno track so loud the glass was vibrating.

I put my ear to the glass and heard a woman scream, "No!"

"Come on!" a man's voice called gruffly.

"No," she cried. "Don't make me!"

"Do it!" he said. "Just do it, you spoiled bitch!"

I slammed my elbow against a glass pane in the French door and reached in through the broken glass to turn the lock. The doors opened onto a sunken family room, with leather couches and recliners grouped around a floor-to-ceiling entertainment centre. The screams had come from somewhere behind this room. I stood and listened and then heard her cry out again, "I can't! I can't do it!"

I raced across the room and through an open archway into a large bedroom set up as a home gym. A treadmill, a stairclimber, a heavy bag and a man straddling a woman who lay on her back on a weight bench, red-faced, struggling to press free weights up in her gloved hands while the man urged her on. "Come on," he said. "Two more!"

"Get off me, you big shithead," she cursed.

She saw me then and dropped the weights so fast the man had to hop away to avoid getting a toe mashed.

"Who the fuck are you?" she said.

Jonah Geller to the rescue.

The man turned too. About my height but a lot heavier. Built-up pecs and delts that gave him the classic V-shape. Bulging biceps and triceps. Fists curled at his sides.

"I'm sorry," I said to the woman. "I heard you scream and I thought . . ."

"You thought what?" she smirked, getting up off the

bench. "That Perry was having his way with me? Not too likely, I'm afraid. Anyway, you didn't answer my question."

"My name is Jonah Geller."

"And you were lurking outside why?"

"I wanted to speak to you about your stepdaughter."

"My step—oh, Maya, you mean? Sorry, I never exactly thought of her that way. What about her?"

"Could we talk privately?"

"Maya's not really my favourite subject," she said.

"Why don't you take off?" Perry said. "The lady still has work to do."

I ignored him. "I just need a few minutes, Ms. Cantor."

"What are you, her lover? I didn't think she had time for men."

"I'm an investigator."

"Working for who?"

"Maya's mother."

"Marilyn? Another not-so-favourite person. So do I bill her for the broken window or you?"

"Tell him to split, Nina," Perry said. "You don't want your muscles to stiffen up."

"Maybe I want to see *his* stiffen up," she said. "He's kind of cute, you have to admit."

She was a wearing a form-fitting, canary-yellow tank top over spandex pants. She put her hands on her hips, cocked one hip and thrust her chest out. Her figure was nothing short of magnificent, possibly even natural. But she did nothing for me. If eyes are the window of the soul, hers would have been papered over with signs saying Room for Rent.

"Come on. On your way," Perry said. As he came toward me, he slammed his fist into the heavy bag, sending it into a wide circle. Maybe I should have cringed with terror or wet myself. But hitting a bag is a lot easier than hitting a trained fighter who is getting more annoyed by the minute.

"Call him off, Nina," I said.

"You've got to be kidding," she grinned.

I sighed and waited for Perry to throw a punch. I didn't want to disable the guy for doing what he thought he ought to be doing, if indeed a thought had flitted through his head. He put up his hands and tried a left jab, which I blocked easily, then a right cross, which I slipped. While he was thinking about his next move, I slapped him across the face.

"Back off," I told him. "No reason for you to get hurt."

"You bitch," he said. "I'm gonna tear you ap—"

I slapped him again. Both his cheeks were flaming red. He came after me again. I blocked everything he threw and kept slapping him.

"Don't you ever close a fist?" Nina complained.

"Call him off," I said again.

"Why? Maybe you'll train me from now on."

Someone should have trained her a long time ago, in the art of human decency. Or at least keeping her yap shut.

Perry tried to kick me in the groin. This I took personally. I shifted to sidekick position and stomped his shin as it rose toward me. He howled in pain and dropped to the floor, clutching his leg.

"That could have been your knee," I said. "You'd be looking at total reconstruction."

"Oh my God," he moaned. "You fucking asshole, you."

"You're welcome," I said. "Now please go away and let me and the lady talk."

He looked at Nina, who shook her head and grabbed a towel that was hanging on the handlebars of the treadmill and threw it at him. "Go on, Perry," she said. "Dry your eyes and beat it."

He pulled himself up and gave me his best death stare. Not quite Dave Stewart in his Oakland prime, but not half bad.

"Wait here," she said to me.

She helped Perry gather up his things and escorted him out the French doors. I heard him say something to her; I heard her laugh at him in response. I guess she had no salt to rub in his wounds.

"So you're an investigator?" Nina said. "Got a gun?"

"We don't carry guns," I said. I still had a Beretta Cougar hidden in my apartment—a present from Dante Ryan—but hadn't so much as looked at it since last summer's crisis had ended.

"And what exactly are you investigating?"

"Why Maya Cantor died."

"Isn't it kind of obvious? She threw herself off a twelfth-storey balcony."

"Why she did it, then."

"And you're asking me? What, did you run out of other people?"

"Kind of."

"I barely knew the girl," Nina said. "She didn't come around much. I got the feeling she didn't approve of me. Go figure."

"She was here the night she died."

"Yeah, Rob invited her and Andrew for dinner. Not exactly Brad and Angelina as company goes, but they were his kids so I went along."

"I heard there was a disagreement."

"From who, Marilyn?"

"Yes."

"The first Mrs. Cantor," she said, twirling a permed blonde curl around her index finger. "You can see why he got tired of her. I mean, besides her age. Rob might be older than me but he's young at heart. She's, like, fifty at least and looks it."

Personally, I had found Marilyn to be an engaging, naturally attractive woman. Nina was admirable in the way thoroughbreds are, with a glossy mane and highly toned muscles, but she had all the class of a hyena tearing at a carcass.

"About that night . . ."

"Look," she said. "Maya could be very—what's the word I'm looking for—judgmental. She had a way of letting you know what you were doing was all wrong. Me, for instance. I threw a wine bottle into the trash instead of the recycling bin and she goes over and takes it out of the trash and puts it in the bin. Okay, so maybe I should be more conscientious about that stuff, but really, in the end, it's one fucking bottle. Who gives a shit, right? No, she has to put on the big show. Never says a word to me even, just plucks it out of here and puts it into there. Disapproval all the way."

"Why was she mad at Rob? Was it something to do with the Harbourview project?"

"Why would she be mad about that?"

"Because of its impact on the environment."

Nina rolled her eyes and drained her sparkling water. "It is so easy for some people to get all worked up about their causes. Their big issues. It makes me laugh, I swear. Where did she think she'd be without Rob's money? You think Maya paid for her apartment or her car or her trips down south with her friends at March Break? If it wasn't for Rob's new building, or his other buildings for that matter, she'd have been living at home and getting around on the TTC. Buying clothes at Honest Ed's."

"But that is what they argued about?"

"I couldn't tell you. I wasn't in the room at the time."

"Andrew said you were. In the den, I believe."

"What is this, Clue? Nina in the den with a candlestick? Yeah, we had a few words. I told you, she didn't like me. She was still pissed off that Rob left Marilyn. Christ, you'd think she'd have gotten over it already. She wasn't a little girl, you know. She was a grown-up woman, barely ten years difference between her and me. As for what she and Rob fought about, I couldn't tell you. I wasn't there."

"Where were you?"

"In the kitchen," she said with a lazy smirk. "Taking the wine bottle out of the recycling and putting it back in the trash."

CHAPTER 14

What is it about men that causes them to lose their minds at mid-life? How could Rob Cantor ditch an intelligent, down-to-earth woman—not to mention the mother of his children—for someone like Nina, who had all the depth of a pie plate? Why hadn't he simply gone out and bought a Porsche or a vintage Stratocaster or gotten a tattoo?

Mind you, my uncle Phil—my late father's youngest brother—bought a Miata convertible for his fiftieth birthday and had it all of three weeks before he drove it into the back of a dump truck on Major Mackenzie Boulevard. Three surgeries and nearly a dozen skin grafts later, he was back behind the wheel of a sedan, where he belonged.

I was thinking about this as I walked up the path beside the house—how a man must feel when he realizes the lines on his face are only going to get deeper, that his muscle tone, sex drive and hairline are only going to diminish—when I heard footsteps coming up fast behind me. I turned just in time to duck the swipe of a garden spade swung at my head by Nina's trainer. The sharp edge of the spade struck the wall of the house, sending bits of mortar flying.

"Think you can push me around?" Perry snarled. His cheeks were still red from the slaps I'd dealt him. He hefted the spade and advanced on me. "Think you can fucking embarrass me?"

"I already did, Perry."

"Fucking smartass. Let's see how smart you talk without any teeth in your head."

He drew the spade back and swung it at my head like a right-handed batter. The backswing gave me time to move in on him, my head down, my right hand up to protect my face. The wooden shaft of the shovel hit the meaty part of my left arm, up along the bicep. On impact, I wrapped my right arm around his, trapping the spade, spun backwards and delivered a left elbow strike to his chin. As his head snapped back, I spun again and followed up with a knee to his gut, doubling him over. I slammed my elbow down onto his neck and he dropped to the ground.

"I think I just embarrassed you again," I said. He didn't answer, apart from a moan and a dribble of spit from his lips. I pitched the spade into a bed of ground cover and walked to my car, rubbing my upper arm. I'd have a whale of a bruise there, but it beat getting my head stove in. *That* would have been embarrassing.

I had picked up a *Clarion* on the way back to the office and was reading it while pressing an ice pack on my arm. The only tabloid in town, the *Clarion* generally had the best coverage of murders and other crimes. According to the story, Martin Glenn had not been killed in the alley where his body had been found. Lead investigator Katherine Hollinger was quoted as saying the killing had taken place "at a crime scene yet to be determined" and his body dumped in the alley post-mortem. Also quoted was the local city councillor, who said the real crime was that gay men were still targeted by homophobes.

Only the last quote in the story was of real interest to me: Martin Glenn's long-time companion, who told the *Clarion* he was in a "state of absolute shock that someone would harm Martin . . . I don't know how I'm going to make it without him."

His name was Eric Fisk.

I was looking up Fisk's number when my phone rang. I glanced at the caller ID and debated whether to answer it or not. I lost the debate around the third ring.

"What the hell do you think you're doing?" my brother yelled.

Daniel is almost three years older than me and has the Pope beat six ways to Sunday when it comes to infallibility. Or so he thinks.

I said, "I'm fine, thanks for asking. And you?"

"I'm not kidding, Jonah. I passed along a simple job because I felt sorry for you and you turn it into a goddamn mess."

"Why would you feel sorry for me?"

"Because you're getting nowhere in life."

"According to you."

"And Mom."

"She said that to you?"

"Never mind what she said. This isn't about her."

"You brought her up."

"Will you just listen for once? Rob Cantor just called and he is furious—*furious*, Jonah. What the hell were you doing at his house?"

"Talking to his wife."

"And beating the hell out of their personal trainer."

"I was defending myself, Daniel."

"Whatever. I can't believe you're screwing up the one case I sent you—"

"Who says I'm screwing it up?"

"Rob does."

"I'm not working for Rob."

"Rob, Marilyn, it's the same thing."

"Not since he dumped her."

"Look, I referred Marilyn to you because I felt sorry for her."

"I thought you felt sorry for me."

"Cut it out! Her daughter killed herself and she needed some kind of closure. That's it."

"She didn't kill herself, Daniel."

"What!"

"Maya Cantor did not kill herself."

"Says who?"

"Says me."

"Her parents say she did. The police say she did. The goddamn coroner says she did."

"I don't care what anyone says. She did not jump off her balcony."

"This is so typical of you, Jonah. You take something straightforward and twist it around until it's totally out of whack. No wonder your boss fired you."

"He didn't fire me."

"Well, I am."

"You are what?"

"Firing you. You're done with this."

"You can't fire me, Daniel. I'm working for Marilyn Cantor."

"On my recommendation, which I greatly regret."

"Doesn't matter. She hired us. She wrote us the cheque."

"Tear it up."

"Piss off, Daniel."

"What did you say?"

"You heard me."

"Jonah, I am warning you. Call Marilyn and tell her you are done."

"Or what? You going to call Mom and tell on me?"

He sighed loudly into my ear. "You are such a baby sometimes. You have no idea how the real world works."

"But you do."

"Of course I do."

It occurred to me then that there might be another reason behind Daniel's call. "Are you involved in the Birkshire Harbourview project?" I asked.

"What does that have to do with anything?"

"You are, aren't you?"

"My clients are none of your business."

"Yeah? What if Maya died because she knew something about the building site that she wasn't supposed to know?"

"That is totally irresponsible of you to say. Unless you have concrete evidence—"

"But what if she did, Daniel?"

"What the hell are you implying? That Rob Cantor would kill his own daughter to protect his investment?"

"It's a big investment."

"Only someone without children could come up with something like that. You're losing it, *little* brother. You are completely and totally losing your mind."

"So maybe he didn't do it," I conceded. "It doesn't mean that someone else didn't."

"Like who?" he scoffed.

"When I find out, you'll be the first to know." I hung up before he could say anything more.

CHAPTER 15

"Wow," Jenn said, looking at the bruise on my arm.

"You live with a nurse and 'wow' is the best you can do?"

"She's a nurse practitioner, boss, and I'm pretty sure 'wow' would be her reaction too. I trust this Perry looks worse than you do."

"Much."

"Good. You want a painkiller?"

"I'd rather hear something new about Martin Glenn."

"All right," she said, flipping her notebook open. "I spoke to a guy named Ian Kinross at the Ministry of the Environment. He worked with Glenn for years, until Glenn left to start his consulting business. He says Glenn was as straight an arrow as you could find. Ran everything by the book. He said, and I quote, 'If Martin told us a site was clean, that meant it was clean as a whistle.' He'd never had a Record of Site Condition revoked."

"Did Kinross audit the report on the Harbourview site? They're supposed to do that before approval to build is granted."

"*Supposed to* being the operative words. With the number of new buildings going up, they're totally swamped."

"Do we know if Glenn himself did the tests at Harbourview, or could it have been an employee?"

"There are no employees. EcoSys is a one-man show."

"What? How is that possible?"

"Glenn subcontracted the work. Tests were done by an independent lab. If soil had to be dug out and treated, he hired a firm that specializes in that. Same with building underground barriers. He was basically a consultant for hire. His biggest advantage was being able to squire his clients through the bureaucracy."

"Well, something was bugging him about the project," I said.

"Kinross didn't know about it."

"I know someone who might."

"Who?"

I pointed to the last paragraph of the *Clarion* story. "His long-time companion."

The apartment Martin Glenn had shared with Eric Fisk was on the top floor of a pink limestone Victorian townhouse in Cabbagetown, an old east-end working-class neighbourhood that had been revitalized in the eighties. The rooms had been opened up to let in more light; drywall torn away to expose brick walls. The floors were wide oak panels, sanded down and polished until they gleamed. Colourful framed photos of exquisitely prepared food hung on the walls, each illuminated with baby spotlights. There were cut flowers in vases everywhere: gladioli, snapdragons, birds of paradise and others I couldn't name.

Fisk was about five-foot-five and weighed little more than a hundred pounds. His head was shaved and his slight body wrapped in a heavy grey wool sweater. His jeans were cinched at the waist so they wouldn't slide down his hips, held by a belt that had had extra holes punched in it.

The front room had an electric fireplace whose false coals glowed behind an ornate metal grille. We sat in white upholstered chairs draped with cloths that looked Mexican or Central American, striped with the brightest shades of colour in the spectrum.

Fisk wiped his red-rimmed eyes and asked if we had any more news about Martin.

"What have the police told you so far?" Jenn asked.

"Just that he was beaten, and that it happened somewhere else. The woman who interviewed me, she was very nice, but the man with her . . . he suggested Martin had been out cruising. *Cruising*, like it was nineteen-fucking-eighty or something."

"McDonough," I said to Jenn.

"I got the feeling he thought Martin . . . that he deserved what he got," Fisk said. "Who could even think that? Being beaten to death . . . It's the worst way to die I can think of. Someone hitting you and hitting you. And until you go unconscious, you'd be thinking, If they just stop now. If this is the last blow. Or this one." Tears ran down his face and he wiped them with a tissue and then coughed into it: a dry racking cough that shook his body.

"Excuse me," he said, when he could catch his breath again.

"Eric," I asked. "How much do you know about Martin's business?"

"Only how hard he worked."

"Did he ever talk about the man he was working for?"

"Mr. Cantor?"

"Yes."

"I know he was very excited about landing the contract. Working with Mr. Cantor—and a celebrity like Simon Birk— we were both kind of thrilled about that."

"Did he stay thrilled?"

"What do you mean?"

"Did it seem like the relationship had soured at all of late?"

Fisk thought about it for a moment. "Martin did seem tense lately. He didn't talk about work much. And I didn't ask.

Engineering wasn't my thing, to be honest. I'm a chef," he said, waving his hand in the direction of the photos on the wall. "Or was, I should say. I can't really work anymore. I haven't for over two years. Once I started to become symptomatic . . . People I worked with were nice to me and all, very sympathetic, but the bottom line was they didn't want someone HIV-positive working in the kitchen. Even doing beauty shots for magazines, food no one was ever going to eat. It's not like I blame them. I probably wouldn't have wanted me there either. But it was very hard going from two incomes to one. And now without Martin—my God, I don't know what I'm going to do. I'll be just like him, waiting for the next blow to land."

I looked at Jenn then back at the man seated across from us, huddled in his sweater.

"How long since you were diagnosed?" I asked.

"A little over six years. But it's only been for the last two years or so that my health has really started to decline."

"How bad?" Jenn asked.

"Pneumonia, thrush, uncontrollable diarrhea, you name it. Once your CD4 count gets below two hundred, you're a sucker for every opportunistic infection out there. I was taking anti-retroviral therapy, which helped a little, but it was a cock-tail of drugs, three of them, all of which kicked the shit out of me. The side effects were so bad, sometimes, that death seemed the least worst option. But then Martin . . ."

"What?" I asked.

"They've just come out with a new experimental drug in New York. What's called a highly active anti-retroviral treatment—only one pill a day, and a lot fewer side effects—but it hasn't been approved in Ontario yet. Fucking Health Ministry. The Hell Ministry, I call it. So we were arranging to bring it in on the sly through friends in New York. But the cost, my God! Over three thousand dollars a month. I didn't know how Martin was going to manage it but he promised he would."

"Eric, did Martin keep any papers here?"

"Like bills and things?"

"More related to the project he was on."

"No," he said. "Everything was at his office and the police took it. There's nothing here. Nothing anywhere. Nothing left of my useless fucking life."

He started to cry and this time the sobs shook his small frame so hard I thought his bones would break. "What am I going to do?" he moaned over and over again, rocking back and forth as though in prayer.

Neither of us had an answer for him. All I could think of was to wish him good luck; Jenn, being Jenn, put a hand on his shoulder and then hugged him and told him we'd find out who killed Martin.

Walking out his door, I almost wished Perry would spring out and attack me again, so I could hit something—someone—anyone.

CHAPTER 16

"Homicide."

"Only you can make that word sound good."

There was a pause and then she said, "Hey, there." Not exactly warm, but not black ice either. She said, "I'm sorry about last night. Maybe I jumped to conclusions too fast, but you really threw me."

"I know. You feel any different today?"

"Not different enough."

"I was hoping I could buy you a coffee."

"I told you I'd call you. Anyway, I'm on a murder, and you know what they say about the first twenty-four hours."

"What if I can help you with it?"

"How?"

"Your victim. Martin Glenn. I know something that you should know."

"Like what?"

"A motive."

"On the level? This isn't some bullshit way of getting us together?"

"I happened to see him in a screaming match with someone a few hours before he was killed."

"Who?"

"You'll buy the coffee?"

"Jonah, you better not be messing with me."

"I'll be there in twenty minutes. You can decide for yourself."

We met in the lobby of police headquarters at 40 College Street, at the same coffee bar where I'd first looked into those eyes last June, when the cases we were working on converged. We'd agreed to meet here, instead of her office, to escape the prying eyes of her partner, whose dislike for private investigators in general was exceeded only by his antipathy for me in particular.

"Martin Glenn was working for a company called Cantor Development," I said. "They're putting up condo towers in the port lands and his company was cleaning the site."

"But?"

"Something went wrong. I'm not sure what exactly, but I think he was being asked—or paid—to sign off on something that wasn't kosher."

"Details, please."

"Like I said, a screaming match yesterday afternoon with the developer, Rob Cantor."

"You witnessed this?"

"I did. Cantor was warning him, telling him to think about Eric before he did anything rash."

"That being Eric Fisk?"

"I assume."

"What else?"

"Eric needed money. A lot of it, more than Glenn could afford on his regular consulting fees."

"For what?"

"You saw him."

"I did."

"He needs an anti-retroviral treatment that's available in New York but hasn't been approved here yet. He'd have to pay cash for it—thirty-five, forty thousand a year."

"So you think Cantor was paying Glenn to look the other way on something to do with the building site."

"Yes."

"But aside from the spat you witnessed, I don't suppose you have proof?"

First my brother, now Hollinger. What was it with people and their need for evidence?

"I don't have the authority or the means to search Glenn's home or office," I said. "You do."

"We've started on that already," she said. "But this might help narrow our focus."

I said, "You're welcome," just as a loud voice behind me cackled, "Well, if it isn't the cupcake."

Crap. Of all the coffee joints in all the police stations in the world, Gregg McDonough had to walk into this one.

"I was providing information to your vastly superior officer," I said.

"About what?"

"About Martin Glenn," Hollinger said.

McDonough lost a little of his swagger. "What would he know about Glenn?"

"Enough to make it worth listening."

"You know the listening thing?" I asked. "It's when you shut your mouth long enough to hear what other people say."

He was a big redhead and his complexion got redder, like a mercury thermometer heating up. "You know, Geller, I liked you last summer," he said.

"You hid it well."

"For a couple of murders, I mean. Maybe the Super has closed the books on them. Doesn't mean I have." And off he went to join the lineup at the coffee bar.

"How do you work with that lunkhead?" I asked Hollinger.

"I roll my eyes a lot. I sigh occasionally. Once in a while, I snap a pencil."

"There's something else I should tell you," I said.

"About Glenn?"

"Not directly. A couple of weeks ago, the developer's daughter, Maya Cantor, supposedly killed herself."

"Supposedly?"

"I don't think she did, Kate. She went off the balcony of a high-rise and I'm pretty sure someone helped her over."

"I don't suppose you have proof of that either?"

"There's proof she had plans for the next day."

"I doubt that will be enough to open an investigation. Have you seen the coroner's report on her death?"

"I'd like to. Think you could call their office for me?"

"I can call," she said. "But it's really a family member you need to make the request."

"Her mother will," I said.

And then McDonough was back at our table. "I'll be upstairs, boss. Working. Whenever you're ready to get back to it." Then he laid a paper plate down in front of me and walked away.

On it was a cupcake. With vanilla icing and sprinkles.

Hollinger rolled her eyes and sighed. If she didn't snap a pencil, it was probably because she didn't have one.

"You'll talk to the coroner?" I asked.

"Yes." Then she paused, looked into my eyes and smiled.

I said, "What?"

"One last question."

"What?"

"You don't have to answer."

"Try me."

"You going to eat that cupcake?"

CHAPTER 17

The Office of the Chief Coroner was located behind police headquarters on Grenville Street, in the same building that housed the Centre of Forensic Sciences. The phone was ringing at reception just as I arrived. The receptionist gave me the one finger/one minute sign, said "Uh-huh" a few times and jotted a few notes down on a pink telephone slip. She said, "All right then. You have a nice day too," hung up and smiled at me. I showed her my ID and told her Detective Sergeant Hollinger might have called on my behalf.

"Well, isn't your timing perfect," she said. "That was her calling. And a Marilyn Cantor called as well. Have a seat and I'll check which coroner handled the post-mortem exam."

I sat in a grey padded chair, under a framed motto that said, "We speak for the dead to protect the living." I was afraid to even look at the magazines on the table. What would be on display: *Canadian Autopsy? Bone Saw Monthly? Better Hose and Table?*

About ten minutes passed before the door opened and a tall, white-haired man in his sixties peered down at me. He had a smooth, kindly looking face and a firm handshake. "I'm Brian Morrison. I understand you have a question about one of our cases."

"A young woman named Maya Cantor."

"Normally, we require an access to information request to disclose the results of a post-mortem exam," he said. "But I spoke to the mother of the girl just now. And I understand a homicide detective called as well."

"Will that suffice?"

"I asked Mrs. Cantor to fax a signed request. Meantime, come on back and we'll see what we can do."

He led me through a quiet, carpeted hallway to an office that was too small and too hot for comfort. The bookshelves were packed so tightly with binders and books that he probably couldn't have squeezed one more sheet of paper into them. Piles of papers were stacked knee-high around the perimeter of the room. A human skeleton hung from a planter's hook in the ceiling, twisting ever so slowly in the current of air coming from the HVAC system.

Dr. Morrison opened a file cabinet and thumbed through files beginning with the letter C. "One day," he said, "this will all be computerized. Until then, the floors shall groan under the weight of all this paper. Ah, here we are. Cantor, Maya Arielle. Lovely name. Lovely young woman, as I recall. Or was before the fall. So unfortunate. So young to have taken her own life. You have to wonder what goes through their minds these days. One would think they'd find the world as exciting a place as we did in our twenties."

Personally, my world had been too exciting at that age. I was twenty-three, just a year older than Maya, when Dalia was killed by a Hezbollah rocket. Twenty-three when I enlisted in the Israel Defense Forces in a misguided search for revenge.

"What was your question, Mr. Geller?"

"Was there anything to suggest a finding other than suicide?"

He frowned. "Well, we discounted accidental death from the start. Her tox results showed the presence of alcohol, but she was well below the legal limit of impairment. And given the height of the balcony wall, it didn't seem possible that she could have fallen over. So the question then became suicide or homicide."

"How do you make that determination?"

"We look at several things. The injury pattern, of course. Placement of the body in relation to the takeoff point. Presence of a note or other communications at the scene."

"You examined her apartment?"

"The Coroner's Act gives us that authority. There was no note found in this case. No signs that violence or any sort of struggle took place."

"What about her injuries?"

"You have to understand, when a body falls from that height, the trauma of the impact is so severe, so widespread, that it's almost impossible to determine whether there were ante-mortem injuries. But there has been some notable research in the field of kinetic motion analysis of late."

"In what?"

"In layman's terms, how variables such as height and velocity at takeoff determine where a body ought to land in relation to a building, bridge or what have you. If you give me a moment or two to call it up, we can review things from that point of view."

He tapped away at his keyboard for a few minutes then said, "Ah."

"Ah?"

He swivelled his monitor toward me. The screen showed a number of parabolas and bell-shaped curves. I looked hard at them—I really did—but they meant nothing to me. That's what I get for sleeping through high school math, when the only bell-shaped curves that interested me were the ones under Sandy Braverman's sweater.

"Rather ingenious, this study," Dr. Morrison said. "They employed trained gymnasts, divers and athletes to establish the values we use to determine whether a victim simply stepped off into thin air, jumped from a standing position, took a running jump or executed a swan dive, as it were."

"And?"

"In Ms. Cantor's case, given the distance from the building and the position of her body, we know she didn't step off and she didn't jump feet first."

"She dove."

"Yes. Not with a running jump, of course. The waist-high balcony would have precluded that. But she did land a considerable distance from the building."

"So she could have been thrown off?"

"No one could say that with any certainty. A lot of this research—and perhaps I should have mentioned this earlier—was done with divers landing in water. They tended to hit the surface head first or feet first. With actual jumpers, another part of the body may hit the ground first, which influences the distance from the building itself. In Ms. Cantor's case, the distance wasn't conclusive either way."

"Hypothetically, then."

"You have to understand, Mr. Geller, that this office has been through a very difficult time since the revelations of the Pappas Commission. We're rather loath to speculate on anything that can't be proved."

Just a few months ago, Justice James Pappas had been asked to investigate how one rogue pathologist with an agenda of his own had been responsible for dozens of people being accused of killing children in their care, when in fact the deaths had been of natural causes. Some had lost custody of their children while under investigation; some had been convicted of homicide and served hard time before their cases were reopened.

"Let me rephrase it then," I said. "Is it possible, given the position of her body and the distance from the building, that she could have been thrown or pushed off her balcony?"

"I think I can grant you that much."

CHAPTER 18

Technically speaking, I still had an appointment with Rob Cantor that afternoon. But I saw no point in keeping it. He'd have nothing to say to me, and I needed more proof—something, anything—before confronting him further. Maybe once I'd spoken to Will Sterling, I'd have what I needed.

I stopped at the New Yorker Deli on Bay Street and picked up sandwiches, potato salad and coleslaw and drove back to the office. I figured Jenn would be hungry and I certainly was, since Hollinger had commandeered my cupcake.

I parked in back of our building and took the stairs up, carrying two bags of food. The front door of our office was locked and I wondered if Jenn had gone out. I gripped the bags in one hand and unlocked the door. There was no one in the front room.

"Jenn?"

There was a pause before she said, "Back here."

"I've got lunch," I said. "And news."

I went into the back office and saw Jenn sitting stiffly in her chair. A thirtyish man in a hoodie and jeans too tight for his thick build was standing behind her, his fist curled in her hair. His other hand held the edge of a hunting knife against her throat. The door closed behind me and I saw another man, older, more my age, in a leather coat pointing a gun at me. His jet-black hair was greased back from a widow's peak halfway down his forehead and he wore a thick gold cross on a chain that hung down to his sternum.

"What's for lunch?" he said.

Eidan Feingold had taught me ways to take a gun away from a man. But the lessons had never included a scenario where your partner was being held at knifepoint.

"Put the bags down," he said. "On the desk."

I set them down. "There's roast beef," I said, "or tuna salad. Take your pick."

"Shut up," the gunman said. "We're all going to go out that door now. Down the hall to the stairs, quiet as mice. Out into the parking lot and into the car on a drive. You got that, lunch boy?"

"Crystal clear."

"You act nice, you won't get hurt. We'll go somewhere, we'll talk to some people, then we'll let you go."

Sure they would. And a fairy godmother would pave the way back with candy.

"You do anything stupid," he said, "and Blondie's gonna get sliced."

"I'll cut her fucking tits off one at a time," his buddy said. He had angry red blotches on his face and bad teeth that showed when he grinned. He slipped his free hand inside Jenn's blouse and cupped one breast. "And wouldn't that be a shame. She has nice ones. A real handful," he said and squeezed her breast hard. She grimaced and bit her lips rather than let him see her in pain.

"Where we going?" I asked.

"Does it matter?" the gunman said. He stepped back and levelled the gun at my chest. "Don't even think about it."

"No thinking," I said. "Not me."

He opened the door and backed out into the anteroom. His partner took his hand out of Jenn's blouse and stood her up roughly.

"Walk," the gunman said to me. He backed his way to the front door and felt for the handle. "Just remember what happens if you fuck around."

He kept the gun on me as he opened the door. I tried to keep the surprise out of my eyes.

Eddie Solomon was standing there with a tray in his hands. It held a steaming carafe and three coffee cups.

"Ahem," Eddie said.

When the gunman wheeled, Eddie threw the tray in his face. The gunman screamed as the hot coffee splashed over him. The heels of both hands went up to his eyes and it was easy for me to grab his gun hand, turn the arm toward the floor, pivot and drive my opposite knee down into it. It broke with a lovely snap, better than I could have hoped for. The arm wouldn't move again till spring. The gun fell to the floor. I grabbed it before it could bounce and turned to point it at his buddy.

No need.

While he gaped at his partner going down, Jenn pinned his knife arm against her chest with both hands, leaned back into him, lifted her heels and brought them down hard on the thigh of his front leg. He howled, charleyhorsed but good, and fell to the floor on his back. The knife clattered away and as he writhed on his side, she rolled onto her knees and socked him hard where his jaw met his chin, all her weight behind it. His eyes closed and his mouth formed an oval. When he tried to stand up she put her boot on his shoulder and sent him sprawling into the chair she'd been in.

"Who's the bitch now?" she asked him. "Who's the bitch now?"

"Jonah!" Eddie cried.

I turned to see the gunman barge past him and run for the stairs, cradling his broken arm. I could have shot him, I suppose. But the carpet was already stained from Eddie's spilled coffee.

"Lock the door," I said to Eddie. "And get behind the desk."

"You know how much that coffee cost a pound?" he moaned. "That was the Javanese monkey shit."

I picked the knife up off the floor and placed it on the desk in front of Eddie. I checked the load in the gun and handed it to Jenn. "If he tries anything," I said, "shoot him in the balls."

"One at a time?" she asked. "Or both in one shot?"

"Depends how little they are."

"One should do it."

"Give me your wallet," I told the guy. He fumbled it quickly out of his back pocket. I shoved him back into Jenn's chair and looked at his driver's licence. His name was Sonny Tallarico. "Okay, Sonny," I said. "Who sent you?"

"Man, I can't tell you that."

I said, "Let's try that again," and drove the palm of my hand into the bridge of his nose. Not quite hard enough to break it, but it drew both blood and tears. When he brought his left hand up over his nose, I grabbed his wrist and cranked his ring finger back and counter-clockwise.

"*Jesus fucking Christ!*" he screamed. "You broke my fucking finger! You broke my fucking finger, you motherfucking prick!"

"I did not," I said. "I dislocated it. And as soon as some-one pops it back in, the pain will go away."

"Do it," he panted.

"Do what?"

"Pop it!"

"Me?"

"Come on!"

"Who sent you?"

"Christ, man, they'll fucking kill me."

"You think we won't?"

"You touched my tits," Jenn said. "Without asking."

"Jesus Christ," he moaned.

I grabbed the ring finger on his other hand. "You want the two-for-one special?"

"No!" he screamed. "Don't! Don't, please."

"We're listening."

"Just a guy we know."

"What guy?"

"I can't."

"Last chance, Sonny," I said. "I do both hands, you'll need someone else to hold your dick when you piss."

"Lenny! Lenny's his name."

"Lenny what?"

"Corazzo."

"And who is Lenny Corazzo?"

"Just a guy we do stuff for."

"Yeah? What else did he ask you to do this week?"

"This week? Nothing, man."

"He didn't tell you to beat up a guy?"

"What guy?"

"A blond guy. Martin Glenn."

"No," he panted. "No blond guys."

I started to bend his finger back but he just closed his eyes in anticipation of the pain. I had to believe he was telling the truth. I let go of it. Jenn looked disappointed.

"Please," he said. "Put my finger back." His injured hand was trembling like a morning drinker's; he had to clutch it in his good hand to make it stop.

"One more thing."

"Come on, man. You promised."

"This isn't Boy Scouts, Sonny. What's your partner's name?"

"My partner—"

"The guy with the gun. The one whose arm I broke."

"Oliviero," he groaned. "Sal Oliviero. Sally O he goes by."

He'd volunteered something. It told me he wasn't holding back.

"What do they call you?" I asked.

He looked down.

"I'll find out anyway. Don't prolong this."

"Sonny the Gun," he said.

Jenn hooted. The best revenge.

"All right," I said. "Stay still." I took hold of his shaking hand and told him to look away.

"Away where?"

"Anywhere but your finger, Einstein."

He looked down at the ground, then closed his eyes and sucked in his breath. I grasped the injured finger. Fixing a dislocated finger is not as easy as it looks in televised sports, where they yank it, tape it and send the guy back in. You have to bend the finger backwards, like you did in hurting it, grip it from behind and push the base forward. In lay terms, it hurts like fucking hell. I told Sonny to count to three and at two and a half I put his finger back into place. His eyes went wide and a guttural sound escaped his clamped jaws. Pain ran through his body like a tremor.

I took all the cash out of his wallet and handed it back to him.

"You're taking my money too?" he whined. "After what you did?"

"For the coffee stains," I said. I told him to stay seated and used a digital Nikon to take his picture, then told him he could go. "Ice your finger and take a few Tylenol," I said.

"Fuck you," he mumbled.

"I could just as easily have done your thumb," I said. "Then you'd need a surgeon."

"Fuck you again."

Some people. You just can't please them.

Once he was out the door, Eddie said, "Things were a lot quieter when there was a photographer here."

I said, "Who's the hero now?"

Jenn came over and put her arms around Eddie. He was a foot shorter than she was and his head nestled nicely against her breasts. She patted his back and held him there.

"Jenn?" he said.

"Yes, Eddie?"

"You going to shoot me for this?"

"No, Eddie."

"Not that it matters," he beamed.

CHAPTER 19

The lunch trade at Giulio's had ended and the restaurant was closed as the staff prepared for dinner. As I sat in Dante Ryan's small office, the smell of tomato sauce, garlic, frying onions, simmering broth and sizzling meat filled the air. I had never gotten around to the lunch I'd brought back to the office and regretted it now as the fragrant smells had me all but salivating.

"Okay," he said. "Let me just double-click . . . here we go." Up came a photo I had emailed him of an unsmiling Sonny "the Gun" Tallarico. "He said he worked for Lenny Corazzo?"

"Yes."

"Didn't tell you who he is?"

"No."

"I'd have gotten it out of him, you know."

"Even if he didn't know it?"

"Even if. And the other guy was Sal Oliviero."

"That's what Sonny called him."

He stared at the photo a little longer then shook his head. "Let me make a call," he said.

"Okay."

He looked at me.

"What?"

"I can't make it with you sitting here."

"Oh."

"Take a seat outside a minute. You want a plate of some-thing? Mimi can probably scare up some cannelloni or something."

"I could manage cannelloni." Manage it? I'd eat anything put in front of me and the plate it came on.

"Mimi?" Ryan called.

An attractive, dark-eyed, young woman poked her head in the doorway. "You bellowed?"

"Mimi, darling, fix my friend Jonah up with some cannel-loni before he drools on my computer. Spinach and ground veal okay with you?" he asked.

"Oh, yeah."

Ten minutes later, Mimi brought me a plate with four steaming pasta rolls smothered in a rich tomato sauce. "Can I get you something to drink?" she asked.

"A glass of water would be fine."

"Sparkling or plain?"

"Sparkling, thanks."

"Perrier or San Pellegrino?"

"Whatever's open."

"Natural or flavoured?"

"You're killing me, Mimi."

"It's just you're a friend of the owner's," she said. "He said to treat you real good."

"Plain San Pellegrino is fine."

By the time she returned with my drink, two of the can-nelloni were history. The other two had joined them by the time Ryan summoned me back into his office.

"Close the door," he said.

I did.

"You piss someone off in construction lately?" he asked.

"Entirely possible."

"Lenny Corazzo is a son-in-law to a guy named Mike Izzo."

"As in Izzo Construction?" The trucks working the site at the Birkshire Harbourview had all been emblazoned with his orange and black logo.

Ryan nodded.

I couldn't believe it. Rob Cantor had sicced goons on us. And if he was capable of that, maybe the horrible thought that had been crowding my mind—that a man could kill his own daughter to protect his business—was also true.

"Listen, Jonah," Ryan said. "Everything that went down last summer, everything you did for me, you remember what I told you? I said I owed you and you could call on me for anything, anytime. You remember that?"

"I do."

"Now construction, as you may know, is a rotten fucking business. Mobbed up, I mean. Doesn't matter where you're talking—here, New York, Chicago—any big city, it's the same. Every truck that rolls, every load of soil dumped, every ton of concrete poured, there's a tax. Sometimes ten per cent of the total cost. The Gambinos, the Bonannos, all the big crews and their affiliates, they've been mixed up in it since forever. So if Mike Izzo doesn't like you, don't think he'll stop with those two low-lifes. What I'm saying, I guess, is that even though I'm technically retired from the life . . ."

"Stay retired," I said. "You worked hard to get out, I don't want you going back in on my account."

"I could make a call or two. Find out how big a hard-on Mike has for you."

"All right. And maybe one other thing."

"Shoot."

"You may want to rephrase that." I took out the gun that Sal Oliviero had dropped in the office. "Can you get rid of this for me?"

He examined it closely. "You kidding? A Beretta 92FS? That's one fine pistol, man, replaced a lot of revolvers on a lot of police forces. The army didn't like them 'cause they sometimes broke down under extreme conditions, but for the streets of Toronto they're just fine. This one is already broken in but not abused. The guy you took it off will be kicking himself."

"That's fine. I only got to kick him once."

"You should keep this, you know."

"I already have one I never carry."

"The Cougar I gave you?"

"Don't give me that look."

He hefted the pistol, turning it back and forth, letting light play off its chrome finish.

"You sure you don't want it?" he said. "One at home, one at work kind of thing?"

"I'm sure."

He took a ring of keys off his desktop and opened a drawer, from which he extracted a grey metal strongbox. A second, smaller key opened this. He took out an envelope full of hundred-dollar bills, counted off five and offered them to me.

"That seem fair? Brand new, it retails about six bills in the States."

"You're the expert," I said, taking the bills. Found money for World Repairs.

"Doesn't make sense to me, giving up a fine weapon like this," he said. "Why don't you give it to your partner?"

"We've managed without them so far."

"*Managed*," he said. "The woods are full of people who manage. Most of them in shallow graves."

CHAPTER 20

Will Sterling's place was the main floor of a small semi at the southern end of Markham Street in the Portuguese enclave known as Little Azores. A realtor might have tried to get away with calling it South Annex but only someone dim enough to believe a realtor would have fallen for it. The house was more than tired-looking; it was spent. The grey porch sagged like an old couch and groaned under my feet as I stepped up to the door. The front eavestrough hung like a broken limb that hadn't been set. Recycling bins overflowed with pizza boxes and old *NOW* magazines and empty two-litre pop bottles. The sharp stink of cat spray filled the air.

The doorbell was taped over with a note that said Knock Loud. I did. First with my knuckles, then with my car keys.

No one answered. I checked my watch. It was five-thirty. Will had said he'd be home by four—five at the latest. I used my cell to call his number but it went straight to voice mail. I peered through the front windows and saw lights on and a TV flickering in one corner. There were textbooks open on a coffee table facing the TV, with a pen and highlighter next to them.

I walked down the drive between the house and its neighbour to a side door that I figured would lead up to the kitchen and down to the basement. I knocked several times; no one answered there either. That left the back door. I walked through an unkempt yard, the grass long and matted and covered by rotting leaves. A small concrete patio was breaking up, having heaved through many a frost and thaw since it was first laid. I climbed three steps to a wooden porch that held a barbecue pitted with rust and peered through the kitchen door. All the lights were on. The counters were covered with fast-food wrappers and plates caked with old food. The sink was piled high with glasses. I could see two slices of bread in a toaster and a peanut butter jar next to it, its lid off, a knife planted in it like a flag.

Someone was home. They just weren't answering.

Had Will changed his mind about talking to me? Or had someone changed it for him?

I tried the kitchen door. It was locked but didn't feel too sturdy. What the hell: I'd already broken into Rob Cantor's house—might as well make it a double-header. I picked up a piece of broken patio stone and smashed a pane in the kitchen door. I reached in carefully and felt for the lock.

Damn it. A deadbolt that could be opened only by a key. I felt around the door jamb around eye level. Sometimes people left a key there on a nail in case they had to get out fast. Nothing. I took a step back: in for a penny, in for a pound. I tensed my core muscles and kicked the door handle. It broke away from the strike plate and swung open. I moved into the kitchen and closed the door behind me.

"Will?"

No answer.

There was no one in the kitchen. No one in the dining room, which had been turned into a makeshift bedroom. No one in the front room where the TV was tuned to Much Music. A video by Arcade Fire was playing with the sound off. There was no one in the bathroom.

That left one more room on the ground floor, a bedroom at the back next to the kitchen. I eased the door open and found

Will Sterling at the foot of his bed with a pillow over his face. The pillow was stained with blood. At the centre of the blood-stain was a black hole. Bloody feathers fanned out around his head like a headdress.

I felt his neck. It was cold but not icy and moved easily enough. Rigor mortis had not yet set in. He'd been dead less than an hour or two. I looked at his body, a cold black rage building inside me. Three dead now. Three obstacles removed. I wanted to go back out the rear of Will's house, race down to Rob Cantor's plush office, pull him out of his padded leather chair and dangle him out a window over Queen Street.

All the drawers had been pulled out of Will's dresser, all his clothes thrown out of his closet and his school papers strewn everywhere. If there was anything to find, whoever had killed him had probably found it. I prowled around anyway, without knowing what I was looking for. I was about to leave when I noticed the white stains on his pant legs: this morning, I had figured they were paint or plaster, but there was no sign that any work was being done in the flat. I looked closer.

It was bird shit. Gobs of it, with feathers stuck to it—feathers that didn't match the ones from the pillow that had been put over his face.

I backed out of the room to the kitchen, where I used Will's phone to call Katherine Hollinger's office.

"Jonah," she said, "I keep telling you I'll call you when I'm ready."

"This isn't personal," I said.

"What then?"

"Business."

"About Glenn?"

"No."

"Then it'll have to wait," she said. "I've got a murder to clear."

"Got time for one more?"

CHAPTER 21

She came without McDonough, as I'd asked. Instead, she was accompanied by two other detectives, Graham Neely and Todd Gavin, who'd been assigned the case. I walked her through the flat, showing her everything I'd done, every item and surface I'd touched, as the detectives and crime scene officers examined Will Sterling's body and set up their equipment.

"You wanted proof that Martin Glenn's murder was tied into the Harbourview project?" I said. "This is it."

"How?"

"Will Sterling knew something about the project that was going to stop it cold."

"You don't know that for a fact."

"He knew Maya Cantor. She was trying to help him. I think they found out something they weren't supposed to know."

"You think."

"Will said this morning it had something to do with PCBs."

"But he didn't tell you what exactly."

"Because they killed him first."

"They who, Jonah?"

"How about Mike Izzo?"

"Who is . . ."

"He owns Izzo Construction. They're building the Harbourview condos."

"What connects him to this?"

I gave her an abbreviated version of what happened when the two goons accosted Jenn and me in our office.

"You don't have any proof that Izzo sent them."

"They were working for Lenny Corazzo and he's Izzo's son-in-law."

"I work in the real world, Jonah. You think I can bring in someone like Izzo for questioning or get a search warrant based on that? You should have called us when you had Tallarico in your office."

"He told me everything he knew. And I have his address."

She copied it into her notebook then flipped it closed. "All right," she said. "We'll bring him in for questioning. See if he has an alibi for Glenn's murder. Now let us do our work here. If there's a connection between these two killings, we'll find it."

"Three killings," I said.

"Maya Cantor's death was ruled a—"

"I know damn well what it was ruled."

One of the crime scene techs lowered his camera and looked at Hollinger. She grabbed my elbow and steered me into the kitchen. "Listen," she said in a low voice. "I value your opinions, I do. I respect your judgment. But don't raise your voice or second-guess me in front of my team. I'm a Homicide detective, Jonah. I have to let the facts speak for themselves. Facts, not guesswork or theories. The most the coroner did was concede Maya could have been—*could have been*—pushed. Not that she was, not even that it was likely. We are actively investigating the links between Glenn and his work for Cantor Development. We're looking into his bank records, his phone calls, his email. If there's a connection to Maya, we'll find it. And we'll do the same thing here. If Will Sterling was killed because of something he knew, we will find evidence of it. Evidence, Jonah."

Her arms were folded across her chest, her lips tight, and her eyes, those eyes, whose colour always seemed to fall in the warmest part of the spectrum, looked flat and cold.

"Are you done with me?" I asked.

"Is this you pouting?"

"No, this is not me pouting. This is me asking if I'm free to go."

"I'll have to check with Neely," she said. "He's the lead on this one."

Neely was about forty and had a brush cut that would have made a drill sergeant stand up straight. He made me go through everything from the start again: why I had been there, why I had broken in, why I thought Will's death was linked to other deaths. He took no notes, just stared at me while I spoke. After he'd heard it all, he said to Hollinger, "You buy any of this crap?"

"We'll check it out," she said.

"You know where to find him?"

"Yes."

"All right," he said. "He can go."

"Thanks," I said.

"After we test him for gunshot residue."

CHAPTER 22

At nine o'clock the next morning, I was back at the Earth Sciences Building on Willcocks. News of Will Sterling's murder had hit the students and administrators hard. I approached a group of people who were crying and consoling one another. One red-eyed young woman walked me over to a man in his early twenties with a mass of dark curly hair pulled back in a ponytail and a soul patch that grew two or three inches past his chin. He wiped his eyes with his sleeve when we were introduced. His name was Jason Eckhardt and he had been Will's lab partner in their analytical chemistry course. We walked slowly down a polished hallway to a brightly lit lab with white walls, white countertops and white fluorescent lights buzzing in the ceiling like trapped, angry flies.

He sat next to some kind of spectrometer and told me to pull up a chair. "Before I say anything," he said, "I want to know everything Will told you."

"That won't take long."

"I'm listening."

"I know that there is something wrong at the Harbourview construction site. Will all but confirmed yesterday that it has something to do with PCBs."

"Not just any PCB," he said. "One of the most toxic of all,

something called Aroclor 1242. Extremely dangerous for people and other animals. A known carcinogen—that means it causes cancer—the liver being the most common target organ. It's also a developmental toxicant, meaning it's very bad for unborn children. And it's suspected of causing a host of other illnesses or symptom clusters in shore birds, reptiles, amphibians and most likely humans as well."

"Where does it come from?"

"Most commonly from coolants in electrical transformers and turbines."

I thought of the decommissioned generating station across Unwin Avenue from the Harbourview site, the transmission towers along Commissioners Street and the other heavy industries north of the site, and wondered whether long-buried toxins could have seeped into the earth.

Jason showed me a printout from a gas chromatograph. It looked like the results of a polygraph done on someone who made wild swings between truth and lies. "Our course requires us to collect and compare soil and water samples from different sites, one clean and one dirty, analyze them and report the results. Will did most of the collecting." Jason looked away and swallowed and sucked at the inside of his cheeks. "We were perfect lab partners," he finally said. "I love the machines. The mass spectrometer, the gas chromatograph. Loading up the tubes and watching them cycle around. Interpreting the results and confirming the hypothesis. Will was the outdoorsman. There's nothing he liked better than collecting samples, getting all muddy and buggy. I used to wonder if he actually rolled in the muck like a dog, he'd come back so dirty. He didn't have as much patience for the tech side, which was cool, because that's my thing.

"This first sample," he said, "came from soil we knew to be contaminated with this stuff, on a site that once housed an oil refinery but hasn't yet been cleaned. As you can see, it clearly identifies a high level of Aroclor 1242. Dirty, dirty soil, not the kind you'd ever want to build on, not without extreme remediation."

He laid a second sheet of paper beside it. "This was supposed to be the clean sample, the one we compare the polluted soil against. But look at these peaks and valleys, the way they scan from left to right. It's Aroclor 1242 again."

"Where did this one come from?"

"Down along the lake, near Tommy Thompson Park."

"At the Harbourview building site?"

"Yes."

"The lakefront parcel, where the park is going to be."

"That's why I thought there must have been a mistake, that maybe I had gotten the samples mixed up. I told Will we should collect new samples and run them again. He didn't want to. He wanted to call the developer of the site and get in his face about it—he's a lot more confrontational than me—but I told him our final marks depended on it. So he collected another sample. It took time to run—there's only one chromatograph here and it's constantly in demand—but in the end the same results came up. That's this third sheet here. Same chemical makeup as the first two. Confirmed presence of Aroclor 1242."

"When did you tell him?"

"Yesterday morning at class."

Will had told me before class yesterday morning that he could guess what Maya and her father had been arguing about . . . that he'd know more about it later in the day.

"Did Will ever mention Maya Cantor to you?"

"The girl who killed herself? Sure. Her father is the one building those condos."

"Did he tell her about the samples?"

"Definitely. He was hoping she could—I don't know, pressure her dad into doing something about it. That's why he was so bummed when he heard she died. I think he felt like she bailed on him just when they were getting somewhere."

Neither of them knew how close they really were, I thought. And that's why both were dead.

CHAPTER 23

"According to the Record of Site Condition that Martin Glenn filed," Jenn said, "the southern end of the site was squeaky clean."

"But according to the samples Will took, it's anything but."

"Which provides somebody with an excellent motive for killing him."

"And Glenn. And Maya."

"You honestly think her father killed her?"

"Why not? I read somewhere that the vast majority of children who meet a violent end are killed by their own parents."

"How could he live with himself?"

"Let's ask him," I said.

"Where would we find him this time of day?"

"His office or the work site."

"And?"

"The site is out of the question," I said. "Full of guys who could throw us out with one hand and eat their lunch with the other. The office has a receptionist or two to get past, but I think we could handle them."

Jenn thought about that then broke into a smile that would charm anyone who didn't know her like I did. The smile of a fox who'd just discovered an unguarded henhouse.

"Want to mess with his head?" she asked.

"I'd rather thump it a few times."

"Want to mess with it first?"

Half an hour later, she dialled Cantor's office and asked, in a voice dripping both milk and honey, if Rob was in. "No? Well, can you get an urgent message to him? Tell him I need to see him right away. At my apartment. My name? Look at your caller ID," she said, and hung up.

We were calling from Maya's apartment. Jenn had played Maya's outgoing message a few times and practised pitching her voice in a similar range. Not as spot-on as her Scary Mary impression, but it got better with each try.

It took Rob all of three minutes to call back.

Jenn picked up the phone and whispered, "Hello?"

I heard his voice blustering over the other end, asking what the hell this, who the hell that.

"Please come, Daddy," she whispered, and hung up.

"You're creepier than you let on," I said.

"Who isn't?" Jenn grinned.

Jenn and I stood on Maya Cantor's balcony, watching a long V-shaped formation of geese fly south toward the lake. The wall around the balcony came up to my waist. I was a few inches taller than Maya. It felt safe to me. Probably had to her too, until someone hoisted her over.

How many seconds to fall from twelve floors up, I wondered. Probably three or four at the most. What did she feel in those last moments of her life? Did she see scenes of her brief life flashing by? Or was she just gripped with the terror of falling, the ground rushing up at her, unyielding black pavement ready to claim her broken body?

No. It would be the horror of knowing it was her own father who wanted her dead. Whether he had done it himself, or hired it out, she had to have known in the last cold seconds of her life that he was the one behind it.

My own father had died when I was fourteen, felled by a massive heart attack no one had foreseen. Unlike many of my friends, I never had the chance to see my dad grow old and weak. I had been spared the feelings a young man endures as his father is transformed from a giant, a hero, into an ordinary man—sometimes less than ordinary—flawed, fallible, unsure of himself. Buddy Geller would always be forty-four to me, with a full head of black hair, seemingly strong and robust. He would always be warm and loving.

He would never be my murderer.

I went back inside, leaving the sliding glass doors open, and stood facing the balcony. How had they done it? Grabbed her collar and waistband and heaved her over? Stood her up on the balcony wall and given her a strong shove?

I went back outside. "Let's try an experiment," I said to Jenn.

"What kind, doc?"

"Face the wall."

"Like this?"

"Perfect." I took hold of her belt and jacket collar and felt her whole body tense up.

"Relax," I said.

"Yeah, right."

"Maya was, what, five-seven? A hundred and thirty pounds?"

"Something like that."

"And you're six feet."

"Ask me my weight and you're a dead man."

"I don't have to ask. I can feel it."

"Was that a shot?"

"A statement. Now Rob Cantor is my size . . . a little taller than me."

"In shape?"

"He works out." I bent my knees and hefted Jenn a few inches off the ground.

"Jonah . . ."

"Don't worry,"

"Jonah!" she said.

"I'm not going to throw you off."

"I know that," she said. "I just wanted to ask what kind of car Rob drives."

I remembered a silver Mercedes parked at the job site: the only luxury sedan amidst a bunch of muddy pickups and SUVs. "Grey or silver Mercedes, I think."

"Then let go of me, doc. I think that's him down there."

A few minutes later, a key slid into the lock on Maya's front door. The door opened and Rob Cantor stepped inside. He stood in the doorway listening, looking around, then closed it behind him. He wore glasses with transitional lenses, darkened by the outside light, but slowly lightening to reveal the eyes behind them.

Roger Daltrey sings a Who song about a bad man behind blue eyes: how no one knows what it's like to be him. Could Cantor be that hated man, fated to telling only lies?

I stepped out of the kitchen, where I'd been crouched behind a counter.

"You," he said. "I should have figured you were behind this. I thought maybe your brother straightened you out, but I can see he didn't. Well, this is one sick fucking joke, calling me from here, pretending . . . How did you get in here anyway? No, don't tell me. Marilyn, right? She's in on this too. Was that her on the phone? I mean, if it was, she's even sicker than you are. You're doing it for the money, I can almost understand that, but what the fuck is wrong with her?"

"Not Marilyn," Jenn said. She'd been in the doorway of Maya's bedroom. "Just me, Daddy," she whispered.

"Who the hell are you?" he said.

"My partner," I said.

"It figures." He took out his cellphone and flipped it open. "Well, you're both fucking with the wrong guy. I know a lot of people in this town, Geller. Big people. And all of them are behind this project, including your brother. They want to see it happen. And when I get through with you, you'll be unlicensed and fucking well unemployable."

"Are you through?"

"I'm not the one who's through, you thick-headed—hey!"

I clamped his wrist and dug my thumb into the ligaments there. His hand opened and the phone fell into my hand. I flipped it to Jenn, who caught it and snapped the lid off.

"Normally, she rips phone books," I said. "But sometimes a phone will do."

"Are you out of your mind?" he said. "You just assaulted me."

I stepped forward and slapped him hard across the face. It felt even better than slapping Perry had. "*Now* I assaulted you," I said. Then I shoved him hard in the chest. He staggered backward, arms flailing, and landed on a brown corduroy couch.

"Three people are dead because of you," I said.

"You're crazy!"

"Shut up and listen," I said. "I am this close to beating the living shit out of you."

"You can't!"

"I think he can," Jenn said. "Hell, I could and I'm the minority owner."

His mouth opened. I raised my hand. He shut his mouth. He looked at Jenn, then back at me. He looked at his broken phone, as if willing it to ring so he could take a call and end this nightmare.

"Martin Glenn was murdered," I said, "because he didn't want to fake a Record of Site Condition. It wasn't a random act of violence, a mugging gone wrong, a gay-bashing or a lovers' quarrel. He was murdered because of what he was doing for you. Last night," I went on, "Will Sterling was shot to death—rather professionally, from the looks of it—because he took soil samples from your work site and they have enough PCBs in them to give liver cancer to kids who aren't even born yet."

"Will Sterling is dead?"

"That's right. Two people murdered in two days to keep this precious building of yours going."

"And you think I killed them?"

"I don't know that you'd have the guts to do it yourself, but you're awfully good at picking up that phone of yours when problems crop up. Yesterday, for instance, two goons showed up at our office and threatened bodily harm against my partner and me."

"Grievous bodily harm," Jenn said.

"I didn't send anyone to hurt you," he said weakly. "I wouldn't know who to send."

"But Mike Izzo would. Maybe you called Mike, who called his son-in-law Lenny, who called the two morons who stuck a gun in my face and held a knife to my partner's throat."

Rob stared at Jenn as if picturing the blade itself; a latter-day Macbeth envisioning the dagger before him.

"They threatened to cut off my breast," Jenn said.

"But you're okay."

"I'm terrific," she said. "Thanks a bunch."

"Look," he said. "You've got all of this wrong. I was upset with Martin because we had agreed on something and he wanted to go back on it. But I didn't kill him or ask anyone else to kill him. And this Sterling kid, I spoke to him once on the phone. Maybe twice. I don't even know what he looks like. I honestly have no idea what happened to him. I swear on my life."

"Like that's worth a lot right now," Jenn said.

"I'm telling you I haven't done one thing wrong!"

I leaned in close to him and grabbed his tie and pulled his face so close he felt the spray when I hissed: "Three deaths, Rob."

"That's what you said before. But you never even said who the third person is."

"Like I have to, you worthless sonofabitch."

I pulled him up by the tie and grabbed hold of him, just like I had done to Jenn moments before. She came around and took his other arm and together we frog-marched him through the doors and out onto the balcony. "Look down!" I said.

I held the back of his neck so he had no choice. "See the pavement?" I said. "Imagine it rushing up to meet you, Rob. Knowing that when you hit, it's all over."

"You going to kill me?" he said. "It won't change anything. I didn't kill Martin. I didn't kill Will. I didn't do it and I didn't ask anyone else to do it."

"But you killed her, didn't you?"

"Who, goddammit?"

I hoisted him up off the ground, bending the upper half of his body over the balcony wall. His glasses fell off and sailed down to the parking lot where they landed with barely a sound.

"Your own daughter, you bastard."

"No!" he yelled. "No. Please. I didn't. Don't let me go. Please don't let me go."

"Was it like this?" Jenn whispered. "Huh, Daddy? Is this how you had her before she went?"

"I loved Maya, you sick bastards. Loved her. I cried all night when she died. Ask Nina. I cried like a baby, like an animal."

I looked over at Jenn behind Rob's back. She shrugged.

"Pull me up," he pleaded. "I'll tell you everything. I will, I swear. I'll tell you about Martin. About Sterling."

"And Maya?"

"I never touched her. She killed herself."

I leaned in close and said, "Rob, your daughter did not kill herself. She was murdered. She was thrown from this balcony. And if you didn't do it, you better help us find out who did."

Tears ran down his smooth cheeks, and fell like rain toward the pavement. "Please pull me up," he said softly. "I think I'm going to be sick."

CHAPTER 24

"This piece of land," Rob Cantor said. "This beautiful piece of land, all south of the channel, adjacent to the park." He cleared his throat and scowled. He'd been prodigiously sick in the bathroom after I'd hauled him up over the balcony wall and clearly still had the taste in his mouth. "From the minute the Olympics went to Beijing instead of Toronto, and I knew the city was going to put the land up for sale, I started working on it."

He was sitting on his daughter's couch. Jenn and I sat across from him on kitchen chairs. He said, "People like Gordon Avrith, sore losers all of them, they all implied— hell, they damn well *said* I got the land under the table some-how. That I paid people off, whether at the OMB, council, Committee of Adjustment, whatever. And it's all bullshit. What I did was what they should have done. I worked like a goddamn dog, came up with the best design—the grandest design—of anyone and made the presentation of my life. I outmanoeuvred everyone and they can't bring themselves to admit it."

"No payoffs?"

"I never had to. You know what Toronto's like. Everyone is so ready, so desperate to be in the rank of world-class cities.

But the waterfront is such an eyesore. When people saw my plans, they were impressed. And when Simon Birk came on board, they rolled over like puppies."

"So what went wrong?"

"The only thing on the property—that had ever been on it—was a dairy factory. I thought, This isn't heavy industry. This isn't a tire manufacturer, like on the north side of Unwin. It's not an oil refinery. Not a malting plant. It's a place that made fucking milk."

"But?"

"First there was a problem with heating oil. The tank in the factory had been leaking for years, oozing all this sludge into the ground. When I brought Martin in to test the soil and the water, he found problems right away."

"And you didn't want to clean it?"

"No! I mean yes. We did clean it. Dug up all the soil, trucked it out for treatment, brought it back. It cost a fortune, and we were only able to recoup part of the cost from the city. Worst of all, the whole park area, which we thought we could leave wild, had to be dug up and cleaned, then replanted. It took two years of site prep before we could even break ground. That's longer than it would take to build the towers themselves. But we did it all, and by the book. A textbook example of brownfield remediation."

"Then what did Will find? What was freaking Martin Glenn out?" I asked.

"When you build a tower like this, you dig way down for the foundation. Six storeys down."

"Plus the caissons," I said, "which went right down to bedrock."

"Yes. The initial problem, the oil, had never penetrated that far down. But somehow, after we dug the caisson holes, this other substance turned up."

"Aroclor 1242."

"Yes. It was like—I don't know, one of those Godzilla movies where you awaken some monster by blasting a hole in the ocean floor. Martin said when we excavated all that dirt, sediment must have been disturbed, and the Aroclor was released into the water table."

"So a site that's supposed to be clean suddenly isn't?"

"Yes."

"And Will Sterling called you on it."

"Yes. He found traces of Aroclor 1242 along the shoreline and followed it to us. And I talked to Martin about what it would take to clean it up."

"And?"

Rob lowered his head. "It couldn't be done. Not without threatening the whole project. We would have had to do the remediation all over again. Go through the approval process again. It would have thrown us so far off schedule, our bankers—and our other backers—might have pulled out. He said it was out of the question. We had to keep going."

"Who did?" Jenn asked. "Martin?"

He shook his head. "Not Martin. Birk."

"Simon Birk told you to keep going?" I said.

"He said I had to."

"If anyone has enough money to cover an unforeseen expense, wouldn't it be him?"

Rob laughed bitterly. "You really don't understand this, do you?"

"Enlighten us."

"Simon Birk," he said, "doesn't put his own money into any-thing. Not a nickel. It's all leveraged. All of his buildings, all his grand creations, he gets other people to put up the money. Birk doesn't give, understand? He takes. He grabs. He milks." He was getting flushed as he talked, loosening his tie, rubbing his mouth with the back of his hand. "When he offered to partner with us on this project, I thought it was the greatest day of my career," he said. "Me—little Robbie Cantor, the squirt who started out as a janitor for his father—landing the great Simon Birk as a business partner. I thought God himself had reached down from the sky and patted me on the back. Well, it wasn't God, it was Birk, and it wasn't a pat on the back. It was a knife slipping in."

"What did he do?" Jenn asked.

"Simon insists on having the best of everything even if he can't figure out how to pay for it all. For every demand he makes that can't be met, there's also a promise that can't be kept. Money flows between projects like he's robbing Peter to pay Paul."

Jenn asked, "How does he do it?"

"Financing in our business always comes in stages that match certain milestones. When you acquire the land, when plans are approved, when ground is broken, when you reach a certain percentage of occupancy. As our financing was coming in, his building in Chicago, the Millennium Skyline, was in trouble. Again. Christ, it was from the very start. You think I had problems? When they started excavating that site, they found the worst thing a developer can find, worse than PCBs."

"And what's that?" I asked.

"Bones. Old ones. Possibly from the Fort Dearborn massacre, back when settlers first came to the region. Birk had to stop construction while anthropologists sifted through the dirt like prospectors. There were huge delays, which means no money in and lots of money out. Then about three months into construction, there was an accident. A bad one. You might have read about it. Three men were killed, seven injured, when a crane dropped a load of girders on them. That brought more delays and lawsuits he might actually lose for a change. Birk started springing these accounting tricks on my financiers, moving money out of this project over to the other one. He said it would get straightened out once the Millennium Skyline was at full occupancy. And if I didn't play along, he said he'd not only pull out, but make sure I was ruined in the process. So when this problem cropped up on our site, with the Aroclor, there was no money for a second round of remediation. I told Martin we'd have to . . ."

"To what?"

"Bury it. Forget about it. Walk away."

"Even though people were going to be living on top of it. Kids were going to play in that park."

"Look, I know it sounds bad—"

"*Sounds* bad?"

"Okay, it is bad. I can see that now. I really can. I didn't before. I couldn't. I was so caught up in everything. In trying to keep this dream alive."

"But Martin told you he wouldn't go along with it."

"Yes."

"And you told Birk?"

"Yes."

"And Will Sterling? Did you tell Birk about him too?"

"Yes."

"You signed their death warrants."

"If he killed them. You have no proof."

"They were murdered within twenty-four hours of each other," Jenn said.

"Even if he had something to do with it, how was I supposed to know? And Maya died more than two weeks ago. I never said a word to Birk about her. Never told him she was upset about the site."

"She did," I said.

"What!" He pushed himself up off the couch and stood above me with his hands clenched so tight they started to turn white. "When? How do you—"

"We found his number listed in her cellphone's outgoing calls," Jenn said. "And we found this."

She handed him a copy of the email Maya had sent Will Sterling the day she died. He read it, holding the paper as if it were the only thing tethering him to earth, his blue eyes scanning quickly down and then back to the beginning.

Jenn put her hand on his arm and said, "There is no way she killed herself. You understand that now?"

His chin trembled and his hand went to his eyes. He pinched the bridge of his nose. Tears fell anyway. His chest heaved and his voice broke as he said, "Yes."

"And if she didn't kill herself, and you didn't do it, who else had an interest in shutting her up?"

He barely breathed out the name: "Birk."

"This is what you are going to do," I said, my voice a lot sharper than Jenn's. "You listening?"

"Yes."

"You're going to write it down," I said. "All of it. Everything you can remember from the time you first spoke to Simon Birk until now. Every transaction, every conversation, every email. When it is all written down you are going to give a copy to Jenn. Depending on what you come up with, she can share it with the police. I'll leave that to her discretion. Got that?"

"Yes."

"You have a chequebook?"

"Yes."

"On you?"

"Yes."

"Write me a cheque for two thousand dollars."

"What for?"

"Travel expenses."

"Travel?"

"Yes. I'm going to Chicago and I don't see why your wife should have to pay for it."

"Why would Nina—"

"Your ex-wife, goddammit."

"All right, all right. I'm sorry. Two thousand, you said. To go after Birk?"

"Somebody has to," I said.

He filled out a cheque and handed it over. It was for five thousand. "If he did what you say he did . . . if he had anything to do with my daughter's death . . . then do anything," Rob Cantor said. "Spend anything. But above all *do* anything to bring him down. All the way down. I don't know you, Geller, I don't know what boundaries you have—"

"I'm still figuring that out myself," I said.

"Go farther," he said. "If you have to. Do whatever it takes to bring him down."

CHAPTER 25

I made the easy phone calls first: flight, hotel and rental car.
Then I called my mother to let her know I'd be out of town—Jewish mothers must be kept apprised of such things—hoping to get her machine so I could keep it short and chipper, but I got her live instead and had to listen to an overlong lecture about upsetting my older brother.

"What happened?" she said. "You were going to call Daniel and thank him for sending business your way."

I said, "The case he referred to me, *through his assistant*, the simple family matter, turned out to be not so simple. And I had to push Marilyn's ex around a little and he complained to Daniel and Daniel butted in where he shouldn't have."

"I wish the two of you would just get along better . . ."

"This is not about us getting along, Ma. It's about me finding out what happened to Maya. I don't bill what Daniel bills, but my hours matter too. My days count."

"Doing what?" she said. "I don't know what you do anymore. At least when you were with an agency I had some idea."

"World repairs is what I do. Like it says on the door."

"Which means what here on earth?"

"Giving Marilyn her daughter back. Whether Daniel likes it or not."

—

I had to take a few moments to breathe and think my way through my story before I made the next call. Marilyn Cantor had come to World Repairs to find out why her daughter had killed herself. Now she was about to learn that Maya had been murdered. Never having been a cop, only a soldier, I had no experience at breaking this kind of news—only of living it. So I started by telling her that I was going to Chicago. "But don't worry about the expense," I said. "Your ex-husband is paying."

"What does Chicago have to do with my daughter?" she said. "And why is Rob paying for you to go? He didn't even want me giving you his number."

"Maybe you should come down to the office. It might be better if I explain it in person."

Such a smart guy: I couldn't have thought of this before I called?

"What is going on?" she demanded. "What have you found out?"

"This might not be easy."

"I didn't come to you for easy. Please. Spit it out."

I took a deep breath; deep enough for snorkelling. "Maya didn't kill herself, Marilyn. We believe—strongly believe—that she was murdered."

"Murdered . . . who would murder my daughter? She didn't have an enemy in the world."

"She made one," I said.

"A boyfriend?"

"No."

"Then who? And what the hell does it have to do with Rob?"

"I'm going to tell you what I know, but I need some assurance from you first."

"The hell you do."

"Please. I need to know that you'll wait until we find

enough evidence to back up our theory before you do anything about it."

"Do you know what happened or not?"

"All right," I said. "Let me explain it as best I can. Everyone we spoke to had a hard time believing Maya had killed herself. No one thought she was the type to do it."

"I told you that myself."

"I know. And the more we looked into it, the more a different scenario began to emerge."

"Based on what?"

"Phone calls she had made and received before she died. An email found on her computer. A conversation I had with the coroner."

"He agrees she was murdered?"

"He acknowledged that it was possible."

"That doesn't sound very—"

"I'm getting there. We know Maya and a friend named Will Sterling had serious concerns about the Birkshire Harbourview development."

"Oh my God. Where are you going with this?"

"Hang on. They believed there were problems with the land itself—the level of PCBs in the soil."

"But Rob had all that cleaned."

"But a new problem cropped up that couldn't be cleaned. Not on time or within budget."

There was silence on the other end. Then she said in a tight voice, "Who are you working for now? Me or Rob?"

"You," I said. "And only you."

"Then why did Rob—"

"I'm getting to that. We talked to him today, Jenn and I. We got him to admit this problem. And that there have been casualties because of it."

"Casualties? What does that mean? Someone killed Maya over this?"

"Not just Maya. We think two other people were killed over it, to keep Birk's projects in Toronto and Chicago going."

"Not my husband, please," she said. "Don't tell me—"

"Simon Birk is the man we believe is responsible," I said. "That's why I'm going to Chicago. And that's why Rob is paying. He brought Birk into the mix. He bought into Birk's plan to pave over the problems. And he wants Birk held accountable."

A loud clashing noise rang painfully through my ear—the phone being dropped—and I could hear Marilyn crying on the other end. Wailing. All the anger she had been directing in at herself was seeking an outlet now, a place to lodge like an arrow. There was nothing to do but wait until she could gather herself and return to the phone. I made myself listen for moments on end as she gulped and cried and tried to speak and then cried more, apologizing to me as tears welled in my own eyes. I wanted that anger inside me when I got to Chicago. Wanted the fuel it would provide.

When she was finally able to talk, she spat, "That idiot."

"Birk?"

"My stupid fucking ex-husband, that bastard, that heartless fucking prick . . . I'm sorry, I shouldn't speak like that to you."

"Please. I've heard worse."

"It's all part of the same stupid need of his. Having a family and apartment buildings wasn't enough for him. He had to have the young girl, the big phallic towers, the world-famous partner. And look where it got him. Where it got his own daughter."

She asked if Rob had told Andrew. I said I didn't know. She asked what the police thought. I told her we'd been trying to make our case with Homicide. She asked how long I would be in Chicago. I said as long as it took.

"There's more money," she said. "If Rob's runs out."

"It won't," I said. "He's on the hook for every dime."

"Jonah," she said. "How sure are you he had nothing to do with it?"

"You were married to him half your life. Does he have it in him?"

She took her time before saying, "No. I don't think he could. Whatever else is wrong with him, and God knows there's a lot, he loved his children. He divorced me, not them. He's a selfish asshole at times, maybe most of the time—and I'm trying to picture it, believe me—I think I hate him enough to want to think he did it, but I can't. I really can't. But if for some reason I'm wrong?"

"Yes?"

"If there's any evidence at all that he had anything to do with it—anything—even if it was not knowing something he could have or should have known to prevent it, then tear up his cheque and I'll write you a new one. I don't care how much it costs."

"You're our client," I said. "Finding out the truth for you is the only job we have. And if Rob is in any way dirty on this, we'll tear up more than his cheque."

CHAPTER 26

"Homicide."

I said hi.

Hollinger said hi.

A moment of uncomfortable silence followed, until I said, "I know what happened, Kate. To all of them."

"You know or you think?"

"I know. All three were murdered by Simon Birk."

"*The* Simon Birk? The developer?"

"Him."

"He's not even in Toronto."

"But he's Rob Cantor's partner on this project. And when Cantor told him about the problems he was having, Birk had them removed. One by one."

I told her what I'd found out about Aroclor 1242 and its presence on the Harbourview site. How Rob had brought the problem to Birk—all the problems—and Birk said he'd handle them. "Even Rob thinks Birk is guilty," I said. "He's paying my way to Chicago."

"There's still no proof his daughter was murdered," she said.

"What about Glenn and Sterling?"

"We're still looking into Glenn's dealings with Cantor. If what you say about the Aroclor is true, it does provide a motive for his murder. But proving that Birk did it, directly or indi-rectly . . . I can hardly fly him in for questioning."

"What about the Chicago police?"

"Everything we're talking about took place outside their jurisdiction."

"So come with me."

"Jonah, please. I don't run my own agency. I report to a new inspector who squeezes budget dollars from a stone. And even if we had the money, there are leads to follow up here."

"What leads?"

"Glenn had other projects on the go."

"Any as big as Harbourview? With PCBs poisoning the site?"

"He also had a $250,000 life insurance policy that Eric Fisk stands to collect."

"You think Eric Fisk beat his lover to death? He barely has the strength to clothe himself."

"He could have hired it out."

"He could have but not Simon Birk? And what about Will Sterling? You think Fisk killed him too?"

"Don't be nasty, okay? I talked to Neely today and they're checking Sterling's background."

"Did he have insurance?"

"Jonah, I don't have to take any shit from you, understand? I have to run my case the way I see fit. I can't freelance like you."

"So let's work together," I said. "Let me be your eyes and ears in Chicago. If there is evidence tying Birk to these killings—any or all of them—I'll find it. And I'll relay it to you, directly or through my partner."

"As long as it's not based on guesswork. No Crown attor-ney is going to indict a murder suspect—especially Simon Birk—without a solid case. He'd have to be extradited here, for one thing, and with pockets as deep as his, he can hire an army of lawyers."

"I'm still going after him."

"Then good luck. And watch your back," she said. "If what you say about Birk is true, he isn't shy about eliminating distractions."

"I'm counting on that," I said.

There was a moment of stunned silence on the other end of the phone when I told Avi Sternberg who was calling. "Jonah Geller?" he said. "*The* Jonah Geller from Har Milah? There's a voice I didn't think I'd hear again."

"*Hineni,*" I said in Hebrew. Here I am.

"In Chicago?"

"No, but I'll be there tomorrow."

"Flying or driving?"

"Flying."

"When do you get in? I'll pick you up."

"A quarter to ten your time, but you—"

"That means ten-thirty at least O'Hare time. Look for me there."

"I booked a rental."

"For what? To get lost in? Cancel it."

"I won't need a car to get around?"

"In Chicago? Unless you're going to the burbs, you can walk most places or take a cab or the El. Where you staying?"

"The Hilton," I said.

"Which one?"

"Right downtown."

"Which right downtown? There's the Palmer House Hilton and the Chicago Hilton. They're a few blocks from each other."

"The one on Michigan."

"South Michigan," he corrected. "There's a lot of north-south, east-west stuff you have to figure out here. Once you get it, it's not too bad. I'd offer for you to stay at the house, but believe me, with three kids, you'd get more sleep under the El."

"Just picking me up is great. You sure it's not an imposition?"

"For Jonah goddamn Geller? Nothing's too much, believe me."

Later that night I sat at my dining room table, using my laptop to scroll through notes Jenn had pulled together and uploaded to our server. Anything new would be posted there for me to download once I was safely installed at the Hilton.

Simon Elliot Birk had been born in Chicago sixty-one years ago. His father, Ralph, had been a lawyer who initially helped businessmen and developers close their real estate deals, before finally seeing the light and becoming a developer himself. Well schooled in the art of local politics, Ralph had always backed the right mayor, which generally meant a Daley, as well as every other politician whose vote could help swing a zoning decision his way. He had died three years ago, aged ninety. Birk's mother, Pamela, was variously described as a socialite, hostess, arts patron and power behind the throne. She had died of an overdose of alcohol and barbiturates, presumably by accident, when Birk was just sixteen.

A lot of the biographical material had come from a *Chicago Tribune* business writer named Jericho Hale. Judging by the tone of his articles, he had no great fondness for Birk. Jenn had also posted a lengthy profile from *Forbes*, another from *Vanity Fair*—which focused more on Birk's marriage, art collection and social life than on his business—as well as dozens of articles dating back to the nineties, when Birk had suffered some of his greatest reversals in real estate, prior to his phoenix-like comeback.

I read it all. I needed a three-dimensional image of the man, a weakness to probe, a gap in the armour, somewhere to stick in a crowbar and heave.

He was a teetotaller, according to press reports. Never touched a drop, not even champagne to toast a new deal. I imagined a sixteen-year old boy, pledging through tears that he would never taste the poisons that had killed his mother.

He had a brilliant mind for numbers, according to both friends and enemies. "He's unbelievable," a former director of construction told the *Tribune*. "It's not just that he can calculate them faster than a machine, which he can, he also grasps the context at the same time. You put a thirty-page prospectus in front of him, he scans it like a dinner menu, and then asks all the right questions, as if he'd had all the time in the world to study it."

He had a gift for languages: at last count, he spoke fluent French, Italian, Spanish and German, and could acquit himself reasonably well in two or three other tongues.

He was an arrogant sonofabitch. An advisor had once prefaced a remark with "If I were you, Simon," and before he got another word out, Birk had retorted: "If you were me, *Thomas*, it would signify the largest single jump up the evolutionary ladder since the first amphibian crawled onto a beach."

He did not suffer fools gladly. According to a *Tribune* story by Hale, Birk fired a long-time employee who mistakenly calculated an offer in Canadian dollars instead of American, even though the mistake wound up *making* Birk money.

He told the *Vanity Fair* profiler that Jack London had been his favourite author as a young boy. "But I always favoured *Call of the Wild* over *White Fang*," he had said. "Far more interesting to see a house dog turn into a dominant beast than to see a wolf tamed to a house dog, don't you think?"

He was married to Joyce Mulhearn, fifty-four, if you could call theirs a marriage. She had been in an irreversible coma for more than two years and was currently housed in an extended-care facility called Nova Place. If he dated other women, no one had written about it.

He and his wife had owned a home on North Astor Street, a Georgian masterpiece designed by David Adler, filled with art collected by Mrs. Birk, whose tastes leaned toward

Impressionists, neo-Impressionists, Fauvists and art deco—stuck in the early twentieth century. Both Mr. and Mrs. Birk had been savagely beaten during a home invasion, in which the house was looted of some of its most valuable art and jewellery. Joyce had suffered grievous head injuries—the cause of her comatose state—and Birk's nose, collarbone and right hand had been broken.

Birk sold the house not long after the attack and moved to the Birkshire Riverfront, where he already had his offices on the upper floors, overlooking the winding Chicago River and the many bridges that crossed it in the downtown area. Though he stood just five-five, he was considered strong for his size and had been an avid boxer in his younger days, and he worked out daily in his private gym.

His net worth was roughly $1.5 billion. Not exactly Bill Gates or Warren Buffett, but you weren't going to see him sleeping on a sewer grate either.

He gave donations to both the Democratic and Republican parties.

He built casinos but never played in them. "I save my gambling for business," he had said, "because in real estate, I have the longest arms in the house."

He had something like six thousand people working for him, or 5,999 more than I did.

Taken together, his holdings amounted to sixty million square feet, which was probably sixty thousand apartments like mine.

He held season tickets for the White Sox, the Blackhawks and the Bears. "I would have bought Cubs tickets too," he had said, "but in this town you go with one ball club or the other and I'm not much for underdogs."

Birk had no children. No heirs to the empire. Finally, a tally I could match.

So: I wasn't going to beat him by getting him drunk,

outfoxing him on numbers, conning him in any of the Romance languages, outspending him or being a bigger prick. I couldn't hire him, then fire him. Couldn't get to him through his wife or kids. I could outbox him, but there'd be the small matter of getting him to agree to put on the gloves. I might prove his equal in Blackhawks trivia—does hockey not course through the blood of every Canadian?—but I had to assume he'd have me beat on the Sox or the Bears, or even the lowly Cubs, for whom he professed no love.

Maybe I'd just have to beat him senseless with a golf club, throw him in the trunk of a cab and tell the driver, "Canada—and hurry."

At ten-thirty, I turned off my laptop and got my suitcase out of the hall closet. I packed enough clothes to last a week and added hats, scarves and accessories I might need for surveillance. I threw in an extra sweater, in case the famous wind off Lake Michigan began blowing as advertised.

I did not pack my Beretta Cougar, much as I might have liked to. No point in starting my trip with a strip search.

Before I went to bed, I went out onto the balcony and stared out at the stunning skyline and thought, Take that, Simon Birk. My view's just as good as yours.

I'm working late at the office, alone, when there's a knock at the door. Just shave-and-a-haircut. No two bits.

I know that knock. I've always known it.

I rush to the door and fling it open and there he is. My father, Buddy Geller, looking the way he did the year before he died. Black hair gleaming, flashing a smile that Willy Loman would have envied on his best day. I open my arms for a hug but he holds out his hand for a shake instead.

"Mr. Geller," he says. "I'm glad you could see me. You won't regret it, I can promise you that."

"Please, Dad," I say. "Call me Jonah."

"Why, thank you," he says. "Jonah it is. That's a good start. Now, Jonah, I have a proposition for you and I think—I know—you're going to like it, so hear me out."

"Of course, Dad."

"I need you to write me a cheque. Not a big one, just a G-note. Wait. Did I say a grand? Better make it two and I'll tell you why. Because I want you, Jonah Geller, to profit on this every bit as handsomely as me. How profitable, you're asking yourself? How about a twenty-to-one payoff? Maybe even better by post time."

"Aw, Dad, not a horse."

"A horse, you say, like it's any horse. Look at the name. Take a good look." He pulls a racing form from his pocket. The name is circled in a great flourish of ink. Chicago Fire.

"Huh?" he says. "Is that not a sign? Tell me you're in, Jonah. A thousand for you and a thousand for me. And if you're not interested for yourself, then at least the thousand for me. Please. I don't ask you for much, do I?"

I have to admit that's true. I write him a cheque—but just for his thousand.

"You're sure?" he says.

"I'm sure, Dad."

"Not the gambling type?"

"Not tonight."

Next thing I know we're at the track. He signs the cheque over to a teller, holding down a fedora against the wind. I don't remember him wearing a hat at my office. Now it's all he can do to keep it on his head. We find our seats and await the start of the race. Then they announce that Chicago Fire is missing, gone from his paddock without a word. His trainer is frantic, his owner demanding an investigation.

"You find him!" my father shouts.

So off I go into the windy night, searching hospitals, police stations, drunk tanks and detox centres. No sign of the horse.

I go into every bar I can find, from upscale piano bars to

raunchy gay bars to sleazy country-and-western dives where last week's beer is still stuck to the floor. I show pictures of the horse to bartenders, drinkers, hustlers, house band players. Nothing.

When I get back to the track, my father is slumped in his seat, tears mixing with a cold rain that's falling hard on the open grandstand. His thousand—my thousand—is gone and he's too ashamed to speak to me.

"It's okay, Dad," I say. "I'm just glad to see you."

"Really?"

"Of course."

"It's not too late for you to be out? Isn't it an hour later here?"

"Where, Dad? We're home."

"Doesn't feel like home." He holds out his hand and we shake. As I start walking away, he calls out, "Say hello to your mother. Tell her I'm sorry I can't make it tonight."

"What about Daniel?"

"Who?"

On my way out, I stop at Chicago Fire's paddock and there he is, safe and sound, munching an apple.

"Where was he?" I ask his trainer.

"I don't know," the trainer says. He's a big man, strong-looking, wearing safety boots and a hard hat. "He won't tell me a thing."

"He cost me a bundle."

"It was your dad that bet," the man says.

"It was my money."

"Who told you to mix in?"

"He's my father," I say.

"Mix out of other people's business," the man says. "Sooner you learn that, the better."

"Goddamn horse," I say.

"Up yours," the horse replies, spitting bits of apple in my face.

"Watch your mouth," I say.

The horse laughs, showing me yellow teeth. "Make me," he snorts, and more bits of apple spray into my face.

PART TWO

"If you owe the bank $100, that's your problem. If you owe the bank $100 million, that's the bank's problem."

J. Paul Getty

Check-in time at the Chicago Hilton wasn't until three o'clock, so I stowed my luggage with the concierge and bought two coffees from a Starbucks concession for me and Avi Stern. "I wish I had time for lunch," Avi said. "Kitty O'Shea's has a great shepherd's pie."

"How far is it?"

"Other end of the lobby," he said with a laugh.

We drank our coffee in club chairs in a naturally lit alcove off the main lobby. He dispensed some lawyerly doubts about my case against Simon Birk—"We have this concept here known as the burden of proof"—but he at least agreed to call a friend who practised real estate law to find out what he could about Birk's recent dealings.

"I know there have been lawsuits against him, but they've all been civil cases," he said. "He's pissed off a lot of people in his time. Business partners. The banks, when real estate swooned in the nineties. But he's won more civil suits than he's lost and there have never been any criminal charges that I recall."

"What about the fatalities on his job site?" I asked.

"He'll pay for those," Avi said. "But in dollars, not jail time. Unless someone can prove he knew that crane was going to tip over and did nothing to prevent it."

He checked his watch and said, "I have to get back to the office. You have dinner plans tonight?"

"No."

"You do now," he said.

"You sure?"

"You're in my town. What am I supposed to do, let you eat alone in a hotel?"

"Your wife won't mind?"

"Let me worry about her."

There was a story in the news a while back about some young men who taunted a tiger at a zoo, throwing bottles and sticks at it until it became so enraged that it leaped over the fence and meted out some jungle justice.

Not the best way to deal with a tiger but better than no way at all.

Armed with a fold-out map and directions from the concierge, I walked north on South Michigan until it became North Michigan.

The city splits its north-south addresses at Madison, east-west addresses at State.

Avi had drilled me on it before leaving.

Even the most mundane businesses on Michigan—Radio Shacks, 7-Elevens, sub shops and T-shirt emporia—were housed in magnificent stone buildings. Many a fluted column, many a looming gargoyle, heroic figures on straining beasts, all free of graffiti and litter. And this wasn't even the Magnificent Mile yet. On my right were the green expanses of Grant Park and beyond it the hard bright water of Lake Michigan. At Monroe, after a stretch of streets named after largely mediocre presidents—Polk, Harrison, Van Buren—I turned into Millennium Park.

It was the perfect example of what Chicago does right and Toronto does wrong. The entire Chicago waterfront was easily accessible, from the southern complex that housed Soldier

Field, the Field Museum and a planetarium, to the northern end, past the restored Navy Pier to Oak Street Beach.

Granted, Millennium Park opened four years late, but it looked like it was worth all the time and money spent on it. Toronto's waterfront is cut off from downtown by the Gardiner Expressway, neglected and hamstrung by a hodgepodge of commissions and different levels of government that want the glory that would go with a revitalized harbour without committing a nickel.

I walked up the Chase Promenade to the *Cloud Gate* sculpture, a giant blob of highly polished chrome shaped like a huge molar resting on two edges. Like a drop of mercury being pulled into two by surface tension. Buildings reflected in its surface looked like they were listing dangerously to one side. Closer up, it was the people themselves who looked warped. There was space enough beneath the sculpture to walk between the supports and gape up at my reflection. A funhouse of sorts. When I craned my neck, I saw a version of myself I didn't much care for. Distorted face, stretched-out head, much too wide for its body.

Another in a long line of selves I had issues with.

I continued up toward the great lawn, past a music pavilion that looked like someone had blown up a campy sixties spaceship from the inside. Every once in a while I stopped as if to get my bearings, read a plaque, take in a sight, all the while looking for goons, gunmen, leg breakers. Didn't see any. Didn't relax either.

There were already a few great buildings that faced the north end of the park: One and Two Prudential and the Aon Centre. The Birkshire Millennium Skyline was going up on a prized lot next to them, much higher now than it had been in the promotional video Jenn and I had watched. An awesome sight looking up from ground level. All glass on the south side. More rounded than the severe Aon Centre, tapering as it went up, the highest floors like the bridge of a great ship setting forth into the lake. The tower appeared to have risen to its full height of eighty-six storeys, the first seventy-five or so fully clad in glass. Through a pair of field glasses, I could see a dozen floors above in different stages of completion. Six with all-concrete floors, copper plumbing set into their undersides. Three more had temporary flooring made of corrugated plastic or metal sheets. The top two or three were nothing but the central column and a bit of flooring and then bare girders meeting at the extremities. And still men walked up there as casually as if stepping out for a smoke. Granted, they had harnesses, but you had the sense they'd walk up there just as easily without them.

I watched a tower crane lift a girder high into the sky and ease it alongside the frame. Workmen hundreds of feet in the air guided it into position, silhouetted by the sun as they hammered rivets into place with heavy mauls. Through my binoculars, I could see hard hats covered in decals—American flags and union symbols—dusty clothes and tool belts hung on hips like gunfighters' holsters. About half the men looked Mohawk. They were legends in the business, had been since tall buildings and bridges first started to rise out of the North American landscape: men from Six Nations, Kahnawake and other reserves who were said to have no fear of heights, who could walk the high iron as if strolling down a garden path. One man, his long black hair in a braid halfway down his back, shimmied down a vertical girder, gripping it with his gloved hands and pressing his workboots against it to control his descent.

Give me terra firma any day.

One route up the east side of the building had not been glassed in but was covered in plywood. A crane was bolted to the bare concrete of every floor and on it ran the workmen's elevator—more of a hoist really, sliding patiently down the side of the building while a counterweight went up the other side.

When it came to rest on the ground, a dozen or so ironworkers exited, then the weight began to descend and the hoist started its slow return run up.

As the men walked through the gate in the hurricane fence that surrounded the site, heading toward a canteen truck parked at the curb, I asked one of them who the site manager was. He shaded his eyes, scanning the site, then pointed at a burly man who wore a shirt and tie under a windbreaker, a canary-yellow hard hat barely covering his skull, talking on a cellphone as he scanned a set of plans spread over a sheet of plywood that was balanced on two sawhorses. When he closed the phone, I slipped through a gap in the fence and approached him with a notebook and pen in hand.

Time to throw the first stick at the tiger.

"Got a minute?" I asked.

He looked like he could play centre for the Bears in nothing more than his street clothes. "Who are you?" he asked, looking at my bare head and then down at my feet. "And where's your hard hat and safety boots?"

"My name's Jonah Geller."

"Good for you. Now get off this site."

I showed him my ID. "I'm a licensed investigator and—"

"I don't care if you're a registered nurse. No one gets on this site without a proper lid and boots."

"I'm already on the site," I said.

"Then get off. Now."

"Just answer a couple of questions about Simon Birk." It didn't really matter whether he answered them. I just wanted Birk to hear that I'd been asking.

"Call his publicist. I'm sure he has one." He thrust his chin out at me. It was a hell of a chin. Hit it with a crowbar and call it a draw.

"He's in a world of trouble," I said.

"What are you talking about?"

"Simon Birk. His Canadian project? It's all based on a fraud."

"What are you, nuts? He's one of the richest guys in town. In the goddamn country, for Chrissakes."

"Cops there are looking at him for three counts of murder."

"Bullshit," he said. "It woulda been in the *Sun-Times* if that was true."

"It hasn't made the news yet."

"'Cause it's all in your head, whackjob." He moved in on me until I could smell his sour breath. "Simon Birk might be a rich bastard but right now he is our rich bastard. He's putting up this building and paying our wages, which means nobody fucks with him till the job is done. So get off the site before you get curb-stomped." He stepped on my right foot, his steel-toed boot trying to mash my running shoe flat and not doing a bad job of it.

"See what happens when you come in here without boots? Without a hard hat, bud, plenty worse can happen." He pointed up to the top of the unfinished steel tower. "Someone drops a penny from that height, it would put a hole in your head. They drop something bigger, like a bolt, your head splits like a melon."

I could have argued the point—could have stuck stiff fingers up under his ribs and rearranged his organs—but I had done what I'd set out to do. I was pretty sure he'd be on the phone as soon as I was gone, my name burning up a line that would lead to Birk's ears. And if this little action didn't do it, the next one would. Or the one after that.

I said, "I think I'll be going now."

"Fuckin' A," he said.

I've never been sure of the origin of that expression. I didn't think it was time to ask.

CHAPTER 28

If you didn't know who the mayor of Chicago was before arriving at City Hall, you certainly knew it after. The name seemed to be on every door, sign and plaque in the place. Everything down to the elevator buttons brought to you by Hizzoner. And what a place: a huge neoclassical structure that takes up an entire city block, its top half dominated by fluted columns. A symbol of the power handed down from the former boss to his son, more in the tradition of Pakistani democracy than the Midwestern American brand. I walked through the building, trying not to look like a gaper and failing miserably. The lobby of Toronto's city hall feels like a giant library; Chicago's is more like a train station or cathedral with its vaulted ceilings and dim brass lamps, the gleaming filigreed brass around its elevators.

The Department of Buildings is on the ninth floor. This is where you come to get zoning permits, arrange inspections, obtain forms, fill out forms, hand in forms. Apply for licences to work as plumbers, electricians, masons and crane operators. To comply, voluntarily or otherwise, with the city's codes regarding repairs and maintenance.

I guessed I was the only one coming here to raise hell about Simon Birk.

The elevator opened onto a long, bright hallway that echoed with every footstep. There was a counter with computer monitors where visitors could look up city maps, real estate lots, city regulations or their horoscope. Beyond that was the entrance to the Department of Zoning and Licensing. On my left when I walked in was a reception area where dozens of people sat in various stages of impatience, boredom and resignation, four rows of them in the mayor's chairs. I took a seat, anticipating a long wait.

"Six fucking inches," said the man next to me, a stocky middle-aged fellow in a Cubs jacket. "That's what I'm here for—six fucking inches."

"I think Urology's down the hall."

He laughed and clapped my shoulder. "My deck, I'm talking about. Back of my house. Building inspector comes around, tells me it has to be torn down and rebuilt because it's five and a half feet away from the interior lot line, and the minimum distance is six feet. I say to him, 'Fella, we're talking six inches, gimme a break here.' You know what he says? He says, 'Measure twice, build once,' the little prick. 'You don't like it,' he says, 'you can always appeal.' So that's what I'm doing here, wasting my time, wasting their time, over six fucking inches. I mean, it's not some landmark building or heritage property, it's my goddamn house. My next-door neighbour doesn't give a shit. Nobody gives a shit. I probably should have offered the guy something, huh? What do you think? A hundred bucks? Five hundred? Gonna cost me five grand to tear it down and rebuild—if I can reuse all the wood—and that's not even counting my goddamn time." He looked at his watch, at the number of people around us waiting, and sighed deeply.

"Enough of my bullshit," he said. "So what are you here for?"

"High-rise demolition," I said.

"I think you're in the wrong line for that," he said. "You want to be down the other end of the hall where the project managers are."

I thanked him and he wished me luck, which I appreciated. Tearing down an empire is bound to require some. Then I walked past three long curved desks, each of which housed three workstations for project managers. People sat in chairs along the wall—architects or contractors, the architects with smooth hands and expensive pens clipped to their shirt pockets; the contractors with dusty clothes, scuffed boots and rough hands with cuts in every stage of healing.

A middle-aged African-American woman with long hair extensions said, "How can I help you today?"

I asked, "Are you familiar with the developer Simon Birk?"

"Honey, everyone knows Simon Birk. What is it you want?"

"Information."

"What kind?"

"Everything. His permit reviews. Zoning variances. Workplace safety. Citizen opposition. Soil and water reports."

"For which building?"

"All his buildings."

There were half-moon bifocals perched at the end of her nose. She gave me a long look over the glasses and said, "You sure that's all? You don't want to know what he eats for lunch?"

I already knew what he ate for lunch. People like Rob Cantor. Suckers who thought they were his partners.

"Well, fortunately for me, it's Developer Services you want," the clerk said. "They process applications for high-rise buildings. Did you have an appointment?"

"Do I need one?"

"Oh, yeah. If you're asking, I'm guessing you don't have one."

"No."

"You can make one now, or apply for one online, which is probably quicker."

"I'm visiting from Toronto," I said. "Is there any way I could just speak to someone—"

"Sugar, it doesn't matter if you're visiting from Tobago."

"So who would I make the appointment with? Who's the most familiar with Birk's new project?"

"The Millennium Skyline?" She had long pink fingernails decorated with glittering pinwheel-shaped swirls. She tapped her keyboard and said, "The project administrator on that was Peter Stemko."

"Can't I just—"

"No."

"What if I—"

"No! Not without an appointment. And Mr. Stemko's only going to tell you what I'm going to tell you: there's not much you can get without a freedom of information request, and that you will not get overnight."

"What if I had information about safety violations?"

Her look was entirely skeptical, but the crane collapse, and the death of three workers, was too recent an incident for her to ignore me. "You said you wanted information. Now all of a sudden you got some?"

"I do. I can say for a fact that a violation occurred not an hour ago."

"What violation?"

"A man on site without proper equipment. No hard hat, no boots, nothing."

"That's not something we handle." She looked over my shoulder and called out, "Next person in line."

There was only one thing left to do in this situation. Get loud.

"Is it because he's Simon Birk?" I said, my voice rising. Other clerks at the counter looked our way—exactly the reaction

I was hoping for. "People have died because of him. And not just those poor workmen."

"Sir?" she said. "There's no need to raise your voice with me."

"The name is Geller," I said. "Jonah Geller. And this department should be looking very closely at Simon Birk. He abuses the environment. His employees. The families of the men who died building his tower. The very process that—"

"Please lower your voice!"

"Lower it!" I thundered. "I'll raise the roof if I have to."

"Kid has a set of pipes on him," a man behind me said.

Everyone was looking our way now. Clerks, other employees, the people sitting and waiting their turn.

"Simon Birk," I bellowed, "is getting away with murder, just because he's rich."

"Hear, hear," an older woman said. "I never did care for his attitude."

The clerk was on the phone now, calling security, no doubt.

I put up my hands in surrender and walked to the elevator. People gave me a wide berth. "All right," I said. "I'm going. But Simon Birk better look over his shoulder because I won't rest until he pays for everything he's done. Jonah Geller is not giving up on this. Jonah Geller never gives up."

When the elevator came, I stepped into it. No one else from the ninth floor got in with me.

As the doors closed, I heard an elderly man say, "I know Simon Birk from the newspapers. But who the hell's this Geller?"

CHAPTER 29

The Chicago Tribune building is inlaid at eye level with stones liberated from some of the world's most recognizable buildings and structures by intrepid *Tribune* correspondents of days gone by. A tile from the Taj Mahal. Stones from the Berlin Wall, the Great Wall of China and the Alamo. Souvenirs of Notre Dame and Westminster Abbey and Lincoln's Tomb. A twisted bit of metal from the World Trade Center next to a stone from the Mosque of Suleiman the Magnificent. Even chunks of the Pyramids and the Parthenon—the ruined temple, not the nightclub.

The *Tribune* newsroom is on the fourth floor. Somehow I'd expected a scene out of *The Front Page:* a clamorous, smoky room filled with hard-bitten Chicago newsmen pounding out copy on clacking typewriters, phones jangling like alarm bells, flasks of whisky at the ready. Instead, the place was strangely quiet. Soft tapping on computer keyboards. Phones burring discreetly. No cigarettes, no cigars, no pipes, no booze. No copy boys running the gauntlet from writers to editors, no pneumatic tubes whooshing stories over to rewrite. It could have been an insurance office or a call centre, except for one glassed-in area where police scanners squawked.

Jericho Hale was a tall, lean black man about my age,

which is mid-thirties. His head was cleanly shaved, which some-how makes black men look cool and white men unemployable. His eyes were focused on the screen in front of him as his fingers thrummed quickly over the keyboard, lips pursed as if he were about to plant a kiss on someone. The man was in a zone. I stood there watching him for several minutes until he stopped typing and without looking up said, "You had some information about Simon Birk."

I said, "Yes."

He said, "Wait."

He resumed typing, his eyes moving from the screen to a document on the desk next to him and back, until he was satis-fied with whatever he had written. He saved his copy, then pushed back from his computer and took me in.

He said, "Birk."

I said, "Yes."

He said, "Sit."

Hale had been writing about Simon Birk for years. He slid open a file drawer and showed me files jammed into hanging holders. "And that's just one drawer," Hale said. "The man has been something of a boon to me. I'm like one of those birds that ride around on the back of a rhinoceros."

"Better above him than below," I said.

"True enough. So what brings an investigator here from Toronto?"

"I'm looking for information on Birk."

"And you came to me?"

"You've written more about him than anyone else."

Hale smiled. "That's because people give *me* information. Not because I give it to them."

"Maybe we can help each other."

"I know I can help you. What I'm not seeing is how you can help me."

I said, "Birk's putting up a building in Toronto."

"He puts up buildings everywhere."

"This one is called the Harbourview."

"I know. I watched the groundbreaking ceremony on TV."

"It's dirty," I said.

"How dirty?"

"Dirty enough to put Birk in jail for the rest of his life."

Hale picked up a spiral notebook and a pen. Said, "You have my full attention."

"But this is quid pro quo, right? We trade information?"

"You give me the quid," he said, "then we'll see about the quo."

I told him about the deadly Aroclor 1242 that had been found on the site. He took notes without looking down at the pad. I told him how Birk had made Rob Cantor cover it up.

"Because he couldn't afford to have it cleaned?" he asked.

"Yes."

"That's according to Cantor?"

"Yes."

"What else?"

I told him Birk had ordered the deaths of three people to keep the project going.

He stopped taking notes and leaned his long body closer toward me. "Are you shitting me? What three people?"

"Before I get into specifics—"

"Uh-oh. Here it comes."

"Here comes what?"

"The part where you tell me you have no proof of this."

"Not directly, no."

"Nothing? No other sources who'd back you up? Police, say?"

"Not officially. Not yet."

He said, "Are you fucking with me?"

"No."

"'Cause this is a newsroom, and we get a lot of nutbars come in here with crazy stories. They're emissaries from another planet. The mayor's bugging their houses. The CIA wants them dead. The country is being run by reptiles from space."

"I'm pretty sure that one's true," I said.

"Look, I got deadlines. I got real stories I'm working on, the kind that come with sources, witnesses, documents. The kind of stuff I can write without getting my ass sued."

"You don't think Birk is capable of this?"

"What I think isn't worth a damn," he said. "I'm not an editorial writer. I am a reporter, and the company pays me to write factual stories that I can back up, line by line, under the scrutiny of the legal department if necessary and I hate when those people review my copy. If they're not space reptiles, they're first cousins. Now if the police in Toronto consider Birk a murder suspect, and someone there is willing to go on the record, I can report that. If Rob Cantor makes some kind of public statement about the Aroclor, I can report that. Until then, you are a guy who came in off the street with a mouthful of cotton candy."

"It's not bullshit," I said.

I had given Hale my investigator's licence when I arrived. He picked it up off his desk and looked at it closely. He said, "You seem halfway normal to me. But even if I believe you— even if my gut tells me that you are telling the truth—"

"Does it?"

"Doesn't matter. I still can't expose my paper to a libel suit, which happens to be one of Simon Birk's hobbies, and which would get me fired or bumped back to rewriting wire copy."

"I'm not asking you to write anything. Yet. Just hear me out."

"Which I've been doing, despite certain time constraints piling up on my ass."

"And help me understand Birk a little better."

"The quo to your quid? All right," he said. "Let's get to the murders. Who is he supposed to have killed?"

"The engineer who was responsible for cleaning the site. He was beaten to death two—no, three days ago. The environmental studies major who found the Aroclor was shot the next day."

"And the third?"

"Rob Cantor's daughter."

"Jesus. What happened to her?"

I told him about Maya's apparent suicide and the evidence we had found that it had been staged.

When I was done, he gave me a long look, tapping his pencil against his pad, his lips pursed again—his thinking face.

"You're not throwing me out," I said.

"No."

"You're thinking it could be true."

"Yes."

"Because you know Birk."

"Because I know—or at least I think I know—things about him I've never been able to print."

"What things?"

He handed me back my ID and said, "Let's get some air."

Two years ago, Hale told me, two men forced their way into Birk's house, beat Birk and his wife unconscious, and made off with a fortune in cash, jewellery and art.

"Joyce was the collector," he told me. "Birk's idea of great art would probably be a portrait of himself. But she put together one of the best private collections in the city. Everything from the Impressionists onward. The cash the thieves got away with was negligible, maybe ten thousand from a safe. The jewellery not so negligible. Joyce had expensive taste and there were at least two or three pieces worth a hundred thousand or more. Each. But the artwork—man, I think the estimate was fifteen to twenty million."

"None of it ever recovered?"

"Not a sketch."

We were standing on the bridge that crossed the river at Michigan Street, looking out at a boat taking tourists on an architectural tour. We could hear the voice of the guide calling out the names of landmark buildings, the Tribune Tower among them.

"So what was it that you couldn't print?" I asked.

"Put it this way," Hale said. "That robbery couldn't have happened at a better time."

Now it was my turn to say, "You have my full attention."

"Birk was going through hell. They had just started excavating the Skyline site when some old bones were found. There was plenty of excitement because they were thought to be from the first white settlers."

"I read your piece on that."

"Then you know everything came to a screeching halt. And stayed there. At the same time, there was a strike by pipefitters that stopped construction on his building in New York. A casino he built in Macau was basically washed away in a typhoon. The tower crane right here snapped. Kind of a perfect shitstorm for Simon Birk. There were rumours that he was financially constrained before the robbery, but not so much after. The insurance payout was huge. And he sold the house, which netted him a little over ten million. The market was pretty hot at the time. And that all came to him, not his company."

"Are you saying the robbery was his idea?"

"Now we're getting into your territory," he said, grinning at me, "where I might think something but I can't prove it. All I know is what my gut tells me, which is it was too damn convenient. Simon cashed in big time, enough to float his boat until he could start building again."

"But he got the shit beaten out of him. And his wife . . ."

"There's something else that bothered me," he said. "His injuries were bad, but not one of them was even close to life-threatening. Broken hand. Collarbone. Nose. Six weeks later, he was all the way back. Every blow Joyce took was to the head. They beat her fucking senseless with a crowbar or something. Her heart stopped three times before the medics stabilized her."

"You think he wanted her dead?"

"I started out as a crime reporter. And one of the first things cops ask at the scene of a crime is, Who benefits? Whether the home invasion was Birk's idea or not, it left him free and clear of a whole bunch of things. He rose like a phoenix out of those ashes—maybe not as pretty as he'd been, but with shitloads of new cash. He moved himself into his own building, which doesn't cost him a dime, and his only expense is keeping Joyce in a nursing home. Ten, fifteen grand a month max. She used to spend ten times that much without buying a single piece of art."

"Did you float this idea past the cops?"

"I asked whether the evidence pointed to anything but a crime perpetrated by persons unknown."

"And?"

"The lead cop on the case looked at me like I was some kind of ghoul for even asking."

"And that's where it ended?" I asked.

"Let me clue you in on a fact or three about the state of news gathering these days. Circulation is declining every year. Ownership is not happy about said decline. And good investigative journalism is the most expensive kind there is. Sometimes you invest days, weeks, months on something that might not pan out."

"Fortunately," I said, "I have no such constraints."

"Knock yourself out, m'man."

"You remember the cop's name?"

"Tom Barnett."

"Where's he work out of?"

"Bureau of Investigative Services. Detective Division. You planning on talking to him?" he smiled.

"Why not?"

The smile got bigger. "Be interesting to see if he likes private investigators any better than he likes reporters."

CHAPTER 30

Once I was checked into my room, I called Jenn and gave her the rundown on my day.

"You think Birk's ears are burning yet?" she asked.

"I'd bet on it. If the site manager didn't call him, Peter Stemko probably did."

"I'm sorry I missed your act," Jenn said. "You being careful?"

"I'm watching my back while hoping he tries something," I said. "Because so far we've got nothing to hang him with. But there is something you could check."

"What?"

"You have good contacts in the art world?"

"I'm gay, Jonah. I can't go to a party without bumping into four gallery owners."

"Good. Simon Birk's house was looted two years ago."

"I remember. It was in the package I put together for you."

I told her what Jericho Hale had said about the convenient timing of the robbery, and his suspicion that Birk might have engineered it himself.

"Jesus. Is there nothing he won't stoop to?"

"For a change," I said, "there's no proof."

"So what can I do?"

"I'm emailing you an article that lists the main items

taken. Find out what they would have been worth on the black market. Ask if any have surfaced. I'll speak to the insurance company and see if they had any doubts."

"I'm on it," she said. "So . . . your friend Avi help you at all?"

"He said he'd make some calls," I said. "I'm going there for dinner tonight, so maybe he'll have something for me."

"It's good you have a friend there."

"Yes."

"What's he like?"

"Very different than he was in Israel—much more corporate—but I guess I'm different too."

"But some things never change," she said. "I'm sure you have more in common than you think."

"We'll see."

"Anything else?"

"That's it for now. Except . . ."

"Except what?"

"Maybe you ought to work from home while I'm away."

"Why? You think more goons might come around?"

"It's possible."

"And you think I can't take care of myself?"

"Don't take it the wrong way."

"I'm not supposed to worry about you but you can worry about me? Of all the sexist crap."

"It has nothing to do with sex, Jenn."

"Then what?"

I was struggling to find the right way to express what I was feeling—how much she meant to me as a friend and partner—when I heard a loud snort and a peal of laughter and realized I'd been had. "Gotcha," she giggled.

"You witch," I said.

"Guilty," she said.

"A guy tries to show concern . . ."

"I'm touched, Jonah."

"In the head, you're touched."

"I'm also at home."

"What?"

"I felt creeped out at the office after what happened. So I forwarded the phones to home and I've been working here all day. In my jammies."

"And still you give me shit."

"I was a little bored here."

"You're toast when I get back," I said. "You know that, don't you?"

"So get back in one piece," she said. "Then you can give me all the shit you want."

I hailed a cab in front of the hotel, the interior ripe with the smell of curry, and told the Sikh driver I wanted to go to West Montana Street—via the Gold Coast.

I could see his face light up in his mirror at the thought of the higher fare a roundabout trip would bring. "Of course," he said.

I gave him the address of Birk's old house on North Astor Street. He took Lake Shore north along Lake Michigan until Division, where he turned left and drove past North Astor to State. "Astor's a one-way south so I must go around this way," the driver explained. The houses grew grander in size and more grandiose in design, hundred-year-old mansions in all the styles popular at the turn of the century: Queen Anne, Georgian, Romanesque. The people who built these houses once ran the city: the publisher of the *Tribune*, the Wrigleys, the mayor, the guys who made money in steel, lumber, real estate and beer. Not many were family homes anymore. Like the mansions that lined the streets of the Annex back home, they were apartments or condos now, or museums or clubs. The biggest of all was the red sandstone home of the Archdiocese of Chicago; the second biggest, the old Playboy mansion.

When we got to the former Birk residence, I asked the driver to wait.

"Take all the time you need, sir," he said.

The house was spectacular. A four-storey Georgian master-piece built of grey stone, with arched windows on the ground floor and Juliet balconies along the top. Footlights bathed the stone in a soft pink light. There were security cameras at either end of the front gate, one aimed at the front door, one at the street. They weren't new—their black casings showed frills of rust along their edges—and had surely been there in Birk's time. The north side of the house was built up against its neighbour, barely a foot between them, and that gap was well covered by old-growth ivy that was dying against a trellis, dry brown twigs and leaves curling into themselves. On the south side, a drive-way went halfway to the back of the house, ending at a side door covered by a small white portico. A camera there too. I assumed there were cameras at the back of the house as well.

I got back into the cab wondering how the thieves had pulled off their robbery without being caught on tape.

CHAPTER 31

Avi's house didn't look like much from the outside—the brick facade needed some tuck-and-point work and the paint on the porch was coming off in strips—but that didn't reflect the interior at all. The ground floor had been fully renovated into an open-concept space with a huge island kitchen and spacious living and dining rooms separated by wooden French doors.

"When we bought the place, we gutted it and opened it up but we didn't put a nickel into the outside," Avi told me. "It only makes you more of a target for thieves. When you want to sell, that's when you worry about curb appeal."

He introduced me to his wife, Adele, a thin woman with dry, wispy brown hair and angry red patches of psoriasis on her elbows. Her hand felt like chicken bones when we shook and she barely made eye contact. Avi then took me down to the finished basement so I could meet his children. Noah was six, Benji was four and Emily was two. They were watching cartoons on a big-screen TV and barely acknowledged me or their father.

I said, "Every two years, eh? When's the next one due?"

"Three was it for me. Had myself fixed after Emmy."

We went back upstairs where Adele had poured us each a glass of chilled white wine.

"Nothing for you?" I asked.

"It gives me a headache," she said.

At her insistence, we took our drinks into the living room while she stayed in the kitchen to finish dinner.

"Check this out," Avi said, kneeling in front of a glassed-in cabinet that held a stack of stereo components. He loaded a CD into the player and pushed play. It was R.E.M. again, this time the album *Automatic for the People*. He must have had it on shuffle, because the first tune up wasn't "Drive"—it was "Everybody Hurts." Michael Stipe had written the lyrics in reaction to a rash of suicide among young people. And here I was listening to it, on a leg of a journey that began with the supposed suicide of Maya Cantor.

"Avi, please!" Adele called from the kitchen.

"Sorry, hon," he said, and lowered the volume before settling his bulk into a black leather recliner that faced the leather sofa I sat on. "She gets headaches," he said to me. "A lot of headaches."

"Sorry to hear that."

"Not as sorry as me."

"The kids look great," I said.

"They are," he smiled. "They're a lot of fun, most days. Their problems are still little problems—scrapes and spats and arguments over what show to watch. But it's draining sometimes, especially when Adele is—when she's not at the top of her game. And they eat into my salary like termites. And wait till all three are in private school. And summer camp. I'll be out on the street with a sign that says, 'Will sue for food.'"

"You look like you're doing all right."

"Yeah," he said. "All right is what I'm doing."

"So," I said, "were you able to find out anything about Simon Birk that would help me?"

"I did make a call or two," he said. "And I think it's safe to say some of his business practises have raised eyebrows in the

building community. He's known as an extremely tough negotiator, a real balls-to-the-walls bastard, according to my friend.
His word is as good as his bond, only his bond isn't worth shit.
He doesn't give a damn about his investors, his employees, his
residents or anyone but Simon Birk. He's litigious as hell. He
sues everyone sooner or later: business partners, journalists,
competitors. And he's been sued more times than I could count.
But there is nothing to suggest he's ever been involved in anything overtly criminal, Jonah. And certainly not murder. Not
even a hint of it in thirty-odd years."

"Doesn't mean he didn't take it up."

Avi shrugged. I took that as a sign he remained unconvinced.

"Let me ask you something else," I said. "You've heard
about the home invasion at Birk's two years ago?"

"Sure," Avi said. "He and his wife were both beaten up.
Crooks got away with a ton of art."

"What do you think of the possibility that he set it up himself? Anyone you could ask about that?"

"Jesus, Jonah. Is there anything you think he's not guilty of?"

"He was on the verge of going broke, then collected millions in insurance and the sale of his home."

"And he and his wife almost got killed. She's never recovered, from what I heard."

"I'm not the only one who thinks he could have done it."

"Who else?" he asked.

"A reporter."

"I've never seen that accusation in print."

"He hasn't written it yet."

"Because he has no more proof than you. You're going to
need a lot more than these off-the-wall theories to convince
anyone in authority."

"I'm still sure about the killings in Toronto."

"Yeah? Why do you think he's guilty and not this partner
of his, this Cantor?"

"Because that's what Cantor told me and I believe him."

"What were his words?"

"Birk assured him he'd take care of distractions."

"So you're making yourself into another distraction, and if he murders you, you'll have your answer?"

"That's not my exact plan."

"You have an exact plan?"

"To enjoy this glass of wine. After that, it's all up in the air."

Dinner was fast and furious. Adele tended to the children, who had hot dogs cut up in baked beans, guiding spoonfuls into two-year-old Emily's mouth and cajoling the other two to eat, while eating almost nothing herself. The grown-ups had baked salmon fillets, roasted asparagus and wild rice. Avi and I finished the bottle of wine. Adele had sparkling water. After dessert—applesauce for the kids, frozen yogourt for us—she bade us good night and marshalled the kids upstairs for baths and books. Avi led me into the living room and turned on a flat-screen plasma TV mounted to the wall.

"You have to see this," he said, popping in a DVD. "A little blast from the past."

It was a concert film: David Broza and friends at Masada, the two-thousand-year-old mountaintop fortress in the Israeli desert. Once King Herod's winter palace, better remembered as the place where Jewish zealots held off Roman troops until a long siege led to their mass suicide. A mesmerizing guitarist who had been trained in flamenco, and also absorbed folk, jazz, rock and blues into his style, Broza has been variously referred to as Israel's Bob Dylan, Leonard Cohen, Paul Simon, Stevie Ray Vaughan, Bruce Springsteen—pretty much everybody but Yngwie Malmsteen. Every year he hosted a sunrise concert in an amphitheatre on the west side of Masada, singing songs in Hebrew, English and Spanish. The DVD Avi played was a more recent event, but it still took me back to 1995, when Avi, Dalia and I, along with others from our kibbutz, went to hear him play. We ascended the mountain in the middle of the night—because of the searing heat, which often topped fifty degrees, the concert started at a quarter to four. Some four thousand people were there, singing along with Broza, swaying in each other's arms, especially when he played "Yihyeh Tov (Things Will Get Better)," a peace anthem he wrote when Israel and Egypt signed their historic treaty in 1979. We watched in awe as he punished his guitar with manic fingers, its surface scarred and practically worn through. By the end of the concert, we were as sweaty and exhausted as Broza himself, but some of us walked up the Roman Ramp to watch the sun come up over the faraway hills of Jordan, the mountains turning purple and rose in the new light of day. It felt like a time when peace might actually be at hand. We had no way of knowing that our kibbutz, Har Milah, would soon be bombarded by Katyusha rockets from Lebanon, and that one of them would end Dalia's life.

The DVD ended, as Broza concerts always did, with "Yihyeh Tov." I watched the footage knowing that good things had not come. Peace had not come, then or now. I felt tears fill my eyes and tried to wipe them away discreetly. Then I stole a glance at Avi Stern and saw that he was crying too.

CHAPTER 32

I was up by six, unable to sleep after a vague but disturbing dream about Dalia in which we had gone to the cemetery on Mount Scopus in Jerusalem and got caught in a downpour without an umbrella. Why did Avi have to show me that DVD? Yes, Broza's Masada concert had been a great moment in our young lives, but watching the film had only stirred up intense feelings in both of us. Surprisingly intense, in Avi's case. He had brushed it off afterward, saying he was tired, saying he missed all the people he'd known on the kibbutz, missed the happy, crazy passion of life in Israel before the bombardment of Har Milah.

I made myself a cup of coffee, taking it black instead of using the powdered whitening product that came with it, then went to the hotel's fitness centre, where I put myself through an intense hour-long workout: thirty minutes on a treadmill, a hundred push-ups—okay, four sets of twenty-five each—and sit-ups until my abs cried *No more*. After a shower, I checked the hotel restaurant's menu and decided no breakfast was worth twenty bucks, even if it was Rob Cantor's money.

I walked over to Dearborn and found an agreeable diner where they piled on eggs, ham and home fries for six dollars and change. Three men at a table behind me got to talking with a group of four at the next table and soon they were comparing their military service. It started with one spotting a screaming eagle tattoo on another's arm, and asking, "Is that for real? You a Marine? Hey, me too." All but one of the seven had been in the army or Marine Corps. None had been in Iraq—they were all in their thirties and forties—but some had seen action in Desert Storm. Soon they were high-fiving each other and offering to buy drinks come evening.

That was one conversation you'd never get in Toronto, where the closest most people get to military service is protesting outside the U.S. Consulate.

I walked back to the Hilton, pondering my first move of the day. A sign outside Birk's old house said that security was provided by a company called Eye-Con. Maybe someone there would be able to tell me how the home invaders had circumvented the system without being seen.

As I walked up the circular drive, a man stepped out of a black Lincoln Town Car parked in front of the lobby doors and said, "Good morning."

He was around six-three and thin but I was betting there was a lot of lean muscle under his black suit. His head was shaved—no, not shaved: hairless. Not one hair on his head, no eyebrows, no sign that he had to shave his face. Alopecia. It made his eyes seem huge, like he was an amphibian of some kind, a Gollum who'd been living in an underwater cave.

"You've been inquiring about Simon Birk?" he said.

There was nothing in his hands. No one else in the car. I said, "Yes."

"He'd like to meet you," the man said.

"Where?"

"His office, of course. He gets to work early."

I hesitated. I wanted to meet Birk, but had no guarantee that's where this man would take me.

"It's up to you," he said, looking at his watch. "He's

offered to make time for you. But he doesn't have all the time in the world."

"You his chauffeur?"

"I provide a range of services to Mr. Birk. Collecting you is what I'm doing now."

I said, "You mind opening your jacket?"

He smiled without showing any teeth and unbuttoned his jacket. No gun in the waistband, no holster under the arm.

"Backside too?" he asked.

"Please."

He pirouetted. Nothing in the back of his pants. "It's a one-time offer, pal."

"You have a name?" I asked.

"I have several," he said.

"Which should I use?"

"Curry."

You get into a stranger's car, there's always a chance you won't come back, or not all in one piece. But I had come to Chicago to meet Simon Birk himself, so I got into the car and fastened my seat belt, hoping it wouldn't be too bumpy a ride.

The Birkshire Riverfront was on West Wacker Drive, on the south side of the Chicago River, overlooking the LaSalle Street bridge. My hairless escort parked between signs that said No Parking and No Stopping. I followed him into an opulent two-storey lobby with travertine floors and water bubbling through beds of stone. Chandeliers formed of opaque cylinders hung over a semicircular desk where two uniformed guards watched feeds from a dozen security cameras. Curry flipped his car keys to one of them then led me to a bank of elevators whose brass doors were so highly polished I could see my reflection in perfect detail.

There were no buttons to push for the penthouse level; access was by key only. Curry produced a ring of keys, chose one that looked like it was for a bike lock, inserted it and twisted. The elevator rose swiftly enough to make my stomach lurch, and reached the sixtieth floor in less than a minute.

The elevator doors opened directly into a reception area with cherry-wood panelling and the same travertine flooring as in the lobby. The woman behind the desk said, "He's waiting," and reached under her desk to press a button that unlocked the door into the inner sanctum of Simon Birk.

His office wasn't much bigger than a soccer pitch, with windows on two sides offering a fabulous view of the Chicago skyline across the river—the white Gothic stone of the Wrigley and Tribune buildings; the Hancock with its spires like the horns of a gazelle. The third wall had framed photos of Birk's buildings around the world, all taken at night. Surrounding his desk like chess pieces were knee-high scale versions of his best-known towers in Manhattan, Chicago, Los Angeles, Dubai, London, Macau and Rio. Birk could walk among them for inspiration, bestride them like a colossus, all five-foot-five of him.

The man himself was standing behind the mahogany desk, hands clasped behind him, looking out at the city. He kept his back to me as he said, "Chicago is a tough city to build in, Mr. Geller. Toughest in the world. You've seen some of the crap going up in Toronto. I assume you have travelled to other cities. Chicago will not stand for inferior buildings, certainly not among its major projects. Skyscrapers were born here—not in New York, as most people think—and the best architects and developers of our time have come to make their mark here. When you build in Chicago," he said, "you're competing against past and present. And if you wish not only to compete, but to stand out? You know going in that there will be challenges. Hurdles and snags. Every project has them. But this one, Geller . . . this one has been a trial. Every step of the way, there have been problems. First the old bones. Then the crane falling. Month after month I've had to wait for it to get back on track and now it is, finally. You were there yesterday?"

"Yes."

"Watching it go up?"

"Yes."

"Wishing perhaps it would come down?"

I let that one pass.

He said, "For every visionary who looks up at the sky and says, 'Why not,' there is a small person somewhere who'd rather tear it down. Are you one of those, Geller? Because you have to understand that after everything I've had to endure to keep the Millennium Skyline going, I'm not in a position, not in the mood, to brook any further delays."

He turned to face me. His blue eyes looked like diamond chips: cold, hard, glittering. He wore a grey suit and a powder-blue shirt and a dark blue tie. Understated and seriously expensive. I could probably have paid half a year's rent with the money he'd spent on the outfit, and that wasn't counting the chunky Rolex on his hairy left wrist.

There were two low-slung club chairs in front of Birk's desk, much lower than the leather chair behind it. "Please," he said, pointing to one of them. I sat in it. Curry remained standing, leaving me the lowest person in the room.

"You've been asking about me," Birk said. "First in Toronto, and now here. My job site, the Department of Buildings, the *Tribune*. Even probing legal circles. Making quite a lot of noise, and all on your first day in town."

Birk was supposed to know I'd been at the Skyline site and the DOB. How did he know I'd been at the *Tribune*, or when I had arrived in Chicago? How had he known about the lawyers Avi called?

"It's my job to know things that concern me," he said, reading my mind. "And to be frank, Mr. Geller, one thing that's beginning to concern me is you. My work, you have to understand, is highly complex. It requires great attention to detail—from the ground up, so to speak. I'm a very hands-on guy, which means I am involved in every aspect: site procurement and preparation, design and construction, right through to the final fittings and fixtures in every building. I choose the stone, the glass, the lights, the rugs, the fabrics and flooring. I even decide the temperature of the swimming pools. I monitor labour contracts, currency exchanges, legal files, requests for proposals and quotations, gambling statutes, food and beverage trends. The point I'm making, and I do hope I'm making it clearly, is that I have enough on my plate without some pissant private investigator making public scenes and dragging my name through the mud."

"I've inconvenienced you?"

"Yes."

"Not a good idea?"

"No."

"Because you're busy and important and lord of all you survey."

"You should take what I'm telling you seriously," he said.

"Or what? I'll end up like Martin Glenn? Like Will Sterling?"

Birk did a nice job of furrowing his bushy eyebrows as if the names meant nothing. "And who might they be?"

"Corpses now," I said. "Before that, one of them was an engineer on the Harbourview job, and the other found evidence of how polluted that land is."

"And you think I had something to do with their deaths?"

"You said it yourself, you're a hands-on guy."

Birk set his cup down on its saucer and leaned across his desk. I could see a bend in his nose where the home invaders had broken it. "I'll admit I'm not completely up on Canadian law," he said, "but the U.S. system offers people like me considerable protection against libel and slander. Make one more unfounded accusation about me in any public forum, and I'll bury you under a ton of legal paper."

"Isn't truth a defence down here?"

"There is no truth to it!" he said. "None."

"You didn't tell Rob Cantor you'd take care of Glenn and Sterling?"

"What I tell Cantor or anyone else is none of your business, understand?" His face was growing dark with anger. He wasn't used to people talking back to him—suing him, maybe, or playing hardball in negotiations, but not giving him lip in his own office. "None of this is your business. You're a nobody, Geller. Especially in Chicago. You have no standing of any kind here. You're a pipsqueak. You're a shit stain on a sidewalk. I've got six thousand people working for me. I've got enough lawyers to ruin you, your partner, your brother and anyone else who crosses me. So here's the plan. Francis will take you back to your hotel," he said, indicating the man who called himself Curry. "He'll wait while you pack your things and he'll drive you to O'Hare. You'll get on the first plane back to Toronto. You'll stop poking your nose into my affairs and quit making bizarre accusations."

"You haven't even heard them all," I said. "In fact, forget Will Sterling. Forget Martin Glenn. Some of my best accusations are yet to come."

"What does that mean?"

"It means poking holes in your bullshit home invasion story."

He slammed his fist down on his desk, rattling his cup and saucer, spilling droplets of coffee. His hands formed fists and his jacket bunched around his thick arms and shoulders. Francis Curry walked languidly toward me. I think he was trying to look menacing. It might have worked better if he used an eyebrow pencil.

I said, "Don't try me."

"Wouldn't dream of it," he said. He reached into his pocket and dangled his keys. "But you'll need these to get back to ground level. Unless you want to save everyone some trouble and jump out a window."

"Like Maya Cantor?"

He said, "Who?"

Cut from the same cloth as his boss.

On the ride down, I said, "You're not just a driver."

"No."

"Ex-cop?"

"Ex a lot of things," he said.

I said, "I think I'll walk back to my hotel, Francis. Everything's walking distance here, right? Got to love that about a city."

He said, "You not going to take Mr. Birk's advice?"

"No."

"You should."

"What can I say? Chicago is too great a town. It's everything they say it is. I am having far too much fun to go home."

"What's that?" he said. "You giving me your Bill Murray? Having a little fun with me? Okay. Have as much fun as you want. Rack up the laughs. Whoop it up on the streets of Chicago."

"And while I am doing that?"

"I'll be covering Simon Birk's ass," he said. "Who'll be covering yours?"

CHAPTER 33

Eye-Con Security's offices were at the corner of Dearborn and Harrison in the neighbourhood known as Printers' Row, where century-old brick buildings had been converted to offices and lofts. The president, Joe Konerko, was a morbidly obese man with thick rubbery ears whose lobes rested against his jowls. He held out his hand, which looked like a glove that had been inflated, and showed me to a chair opposite his cluttered desk.

He said, "Normally, I wouldn't tell you squat about a client but Birk's not a client anymore. And there were always a few things about that job that bugged me."

"Such as?"

"We pride ourselves on our work. We're not the biggest outfit in town, right? We're not going to compete with your ADTs, your Brinks, in terms of volume. So we specialize in offering the best there is to high-end clients. Your multi-camera closed-circuit systems, complete with interactive video, night vision capability, weatherproofing. The whole enchilada. And Birk went for the best. We had him wired up with eight high-resolution colour cameras outside, plus a hidden dome camera inside, all hooked up to a digital recorder. I'm talking about thirty grand worth of equipment and that doesn't include the installation or monitoring fees. When a client buys a package like that, and still gets cleaned out by thieves, we don't look too good. We look like horseshit, in fact. Especially because of what happened to Mrs. Birk. We felt terrible about that."

"So how did they do it?"

"A security system is like a chain," Konerko said. "Only as strong as its weakest link. The way the cameras were set up, there's no way anyone shoulda got into that house. In addition to our monitors here"—he waved an arm at a glassed-in area where a dozen men and women wearing headsets watched closed-circuit feeds—"the Birks had their own monitor right in the foyer of the house. Nice crisp Toshiba twenty-four-inch. They would have seen who was at the door."

"But?"

"But they let them in anyway," he said.

"Two guys?"

"Yup. Want to see them?"

"You're kidding."

"Hey, it's all digital these days, not like when you had to erase tapes and reuse them. And like I said, this one really bugged me. She was practically beaten to death, Mrs. Birk was, and on our watch." He got up from his desk and brought me into the monitoring room, where he eased his great bulk gingerly into a sway-backed chair and searched a hard drive for the recording.

When he had it cued up, he jabbed a thick finger at the screen. "See the time code? It's just after ten at night. Everything's working like it should. Cameras are all rolling. And a truck shows up."

We watched a half-ton cube van pull up in front of the Birk mansion. On the side was a logo that said Carpet Cleaning and Restoration. Totally generic: could have been stencilled that morning. The driver angled out into the street and then backed up the driveway, stopping just short of the side entrance.

Then the rear doors opened and two men got out. Both wore faded blue coveralls, ball caps pulled low and wraparound dark glasses. The doors of the truck blocked them from the view of the gate camera.

They obviously knew where each camera was. You could tell by the way they positioned themselves, every move orchestrated to deny full-face views.

They pressed a buzzer at the side door. Konerko froze the tape. "Based on the height of this model van, we estimate the guy on the left at about five-eleven, maybe six feet. The right, a few inches taller."

"Six-three?"

"Around there."

About Francis Curry's height.

He pressed play: the side door of the house opened wide enough to admit them, then closed quickly. "So now they're in," he said. "From our point of view, there's nothing unusual so far. Nothing that would have made our people sit up and take notice. Far as we can tell, two guys showed up to pick up a carpet. Granted, it's late, but maybe there was a spill, a flood, who knows what. But the inside camera, the dome, should have recorded whatever happened next, because that's where the Birks were assaulted, right in the front foyer. When the cops came, that's where they found his wife."

"And Birk?"

"He'd made it to the den and called the cops from there."

"What was his story exactly?"

"He said he saw the cleaning truck and assumed his wife had called them. He knew he should have checked with her but he got careless and opened the door first."

Simon Birk, the control freak, the man who chose every detail of every tower he built, getting careless at ten at night, beckoning into his intensely private life two unknown tradesmen in dark glasses and ball caps.

"So what about the hidden dome camera?"

"That wasn't on a live feed to us, obviously. Clients don't want outsiders watching their every move. But it was wired to a hard-drive recorder in a utility closet in the basement."

"Let me guess. The thieves took it with them."

"That they did."

"How did they know it was there?"

"Birk told the cops the thieves knew about the camera and forced him to tell them where the recorder was."

"What did the cops think about that?"

"The guy I talked to—"

"Tom Barnett?"

"Yeah, that's him. He took down the details. Said he'd talk to Birk about tradesmen, staff, people who might have had the inside scoop on the cameras. He questioned me and my employees. But no one ever got arrested. And nothing was ever recovered. I wasn't happy about the whole thing, like I told you. But it wasn't my job to ask Birk why he let the guys in. And thank the lord, I wasn't the one who had to hand him an insurance cheque."

"Who did?"

CHAPTER 34

I called Great Midwestern Life from my hotel room and asked the claims adjuster, Gary Herman, if he could spare a few minutes to talk about the Birks' claim.

"There's nothing I can tell you," he said.

"Because there's nothing to tell or because you aren't allowed to tell it?"

"Either way. We signed a confidentiality agreement."

"You did."

"An airtight one."

"Exists on paper somewhere."

"In this very office."

"So even if you had misgivings about the claim . . ."

"Even if I had whoppers," he said. "I still couldn't tell you that. I also couldn't tell you that Simon Birk is one litigious sonofabitch and that it could never on any level be worth the grief to try to deny the claim. Wouldn't matter the case you had. He would take it to the next level and the next. He'd nuke you if all you had was a baseball bat. That I definitely couldn't tell you."

"As one investigator to another," I said, "could you tell me if the police had misgivings?"

"Would have made my job easier if they had."

"Would have given you traction."

"If they had done so."

"Was it Tom Barnett you spoke to?"

"Finally," he chuckled. "A question I can answer."

I called Jenn at home and told her about my visit to Simon Birk's office.

"If he knows you're there, and he knows your every move, I hope you're being careful," she said.

"His bodyguard is a guy named *Francis*, for God's sake. And he looks like a mannequin. A Madame Tussaud version of himself."

"Doesn't mean he isn't dangerous."

Jenn had put together a complete list of the pieces stolen from the Birk house. "I spoke to my friend Patrick," she said. "He owns a gallery called Arles and he drooled over this stuff. At a legal auction, the stuff would have fetched at least twenty-five million. The Modigliani nude alone would have gone for five or six million, the Monet about the same, even though Patrick said it was a minor variation on the water lily theme. At least a million for Picasso's sketch of his mistress. And that's just three items out of dozens taken. If Birk netted even half of what they were worth *and* collected on the insurance, it was quite the payday."

I asked her if anyone had called for me.

"Anyone as in a certain homicide detective?"

"For instance."

"Sorry, chief."

"What about Cantor? He write up those notes of his?"

"Haven't received them yet."

"All right. Turn up the heat if you don't get anything by end of business."

"Will do."

"Anything else on the go?"

"No."

"I'm thinking it might be better if you were down here."

"Chicago!" she said. "I thought you'd never ask."

"Sierra won't mind?"

"Are you kidding? The Magnificent Mile?"

"I'm not asking you down here to shop."

"You also can't work me around the clock," she said. "There are labour laws, you know."

"In the States?" I said. "Get out."

Nailing Simon Birk for murder was looking more and more like an impossible quest. Unless I found something solid I could feed to Hollinger, the best I could do was blow smoke. I wanted to call her, see if she had turned up anything useful in Martin Glenn's financial records, or in the forensics on Will Sterling's apartment. Maybe she was grilling Rob Cantor as we spoke, nodding grimly, taking furious notes, making the connections, saying to herself, "Jonah was right all along."

Or maybe she was eating her lunch.

The home invasion was my best bet now—if I could find something, anything, to persuade this Tom Barnett to reopen his investigation. It wouldn't carry the same weight as a murder charge but the sentence for fraud—especially one that had led to near-fatal injuries to his wife—might put him away for the rest of his natural life.

Who else had been in the van? Assuming the driver was Curry, the passenger was about six feet tall, Konerko had said, way too tall for Birk himself. Therefore, a third man: a thread worth trying to follow, either with Tom Barnett or Jericho Hale.

Hale was less likely to eat me alive so I decided to see him first.

When in doubt, I walk. It clears my head, works my lungs and feeds my blood. So instead of getting a cab to the *Tribune*, I walked up Michigan to Congress and turned right. I took the bridge there across the Metra tracks to Grant Park, its entrance guarded by statues of fierce-looking Natives on horseback.

There were few other people in the park. The apple and cherry trees were bare, the roses already deadheaded. Park workers were raking leaves and blowing debris into bags. The closer I got to the lake, the harder was the bite of the wind blowing in off its waters. Some of the younger runners jogging past me were wearing shorts, their legs bright red from the cold. I was glad I had on jeans and a leather jacket.

Straight ahead was the Buckingham Fountain. Postcards in the hotel gift shop showed its great spume of water rising fifty feet or more into the air but by late October it had been turned off for the season. A city park worker was hosing dead leaf matter off the fanciful marine sculptures that ring the main fountain. A tourist, overweight and overburdened with cameras and other gear, was videotaping his wife as she sat astride a verdigris sculpture of a cavorting sea beast.

At the far end of the fountain are steps leading down to a path that runs parallel to the lakeshore, where waves were crashing against stone jetties. Dead leaves scuttled on the asphalt like crabs. I had just turned north onto the path when I heard footsteps coming up fast behind me, a heavy tread crunching through the leaves. I turned just in time to see him closing on me, a big man in a three-quarter-length peacoat, his right arm close to his body, something held down along there. Something long and black. A lovely pistol-and-suppressor set.

Advantage him.

But to use a suppressor effectively, he needed a smaller-calibre weapon, which meant he had to get close enough for head shots.

Advantage me.

As soon as he raised his arm to shoot, I charged him, my left hand driving his gun arm off to the side. He was a beefy man in his forties, with a wide Slavic face, thick hair and moustache, like a Stalin double waiting for his cue. I grabbed his shirtfront, pulled, and launched a head-butt from my core. Delivering it with neck muscles alone will hurt you more than the other guy. Driving it from your abs gives it shattering force. I broke his nose with the crown of my head. The stunning blow left him dazed enough for me to thumb his wrist into numbness until the gun fell. Then I elbowed the side of his head, felt his knees go wobbly and let him slump to the ground. I threw the gun into a thick bramble of shrubs. Threw him in after it.

I looked north up the path. Saw no one but two young women joggers, both wearing iPods and blissfully unaware of their surroundings. Looked south: an older man who was picking up after his dog.

I set a quick pace north toward the stately Tribune Tower, walking, not running, trying to put some distance between me and my assailant in case he had backup somewhere.

He had worse.

I had taken maybe ten strides when a black Ford Interceptor drove off Lake Shore Drive onto the sidewalk, blocking my path. The driver's door swung open and a burly towheaded man charged out of his car with a gun in hand. But he opened the car door with such force that it swung back at him, knocking him down into his seat, and I had the choice of trying to disarm my second gunman of the day or listen to Eidan Feingold for once and run.

I turned tail and ran for my life.

CHAPTER 35

A t a glance, the second man looked a dozen years older and a lot heavier than me. He had a gun, but handguns aren't nearly as accurate as cop shows and westerns make them out to be. Anything over a hundred yards would be a crapshoot.

I was in shape and built for speed. I ran back into the park, along the one stretch I knew, the oak-lined path that led to the fountain, arms and legs pumping like a wide receiver with a safety on his tail.

I heard no footsteps behind me. Took that as a good thing. Glanced behind me and saw no one. Turned back, heard an engine roar and saw the black Interceptor bouncing up a narrow paved path reserved for park vehicles, cutting me off again. Once more the gunman spilled out of the car, this time steering clear of the swinging door. He crouched and pointed a semi-automatic pistol at me. No suppressor on it; nothing subtle about this dude.

"On the ground," he barked. "On the motherfucking ground."

I stayed where I was.

"Now!" he yelled. "Or I'll drop you where you stand."

I raised my hands high in the air and turned my back on him.

"I didn't say turn around," he said. "I said get on the god-damn ground."

I lowered myself slowly into push-up position. The pavement was cold against my hands, then my chest when the gunman kicked my hands out from under me. Then he knelt on my back, not being shy about forcing my spine down, and told me to put my hands behind my back.

"You a cop?" I asked.

"I'm your angel of fucking death, you don't do what I say."

I put my hands behind me. He cuffed them in metal, not plastic. Then he grabbed the collar of my jacket and pulled me to my feet, shoved me against his car, forced my upper body down on the hood.

"Do I get to see an ID?" I asked.

His gun muzzle pressed into my neck. "This is all the ID I need right now."

He reached into my jacket and found my wallet. His gun pushed farther into my neck when he saw my investigator's licence. "A PI?" he asked. His free hand moved over every part of my body that could conceivably have hidden a gun. "Where's your piece?"

"I don't carry one."

"What kind of PI goes around Chicago without a gun?"

"A Canadian one."

"Weird."

"You know, if you're a cop, this would be the ideal time to identify yourself."

"Shut up."

"I was attacked," I said. "All I did was defend myself."

"I saw you beat a guy down and throw a gun in the bushes."

Then I heard a woman call, "Excuse me."

He looked up. Even with my face pressed down against the hood of the car, I could see the tourist couple who had been filming near the fountain walking hesitantly toward us, the woman the more assertive of the two, urging her husband forward. He seemed more interested in protecting his cameras.

When they were within ten feet of us, the gunman told them to stop and said, "Chicago PD," and took out a leather ID case, flipped it open so we could all see his badge and his name, which I had pretty much guessed already.

Detective Thomas Barnett, Bureau of Investigative Services, Chicago Police Department.

"We saw it. Dennis," the woman said, her breathing laboured from the fast walk over. "Tell him what we saw."

Dennis was about fifty, also out of breath, with fine sandy hair and a great spur-shaped cowlick in the back. "This fellow was attacked," he told Barnett. "The other guy—"

"What other guy?" Barnett asked.

"A big guy with dark hair and a moustache," I said. "Think Stalin."

"It looked like he was going to shoot this fellow but then this fellow—"

"Jonah Geller," I said, wanting my name out there.

"Then Mr. Geller here knocked him out and ran. And then you showed up."

"I got a call," Barnett said. "An assault in progress."

That had to be steaming bullshit. He had arrived on the scene too fast to have been responding to any call. The couple were the closest witnesses and they obviously hadn't phoned it in.

I walked Barnett and the tourists to where the assault had taken place. The gunman was gone but there was a blood spatter on the pavement where his broken nose had gushed. The gun was in the bushes where I said it would be, and Barnett made a show of sealing it in a plastic bag and locking it in a case in the trunk of his car. Having been educated in these matters by Dante Ryan, I guessed it was a .22, either a Colt or a Field King.

"What about these handcuffs?" I asked Barnett.

"What about them?"

"You heard it from them, I defended myself."

"In fact," the woman said, "we got it all on tape."

"You what?" Barnett said.

"On tape," she said. "Play it back, Den. Show him the part you filmed."

Dennis sighed and unfolded the viewer from his camcorder. He played back footage of the fountain: you could hear him instructing his wife to move out of the way so he could get a close-up of the plaque that told who it had been named after. Then you saw me in the background, walking along the path behind the fountain; the other man coming up swiftly; and my counterattack, which I thought even Eidan would have admired.

"You don't have to keep this, do you?" Dennis asked. "It's got my footage of me in front of Soldier Field."

"Sorry," Barnett said. He held out his hand for the cassette, pocketed it and told them they could go. I tried to look contrite for causing them to lose their vacation footage and thanked them for coming forward. It struck me as odd that we weren't all going down to a precinct to sign statements and look at mug books. But mentioning that would have been like asking the teacher why she hadn't popped a quiz.

It was clearly no coincidence that Barnett had appeared on the scene. My guess was he had been there for two reasons: to confirm the kill, and to provide an official version of the events: probably as a mugging or robbery gone wrong. Either way, I knew now that he was in Simon Birk's pocket, which made me more sure than ever that Birk had set up the robbery at his home.

Barnett undid my handcuffs and said, "How many murders a year you get in Toronto?"

"I don't know," I said. "About eighty or ninety, I guess."

"We get at least five or six hundred," he said. "Used to be like a thousand a year. But still. Five, six hundred is a lot of killings. And there's a lot that go unsolved."

"Which means what?"

"That Frank Sinatra had it all wrong. Chicago ain't your kind of town."

CHAPTER 36

"Back so soon?" asked Jericho Hale.

I held out my wrists. "See these marks?"

"I'm a black man in America," he said. "I know cuff stripes when I see them."

"Want to guess who put them there?"

"I don't have to," he said, "because I can see you're dying to tell me."

He had me there. "Tom Barnett."

He leaned forward so fast his chair almost tipped. "You shitting me?"

"I shit you not."

"Detective Thomas Barnett had you in cuffs."

"I think I'm lucky that's all he did." I told Hale what had happened in Grant Park.

"All right, Geller. Walk with me."

I followed him to the far end of the newsroom, where a young Hispanic reporter sat at a desk covered with police band scanners.

"Alvaro," Hale said.

"Sssh." The reporter had his head down, listening intently to one of the scanners. "Damn," he said. "I can't make half this shit out."

"That's the code for armed robbery," Hale said. "South Hermitage, 6000 block."

"How'd you—"

"I started on this desk, man. You'll develop an ear for it, you give it enough time. Alvaro, this is Geller. He has a question for you."

"Make it quick," he said. "I miss a call—"

"I'll listen to your scanners," Hale said. "You answer his question."

Alvaro looked at me. He was in his early twenties, tops, wiry and full of nervous energy, one knee pumping away beneath the desk.

I said, "There was an assault in Grant Park today. Just over an hour ago. Did anything go out over the police radio? Call for assistance?"

He flipped through a notepad. "Grant Park . . . no. Had a shooting in Humboldt Park and an assault in Hyde Park . . . nothing in Grant."

I beamed a pleasant smile at Hale.

"What?" Alvaro asked. "What's that look? There a story in this?"

"No," I said. "Nothing happened."

"Seriously?" Alvaro flipped to a clean page in the notebook. "I haven't had a decent byline in a week."

"Um . . . Alvaro? Better get back to your scanner," Hale said. "You just missed a Homicide call on West 25th. Probably the Latin Kings."

"What? Shit!" Alvaro said.

Hale tugged on my shirt sleeve and steered me back to his cubicle.

"So," he said. "Barnett responded to a call that never went out."

"He knew it was going to happen. So dish," I said. "What do you know about Barnett that I ought to know?"

"Well, his rep is he's a tough cop, even by Chicago standards. Bit of a head-breaker. But honest enough. Nothing too rancid following him. No whispers he was ever on the take."

"Until now."

"The only thing I recall . . ."

"Yes?"

"You know there's another newspaper in this town?" he said. "One without the, uh, high journalistic standards to which we here at the *Tribune* aspire?"

"The tabloid."

"The very one. They go for stories with a certain flavour. The kind their readers can follow without spraining a lip."

"Mee-ow."

"They ran a story about Barnett two, three years ago. He was heading up the mayor's anti-drug task force then. Cleaning up Englewood, other parts of the city that were basic open-air markets for drugs and guns. We didn't run it because it was personal and it didn't strike us as fair game."

"Go on."

Hale turned to his computer and tapped something into a search engine. "I want to call this up because the headline, as I recall, was gutter fucking poetry and I want to do it justice." We waited a moment until the item appeared on screen: "Cop's Kid Caught in Crack Crackdown."

"Barnett's son?"

"Colin James Barnett, age seventeen. He was arrested by police in Brookfield—that's a suburb out west—selling crack cocaine at a strip mall. Nothing big-time. Basically financing his own habit. Buy seven grams, sell six, get one free, that kind of thing."

"What happened to him?"

"First-time offender and white? He got probation and an order to get treatment."

"I'm guessing drug treatment is expensive here?"

"Yeah, we don't have your socialized Canadian medicine. Costs an arm, a leg and a pint of blood for any decent program."

"Which your average detective can't afford."

"Unless he comes into contact with a Simon Birk, who has lots of money and needs a friendly cop."

"You going to look into this?" I asked.

"Like a proctologist."

"You'll keep me posted?"

"That may not be my top priority."

"But you'll fit it in somewhere."

"I told you before, I'm here to gather information, not dispense it."

The tabloid story was still up on Hale's screen. I looked at the byline under the lurid headline. Paul Vrabowski. "All right," I said. "Think Paul Vrabowski will give me the time of day?"

"Think and Paul Vrabowski don't belong in the same sentence," he said. "Let me make some calls and get back to you."

"Book your flight yet?" I asked Jenn.

"Tomorrow morning," she said. "Same one you were on."

"All right. In the meantime, see what you can find out about a Chicago cop named Tom Barnett. Detective with the Bureau of Investigative Services."

"What about him?"

"Everything you can find. His record, who he reports to, details about his son's drug treatment."

"What's the connection?"

"I think he wants me dead."

"Jonah . . ."

I gave her the same précis of the day's events I'd given Hale.

"So you think Birk has Barnett in his pocket."

"Which goes a long way toward confirming the theory that the home invasion was an inside job."

"Which will do you no good if you're dead or in jail."

"For the moment," I said, "I'm safe in my room. Both locks locked and the chain on. Hear from Cantor yet?"

"Yes. He couriered his statement about an hour ago. I read through it and it looks pretty complete."

"Okay. Call Hollinger and—no, wait. I'll call."

"Thought you might."

"Make a copy and ship it over to her on a one-hour service. I want her to have it in front of her when I talk to her."

Hollinger sounded remote and not just because of the hundreds of miles that separated us.

"I'm willing to concede that Cantor's story sounds plausible," she said.

"That's it?"

"It's hardly a deposition," she said. "There's nothing legally binding about it. And it's totally hearsay, not to mention self-serving. One participant in a conspiracy to commit fraud accusing another alleged co-conspirator."

"Call him in."

"I have," she said. "First thing tomorrow."

"What else have you found out?"

"That I'm able to share with you?"

"Katherine—"

"Don't Katherine me. I can't tell you anything I wouldn't tell a reporter."

"You wouldn't have known about Martin Glenn's fight with Cantor if I hadn't told you. You wouldn't have known about Will Sterling's connection either."

I heard her sigh deeply into her phone. "All right, Jonah. There are a couple of things we have that lend credence to your version of things. Your partner forwarded me the email Maya Cantor sent to Sterling the night she died. It would seem to contradict the mindset of a person who was about to kill herself. We're opening an investigation into her death. A forensic team is going through her apartment as we speak and the scope will be far beyond what the coroner did. We've also asked Jenn to bring in Maya's laptop. Our people can probably do a more thorough search of its contents than you could."

"What else?"

"We found phone calls made from Sterling's house to Cantor's office that fit the timeline you suggested. And calls from Cantor to Simon Birk that followed closely on the heels."

"You're starting to believe me, aren't you?"

"I'll follow up any lead that could help me close these cases," she said.

"Anything new on Glenn?"

"Our financial analyst traced payments made from Cantor to Martin Glenn that seem beyond the scope of work billed by EcoSys. Which supports the theory Cantor was trying to buy a clean bill of health for the Harbourview site. What about you?" she asked. "Anything coming out of Chicago I should know about?"

"You could say that. Birk tried to have me killed today."

"What! Why didn't you—"

"Because I can't prove it was him. I also can't prove the sun's going to rise in the east tomorrow, but I know it, just like I know this."

I told her my theory that Birk had staged the robbery at his house when he was at his lowest financial ebb; how he had co-opted the lead investigator, Tom Barnett, who needed money to get his son off drugs; how I had been granted an audience with His Birkness and the naked ape, Francis Curry; how Barnett had appeared on the scene seconds after the Stalin look-alike had tried to gun me down.

"Come back to Toronto," she said. "Let me see what I can do through official channels."

"No way."

"Jonah—"

"Don't you get this way when you're working a murder?" I asked. "Don't you feel like you have to keep going, not stop, not take a step back until you find out what happened and why?"

"I have a badge," she said. "I have a gun. I have an entire police service behind me. I have powers granted by the province."

"I have a black belt."

"Don't joke about it. I know things got off on the wrong foot with us the other night but I want . . . I don't want . . . I—"

"You care about me?"

"Yes, and damn you for making me say it."

"I fully intend to come back in one piece," I said. "And take you to a restaurant not owned by anyone remotely notorious."

"So be careful."

"Everyone keeps telling me that. Even Barnett."

"But are you listening?"

CHAPTER 37

Jericho Hale called and asked if I had an expense account. I said I did.

"Then get ready to abuse it. I've got something on Tom Barnett I think you'll find interesting."

"How interesting?"

"Interesting enough for you to buy me a steak dinner and a glass of red wine and a shot or two of the Macallan for starters. There's a pretty good joint right in your hotel."

"Kitty O'Shea's?"

"Naw, that's more of a lunch place. I'm talking the Buckingham Steak House. Or if you want to get out a little, there's Petterino's over by the Goodman Theatre."

"I wouldn't mind getting out. In the meantime, there's something else you might want to check."

"Like I got the time?"

"Put young Alvaro on it."

"And have to share a byline? Maybe when the lake freezes over."

"Never mind. Run a check on unsolved homicides for the . . . I don't know, three months after Birk's home invasion. See if any were a white male, six feet or so. Ideally he'd have a connection to Birk or Francis Curry. Maybe a security guard

at one of the buildings or construction sites. Hell, maybe someone who worked for a carpet cleaning company."

"You think they bumped off the guy who helped rob
the place?"

"They don't seem to like loose ends."

It was dusk when I left the hotel. I thought about taking a cab—
limiting my exposure to whatever assassins might lurk in the
lowering darkness—then said fuck it. Walking in a city like
New York or Chicago is one of the great pleasures in life and
no one was going to take it away from me.

The restaurant was at the corner of Dearborn and
Randolph, a block or so north of City Hall.

See? Getting to know my way.

Madison is the north-south split, State the east-west. The
lake is on the right going north.

Definitely getting it.

I took Michigan Street as far as Washington, then cut
west across the foot of Daley Plaza, every different angle of the
Picasso statue offering a different possibility, a different beast.
A woman with parted hair or a ram with crushing horns. An
eerie orange glow rose from the fountain tonight, the water
itself bubbling up orange as if contaminated. I was around it,
already looking north for a Goodman sign or banner when I
heard footsteps.

Fast steps.

Thought, "Here we go," and turned to see a man in a
hockey mask running at me, something down at his side just
like the gunman today. Another gun? No, a knife—better than
a gun here, able to go in and out silently, cut through organ
meat and leave a man drowning in his own blood.

As he got close to me, he moved to my left as if to attack
from the side, maybe push the knife through my ribs and into
my lungs—a quick and quiet method. I moved with him to keep

him in front of me and rolled at the last minute into his legs, sending him tumbling down hard onto the concrete surface. He grunted loudly as he hit. A woman behind me yelled, "Christ!" I jumped onto his back and punched him hard in the kidneys. He yowled. I grabbed his hair and knelt on the hand that held the knife. I was forcing it loose when someone jumped on my back and started pounding my head with small fists.

"Let him go," she screamed. "You're hurting him, you fucking asshole."

Of course I was hurting him. Wasn't that the point with knife-wielding assailants in hockey masks?

I got up fast and spun around, grabbed the fists of the woman—the girl—who was trying to claw me. She looked eighteen at the most. And was dressed as a witch, complete with pointy black hat and an alarming hairy wart on her otherwise smooth face.

"He was trying to kill me!" I yelled.

"You're crazy!" she yelled back. "Chris, are you okay?"

I pushed her away and turned to see the man getting up slowly. His mask had come off. He wasn't any older than the girl, a curly-headed kid with a nasty scrape on his chin, grimacing as he held the spot on his back where I'd hit him.

The knife, on closer inspection, was made of rubber.

"Oh, shit," I said, taking in the orange water gushing out of the fountain. The pumpkins mounted on poles. The girl's costume, the other people in the plaza dressed as cowboys, pirates, scarecrows and superheroes.

The festive banners that said "Chicagoween."

The date: October 31.

"I'm sorry," I said, picking up the knife and handing it back to the kid. "I forgot it's Halloween. I thought you were for real."

"Asshole," the kid said. "You really fucking hurt me."

"I should call the cops," the girl said.

I said, "Don't do that." My luck, Tom Barnett would answer the call. I apologized again to him and to the girl. I reached into my wallet and handed him three twenties. "Please," I said. "Have dinner on me."

"Like I could eat after what you did to me." But he shoved the bills into his jeans pocket. Pointed the rubber knife at me. Said, "You're lucky this isn't real."

Didn't I know it.

They walked off toward the fountain. She put her arm around his waist. He winced.

I headed for Petterino's. As I crossed Randolph, a cab nearly rear-ended a car that had stopped without signalling and blared his horn. Maybe that's why I didn't hear footsteps coming up behind me again. Didn't hear anything at all. Just became aware of the car at the curb, the man at my side, the hard press of a gun in my ribs. The shove into the back seat, the door slamming, the car exiting quickly from the curb lane into traffic. The short ride through city streets, just two turns, then over a bumpy terrain that had me bouncing on the floor of the car, a man's knees forcing me down behind the driver's seat, a gun in my neck the whole time.

Then we stopped and for the second time today I had my hands cuffed behind me. This time by Francis Curry.

CHAPTER 38

To call it an elevator was an insult to other elevators. It wasn't even a lift. A hoist, pure and simple, a technology that dated back to the building of pyramids, one weight descending to pull another upward. The higher we went, the harder the wind blew, waves of it rocking the hoist. The view was probably magnificent but obscured by walls of Plexiglas smeared with months' worth of dirt, handprints, dried drops of rain. Maybe even tears.

The car bucked harder as we rose past sixty, seventy floors, the pitch of the wind moaning like a grieving old woman as it whistled through unfinished floors of the building.

When the hoist reached the very top, Curry stepped back and took out a pistol. "You can get out first," he said. "Slowly, if I were you. Not that there's anywhere to run out there."

There was no flooring beyond twenty feet in any direction. Nothing to walk on but sheets of corrugated plastic, bridged here and there by plywood. After that it was girders only.

I stepped out as Curry directed, stopping halfway across the flooring. Not much I could do with my hands cuffed behind me.

"A little farther," Simon Birk said, and Curry waved his pistol to encourage me. I moved two steps farther out.

No walls, no ceiling. Just girders, the steel skeleton of a

rising giant, through which the wind was truly whipping. My pant legs were flapping against my legs, my hair blowing straight back.

Birk said, "I wanted you to see first-hand what I'm building, since you seem so determined to bring it to a halt."

"Okay," I said. "I've seen it."

"Isn't it magnificent?"

Curry was staying well back of me so there was nothing for me to do but agree.

"Walk," Birk said, nodding his head toward the edge of the ribbed plastic floor. The surface seemed solid enough under my feet. I assumed heavier men than me had trod it. I walked. The wind got stronger with every step out.

Below us, traffic rushed through the streets. Cars, buses, trucks and subway trains, all carrying people to their destinations. To better places than I was in.

"It sways more than you'd expect, doesn't it?" Birk asked. "Up to two feet from its vertical axis. All skyscrapers do, of course. There has to be some give in them. If they don't bend, they might break. Some of the sway will be reduced when it's finished and the cladding is in place. The tenants will never really feel it. But you do, don't you? You feel you're not entirely on solid ground, am I right?"

I saw no point in disagreeing.

"There's a lesson in there, Geller. When someone gives you a chance to bend, you should take it. It beats the hell out of breaking, doesn't it?"

"I get your point," I said.

"You should have done that when it counted."

"Boss," Curry said. I turned around to see Curry's hand on Birk's arm, stopping him from moving or speaking, then pointing out ahead of us.

At the end of a girder that extended out into the blackness was the figure of a man, seated with his back to us. Curry moved over to me and stuck the barrel of his gun in my back. He slipped a key out of his pocket and undid my cuffs. "You say a word," he said, "or make any fancy moves and you'll be dead. And so will he."

"Got it," I said. "No moves."

"Be smart."

"Excuse me?" Birk called out. "What are you doing here?"

The man rose up on the girder in one effortless move, as if the girder beneath him was twelve feet wide instead of twelve inches. He turned to face us. "I work here," he said.

"Well, I own the damn thing," Birk said. "Come on in."

He walked toward us along the girder. No harness. No hard hat. Thick black hair in a braid down his back. When he reached a perpendicular beam, he stopped. "Mr. Birk," he said.

"And you are?"

"Told you. I work here."

"Your name, please?"

"Cross," he said. "Gabriel Cross."

"And what were you doing out there? Your shift was over hours ago."

"Watching."

"Watching what?"

"The night," Cross said. "It's a good place to be when it's quiet. Watch the lights. Stars. Clouds. Can't do that during the day. Too much light. Too many people."

"You don't have a harness on."

Cross shrugged.

"You're Mohawk?"

He nodded.

"Mohawks aren't afraid of heights," Birk said to Curry. "Did you know that?"

"I've heard."

"Gabriel," he said. "I wonder if you'd do something for me."

He said, "Sure."

"Walk back out to the end of that girder."

"The one I was on?"

"Yes."

I tensed, wondering if Birk was setting the man up to fall. Get rid of a potential witness to whatever was going to happen to me. Curry must have felt me tense up because he jammed the gun into my back hard enough to send a sharp pain through my kidney.

I felt bad for the kid I had punched earlier, then went back to feeling bad for myself.

Cross turned and walked to the end of the girder. He never looked down. He could have been on a paved road for all the care he showed.

"Now turn around and walk back, please," Birk said.

He did a little pirouette and walked back.

"Amazing, isn't it?" Birk said to me.

"Yes," I said.

"Thank you, Gabriel," Birk said.

He shrugged.

"I'm going to ask you to leave now," Birk said.

"Okay." He came off the girder and crossed the plywood sheet and went over to a spot on the metal floor where his hard hat and lunch box were. He put on the hard hat, picked up the lunch box. Curry moved directly behind me, so Cross couldn't see the gun at my back.

I moved my left hand onto my belt and used my thumb and first two fingers to form a W. Turned it sideways. Implored Cross silently to see it. It was a sign taught to me last year by a Tyendinaga Mohawk, after I stepped in to even up a fight three drunken white boys had picked with him behind a beer store in Belleville when I was working undercover on the Ensign Tobacco case. A warrior greeting of sorts. But Cross turned away and got into the elevator. Either he hadn't seen my sign, hadn't recognized it or didn't give a shit.

I was on my own. Once Cross was gone, I thought, I'd be left to whatever end Birk and Curry had planned for me.

Before he closed the door, Cross said, "Mr. Birk? That thing about Mohawks—that we aren't afraid of heights?"

"Yes?"

"It's a myth. It's bullshit. We are afraid of heights," he said. "As much as you or anyone else. It's just ironwork pays better than anything else we can get."

CHAPTER 39

"Well, that was disappointing," Birk said. "I always believed that about Mohawks, that they had no fear of heights. I suppose I should respect them all the more if they are afraid and still walk out on beams as if they weren't, but the bottom line is, I don't like being fooled. Getting bad intelligence or information I can't trust." He was wearing a tan overcoat and he shivered slightly in the wind then tucked his hands in his pockets. "You, on the other hand, haven't fooled anyone, have you, Geller? You've been as transparent as a soap bubble ever since you got here. Even before that."

I wondered if Jericho Hale had sold me out—if the invitation for a meal had been a ruse to draw me into the open—or if they had simply tailed me from the Hilton.

"You like pirate movies?" Birk asked.

"What?"

"Pirate movies. Not the *Pirates of the Caribbean* crap—although they did make a lot of money for Disney, which I have to respect. The old ones. The classics. *The Sea Hawk. Captain Blood. Treasure Island. Captain Kidd. The Black Swan* with Tyrone Power. I watched them all as a kid. Not you, huh?"

"I saw *Wall Street*," I said.

"Wiseass," Curry muttered.

"Let him have his fun, Francis," Birk said. "What did you think," he said to me, "watching our Indian friend walk out on that beam? Think you could do it? Think you could hold yourself together a thousand feet above pavement?"

I said, "Maybe."

"Maybe. Hardly a vote of confidence in yourself. And confidence, I'm told, is everything in that situation. So let's give it a try, shall we?" He held out his hand as if inviting me into his parlour. "Go on."

I didn't move.

Birk grinned. Whoever had capped his teeth had done a good job. They gleamed brighter than any star in the night sky behind him. "Not so keen? Well, this is where we get to the pirate part. Walking the plank. Francis, would you mind pointing your pistol at Geller's head? That's it. Nicely done. So here's your choice, Geller. Walk the beam. Or take a bullet. More than one if need be."

I looked at the beam stretching out in front of me. I knew I could walk out and back without falling. I was a martial artist. I had good balance—better than good. I had the ability to focus my mind. When I worked on *katas* I often challenged myself to begin and end them on the same spot, like a gymnast nailing a landing.

"As an added incentive," Birk said, "I give you my word. If you can walk out to the end of the beam and back, you'll be free to go."

"Like that's worth anything."

Birk gave me an aggrieved look, drawing his chin in and arching his thick brows. "I've closed billion-dollar deals on my word," he said.

"And had people killed with it."

"You keep saying that, but if you had one shred of proof—"

"What do you call this? Having Francis put a gun on me?"

"Ripping entertainment."

"And the little escapade in the park today?"

"What escapade? Which park?"

"Grant Park. The guy who tried to shoot me in the head. The guy you sent with Tom Barnett."

"Detective Barnett? I haven't seen him in years, not since he led the investigation into the robbery of my home."

"So capably too. Never caught anyone or found anything."

"At any rate," Birk said. "I'm getting chilly. Wind pressure increases with height, of course, but nothing quite prepares you for it eighty-plus storeys up. So what's it going to be, Geller? Come on, it's only twenty feet long. Well, twenty each way, assuming you make it back."

Only forty feet. Only eighty-five storeys to fall. Seven times the height Maya Cantor fell and her body had been virtually destroyed on impact.

"You can't say I'm not sporting," Birk said.

I stepped out onto the beam—Birk watching me like a wolf who'd found a stray lamb trapped in a bed of mint—and immediately had to adjust to a gust of sudden wind funnelled through neighbouring towers. Maybe Mohawks were afraid of heights, maybe they weren't; this Jew was fucking terrified. Look ahead, I told myself. Never down. One foot in front of the other. I was glad I had running shoes on, not loafers with a slick sole. The studded surface of the beam gave some grip. Halfway out, another gust almost sheared me off into the darkness. I put out my hands, wavering like a tightrope walker; heard Curry laugh until I had regained my balance.

"Bravo," Birk shouted. "All that was missing was a drum roll."

I reached the end of the beam, where it joined an I-beam.

"Now let's see the turn," Birk said. "A little tricky, if you're not used to it. But you're doing very well, so far."

"Beats *American Idol*," Curry said.

"Maybe the early rounds," Birk said.

The beam was wide enough, I told myself. Looked to be twelve inches across. I visualized a move that occurs about a third of the way through a *tensho kata*, where the fighter pivots around from front to back. I had done it hundreds, if not thousands, of times. I tried to feel it in my body, how it would take my feet, my legs, my core right around, and did it, breathing out, using the traditional hand movements to keep my balance.

"You learn that in ballet class?" Curry said.

If only he'd been close enough to hit.

I walked back along the beam, watching Curry more than Birk, but so far he was keeping the gun pointed down. I reached the end of the beam and stepped back onto the temporary flooring.

"Well done," Birk said. "You might be short on strategy, Geller, but you have nerve and everyone knows I like that in a man. And so I am going to surprise you, my Canadian friend, by keeping my word. You're free to go. The game is no longer afoot."

I kept watching Curry's gun hand.

"Go on," Birk said. "About your business. Chop-chop."

I started toward the elevator.

Birk said, "Francis."

Curry's gun came up.

"I said you could go," Birk said with a cold grin. "I didn't say you could take the elevator."

CHAPTER 40

"You were watching the workers here yesterday," Birk said. "You must have seen how it's done. Like a monkey shimmying down a palm tree."

I had watched a man climb down a girder wearing work gloves and boots. Wearing a harness that would stop his fall if he lost his grip.

I said, "If I don't?"

"Francis will shoot you. He won't need much provocation either. I don't think he likes you."

"Too many people know why I'm here. If I'm found with a bullet wound, they'll come after you."

"They who? The police? Chicago averages five hundred murders a year."

"So I've heard."

"Your body will be found in an area known for gang activity. They'll chalk it up to misadventure on your part. The naive Canadian who wandered into the baddest part of town and was shot for whatever was in his wallet."

"No one will buy that."

"People have been buying what I sell all my life. Francis will swear I never left my apartment. I'll swear he was with me all night. Tom Barnett will swear I'm Elvis Presley if I tell him to. Anyway, it's a moot point because I don't think you're going to stand there and meekly take a bullet. Be a sport, Geller. I'm giving you a chance to walk away."

"Some chance."

"Come on!" he cried. "Where's your sense of adventure? You're young. You're fit. You've shown us some moves. You certainly have a knack for survival. You climb down four floors, you'll be back on concrete and you can make it to a stairwell from there. It's not inconceivable you could make it."

Not inconceivable. Just the kind of odds you want.

"I'm giving you more of a chance than, say, Basil Rathbone would have given Errol Flynn. More than George Sanders would have given Tyrone Power. There are no sharks in these waters. Your hands are no longer tied."

"Can we move this along?" Curry said.

"Poor Francis," Birk said. "Francis doesn't care for classic movies the way I do."

"I liked *Kiss of Death*," he said.

He would, the hairless fucking waxwork.

"And if I fall?" I said. "How are you going to explain that?"

"Very easily. You've made your little obsession with me quite public. Your scene at the Department of Buildings. Harassing my site manager here. The scenario would be obvious, I think. Having been ejected earlier, you broke into the site, commandeered the elevator, came up here looking for some evidence to support your outlandish theories about me. And fell. Ouch. The end."

"They're not that outlandish," I said. "You did have them killed, didn't you?"

"On the off chance you make it down in one piece, I think I'll decline to comment."

"And the home invasion? You engineered it, didn't you?"

"Quit whistling out your ass," Curry said.

"On the advice of my director of security, I think I'll duck that one too. Now start climbing." His voice had lost the playful singsong tone he'd been using, sounding more like the balls-to-the-wall negotiator he was supposed to be.

I walked back out along the twenty-foot beam until I reached the beam to which it connected. I squatted down, gripped the sides of the girder and hugged it close to my body, thinking of the workman I'd watched through binoculars, gripping with his feet, shimmying down, as Birk had said, like a monkey down a tree. Except a monkey was made for climbing: exquisitely muscled with feet that gripped like hands and a prehensile tail. I started inching down, keeping my eyes fixed on the pale clock face of the Wrigley Building across the ribbon of river that ran in from the lake. It took several minutes to make it down to the next horizontal beam, where I thought I could rest. But as soon as my feet touched it, something slammed into my right shoulder. The shock of it made me lose my grip for a moment. I slid down hard, felt skin tearing off my palms as I gripped the girder trying to stop my fall. I thought I'd been shot. But then something clanged off a girder far below, and I knew that someone above me, Birk or Curry, had thrown something down. A long bolt.

"Just keeping you honest," Birk called.

I swung my body to the outside of the girder and started down the next length. My hands were cramping around the girder. My quads were stiffening. My collarbone where the bolt had hit felt like it was broken. The muscle that connected it to the scapula was going into spasm. I kept going. Six inches, a foot. Stopped to wrap my arms around the girder and flex my hands. But as soon as I did, more bolts rained down. One hit my right forearm. Another just missed my head. I gripped the girder and renewed my descent.

Thought, "This is what you get for trying." A former colleague, the late François Paradis, once told me, "No good deed goes unpunished." Is that how it really is? Is this how it ends? The fall itself would be over in seconds. I wouldn't feel a thing.

I'd be dead a millisecond after I hit the ground, before the pain impulses could travel to my shattered brain.

I descended another few feet. My hands were being rubbed raw by rough steel. My right arm was on fire from my wrist up to the base of my neck. When I got to the next horizontal beam I stopped to rest again, hugging the girder tight to present the smallest possible target. It didn't help. Another bolt hit my right leg just above the knee. I howled in pain.

"Sorry about that," Birk yelled.

"You are not," I heard Curry say.

I wasn't going to make it. They would find me at the bottom. Ship what was left of me home. My mother would be devastated. Jenn would cry her heart out. Hollinger would probably regret the way things had gone. My brother—what would he feel? I had no idea, and somehow that made me feel sadder than anything else.

I felt tears in my eyes. From the wind, the pain, the rage throttling my heart.

I started down again. Two more floors, I told myself. A dozen more cramps. A hundred more breaths. Breathe into your hands, Geller. Into your quads, your knee, your shoulder, your arm. Fill your chest, your head with air. Sharp, cold nighttime Chicago air. Air off the lake. Air whistling through these towers around you. Breathe it. Climb down through it.

Two more bolts came down. Both missed, clanged off the girder. Maybe I was getting harder to see from up there.

I reached another horizontal beam, changed my position so all that was exposed was my hands and feet.

Another bolt hit my left hand. "Fuck!" I yelled. I felt blood spill through my straining fingers but didn't let go. Wasn't going to let go.

What if I just stay here? I thought. What if they find me in the morning, clinging to this post, stuck to it with dried blood, a twisted figurehead on the good ship Millennium Skyline?

Explain that, Mr. Birk.

But my left hand was starting to give way. My right was barely holding on.

What if I just let go? Would a good coroner be able to tell anything about ante-mortem injuries? *"Hmm. These welts on his hand, his collarbone, his knee. Not consistent with a fall from a great height."*

Would it matter? Birk could probably buy off a coroner. He had at least one cop in his pocket. Plenty of room for a coroner—or did Illinois have medical examiners? Didn't matter. Birk could afford either one.

Nearly a thousand feet to fall. A few seconds at most. My entire body was begging to let go. My hands wanted to. My feet did too. My mind, my heart, my will—the pain was sapping them all.

And then I heard a hum—more than a hum, a mechanical whine—something moving off to my right, on the other side of the building.

The hoist was coming back up.

Why would Birk and Curry have summoned it? They weren't through with me yet. The game wasn't over. Unless it meant they couldn't see me from above anymore and would come to the floor I was on and finish me; or go down to ground level and wait for me to fall.

No more bolts were falling from above, which gave me a chance to climb freely. If I made it down one more floor, I'd be on concrete. But I'd also be right where they expected me to be. They'd be standing in the elevator or stairwell entrance and finish it. But there was another choice. Do the horizontal beam walk again. Come in on an unfinished floor above where they'd be waiting. If the wind didn't blow me off, maybe I could find a weapon—the kind of bolts they had been throwing—or a section of rebar or chunk of concrete to drop on Curry's head from above.

My muscles were still cramping and both palms were bleeding. My feet felt frozen inside my shoes. But three floors down from the top, I inched out onto a beam and moved slowly along, summoning every ounce of my training in movement and fighting, staying steady and balanced, getting closer to the corrugated floor: fifteen feet, ten feet, five. When I was close enough I launched myself forward and landed on my side. Pain shot through my shoulder where the first bolt had hit. But I was back on firm ground of sorts, in a place with a fighting chance. I sprinted toward the elevator. It would have to pass me on the way up to fetch Birk and Curry then come back down. I hunted for a weapon, spied a wrench that had fallen between two sections of flooring, hefted it. It was the best chance I had to take Curry out. Break his gun arm, stave in his shiny skull.

And then take Simon Birk apart.

The elevator ground slowly up the side. I could see light inside it, a bare bulb that made the smears in its Plexiglas surface look ghostly, as if it had been wiped by a spectral hand. I'm left-handed but shifted the wrench to my right, which didn't hurt as badly. I breathed in as deeply as I could without sending more spasms through my side. I had two, maybe three minutes to get ready. I looked for a shadowed place to hide, to make them come to me, to shift the game to my terms.

The game. I had enough to hate Birk for already, but turning my life, my death into a game for his amusement, an entertainment of sorts? I wanted to entertain the living shit out of him. I had to focus my anger, not let it get the better of me, at least not until Curry was down.

But the elevator never went up to their floor. It stopped at mine. And when the doors opened the only person in it was Gabriel Cross.

I stumbled into it and fell onto the floor. I would have shaken his hand but I doubted he wanted any part of my blood-smeared lumps of meat.

"You got my message," I said.

"No," he said. "I got Mr. Birk's." And he surprised me by doing a note-perfect impression of Birk. "'Gabriel, I wonder if you'd do something for me. Walk back out to the end of that girder.' Like he's the organ grinder and I'm the monkey. I could tell they were up to no good with you. When I got to my truck, I took a look up through my binocs. And there you were, doing Spiderman. Figured you might need a lift."

He started the hoist back down. They could throw all the bolts they wanted. I was safe inside it.

"You work for a man," Cross said, "that's all it means. Doesn't mean he owns you. Used to, maybe. Not today. Not with all these buildings going up. Not when you're a Mohawk who's not afraid of heights."

CHAPTER 41

Gabriel Cross drove me back to my hotel, by way of a Walgreens on North Clark Street. I stayed slumped in the car seat while he went in to pick up what I needed—extra-strength Tylenol; gauze and tape; peroxide; Polysporin; arnica gel.

Sadly, they didn't sell rocket-propelled grenade launchers.

When he pulled up in front of the Hilton, he said, "My wife has a friend who's a nurse. Lives in our building. I could see if she's around."

"There's nothing a nurse can do for me."

"How you going to wrap your hands? Neither one of them's working."

He had a point.

"Her name's Nola," Cross said. "If she's home when I get back, I'll send her over."

"What should I pay her?"

"Whatever you can spare," he said. "She's a single mother."

"A hundred? Two hundred?"

"Two's all right."

"What about you?"

"What about me?"

"You saved my fucking neck."

"You want to pay me?"

"If you could use it."

"I can always use it. But I'm going to say no thanks."

"Sure?"

"What I did, I did for me, not you. I told you, I didn't like how Mr. Birk spoke to me."

I said, "I'm going to thank you anyway."

He said, "Okay."

I tried to open the car door but my hand wouldn't grip the handle. He got out and opened the door from the outside. I got out slowly, feeling pain in more places than I could count. Cross walked behind me, a hand at the small of my back, as I shuffled into the lobby. He had to press the elevator buttons for me and work the key card into the lock on my door. Once I was flat on the bed, he left and I dozed for an hour until the knocking began.

"My lord," Nola Johnson said. "You look like you were beaten with tire irons."

I was stripped down to my underwear, covered in welts. My palms were burning where skin had been rubbed off. "Close enough," I said.

"Do I have to tell you this might sting a little?"

"That would be a major improvement."

She used peroxide to clean my palms and the oozing cut between the first two knuckles of my left hand. I gritted my teeth and sucked in air. She covered the broken skin with a thin layer of Polysporin and wrapped my hands in gauze. She went out to the hall and filled a bucket with ice and had me sit in the tub while she rubbed ice cubes onto the welts on my arm, shoulder and thigh. Then I lay down on the bed and she rubbed arnica gently onto the bruises.

"I don't think anything is broken in your arm," she said. "As to the rest, you should probably get X-rays. I wouldn't be surprised if your second metacarpal showed a fracture. That bone isn't that hard to break."

"I practise karate," I told her. "I've broken it before."

"Your patella is awfully swollen," she said. "Can you straighten your leg?"

I tried. Couldn't do it.

"And there's your clavicle. Again, I wouldn't be surprised if there was a break. How much Tylenol have you taken?"

"Four extra-strength."

"Any alcohol?"

"No."

She reached into her pocket and took out a small vial. "These are Tylenol 3s. You can take one now and one in four hours."

"Thanks."

"But you have to wait the four hours. Promise?"

"Yes."

"I work at Cook County Hospital," she said, handing me a slip of paper with a phone number. "I start at eight in the morning. If you come in at seven forty-five, I can get you X-rayed."

"I'll see how I feel in the morning."

"You worried about the cost?"

"No."

"You should be," she smiled.

"Thank you."

I told her where my wallet was, and to help herself to her fee.

"Don't forget," Nola said. "Four hours until the next pill."

"I won't."

I didn't wait the whole four hours. But I did wait until the door had closed behind her.

Then I called Jenn at home.

"Cancel your flight," I said.

"Why? What happened?"

"I'll tell you when you get here."

"But you said—"

"I didn't say not to come. I need you to come by car. Tonight."

"Why?"

"'Cause I need you to bring something you can't take on a plane."

"What's that?"

"Dante Ryan," I said.

CHAPTER 42

I must have slept with my hands clenched into fists. I could barely get them open far enough to pry the top off the vial of Tylenol 3s Nola had left. I did, though, and took two. Struggled to make a pot of coffee without burning myself, then limped down the hall wrapped in a complimentary bathrobe and refilled the bucket with ice.

The bruises were ugly. Like someone had rubbed my forearm and knee with blueberries. I couldn't see the one on my shoulder without a mirror and didn't see the point in trying. I lay naked in the tub with ice on my arm and my knee, waiting for the codeine to hit. Pondered the wisdom of taking two more.

One codeine, two codeine, three codeine, four
If that doesn't do it, take a few more.

I wondered if Jenn had been able to find Ryan and, if so, where they were. Still in Ontario? On I-94 by now?

When the ice had melted, I got out of the bath and started filling it with hot water. Nola had said alternating between cold and hot would help reduce inflammation and relax "the insulted areas." I towelled off and slipped back into the robe and managed to open the door locks and retrieve my courtesy copy of the *Chicago Tribune*. I sat on the bed while the bath filled. The news section had nothing about a man in a hockey mask being assaulted in Daley Plaza the previous night; nothing about a man being forced to walk the plank eighty-five storeys above the city; no mention of a corrupt cop throwing his weight around in Grant Park.

I closed the paper and walked stiffly to the bathroom. Didn't take much longer than a bear going over a mountain. I turned off the water, tested it, found it below scalding and steadied myself with my elbows as I lowered my sore self down. Waited for its relaxing properties to take hold.

Yeah, that's me—Jonah the waiter. Waiting for relief from heat and codeine. Waiting for Jenn and Ryan. Waiting for a bright idea that would take me off the hot seat and plant Simon Birk on it.

I was lying flat in the tub in water up to my jaw, my hands up around my ears to keep the gauze wrappings dry, raising and lowering my knee, when I heard a click sound at the door. An entry card going in and out, the lock disengaging, the handle turning.

I used my elbows to get into a sitting position. The bathroom door was halfway open. I must have forgotten to relock the door and set the chain. I could see a tall black woman in a wine-coloured uniform holding a stack of towels. Her skin was coffee-coloured and she was heavily freckled, especially around the eyes, and she was about to see more than she'd bargained for. I called out, "Hello."

"Oh, sorry. Housekeeping."

"I'm a little indisposed," I called. "Can you leave those on the bed, please?"

"I'm sorry," she said. "I thought you were out."

I was sinking back into the water when I realized I hadn't heard a knock. Heard the card whisper into the lock. Heard the electronic click of the lock release. Heard the handle turn, the door brush open against the grain of the carpet.

No knock.

If she hadn't knocked, or called out a greeting, why would she think I was out? I kept my eyes on the mirror as she passed out of view on the way to the bed. Waited. Saw her come back toward the bathroom, holding one towel flat in one hand, the other hand hidden within its fold.

I was on my way out of the tub when she burst through the door, slashing down at my torso with a long, thin blade. Nothing rubber about this one. It was a good old-fashioned knife meant for gutting. I landed on my back and used my legs to push left and away from the thrust. Her hand plunged into the hot water. I grabbed her wrist but couldn't hold it in my injured hand. She pulled it away and slashed down again. I blocked it. She stuck her other hand in my face and tried to push me under water. I kicked out at her and caught her a glancing blow against the head, just enough to stun her a bit. I wrapped my arm around her knife hand and pinned it there and kicked again, this time catching her a good one, the ball of my foot against her chin. Her head snapped back against the tiled wall. As it bounced forward, I wrapped both ankles around her neck and twisted downward. She lost her footing and fell toward me. When she hit the water, a wave of bathwater coursed into my mouth. I coughed it up, planting my elbows on the bottom of the bath, squeezing my legs together until her face went below the surface. Her free hand clawed at my face. I bit her fingers. She tried to bring her knife hand up. I kept it pinned. The water bubbled furiously around her face, as if piranha were stripping an animal of its flesh. I kept squeezing. My quad muscles shuddered. She tried to gain purchase, to back away from the tub, but water had splashed onto the floor and her feet slipped sideways. One knee gave way beneath her with a sickening crack. Her hands stopped trying to attack and tried to push off against the sides of the bath. I kept the knife hand pinned where it was.

Then the bubbles stopped.

I kept the pressure on for another minute. And one more. When I knew she'd been under water too long to be faking it, I let go. She slumped into the tub, sloshing more water out onto the floor. I scrambled back, looked under me to locate the knife and plucked it gingerly out of the water. My bandaged hands were wet but I didn't care. I dropped the knife on the floor. My chest was heaving, my head pounding from the effort. I wanted to stay in the bath but didn't care for the company. I got out, almost wiping out on the slick floor, and stumbled to the bed and fell on it, wet as a seal. I reached for a towel and was drying off when I heard a loud knock on the door.

"Yes?" I called out.

A woman's voice said, "Housekeeping!"

Now *that's* the way it's done, I thought, not knowing whether to laugh, cry or limp back into the bathroom and get the knife off the floor.

"I'm sick," I said. "Come back tomorrow."

"You don't need towels?"

"I've got enough for today, thanks."

When she was gone I locked every lock there was— deadbolt, security bar, chain—and stuck a chair under the door handle.

CHAPTER 43

I was sick to fucking death of Simon Birk's attempts on my life. Even sicker over what the latest one had made me do.

When Stefano di Pietra had drowned, I'd had the luxury of telling myself I hadn't actually killed him. Hadn't physically laid a hand on him or held him under. Had merely eased out the rock on which his neck had been resting until the water rose over his face.

There was no getting around it this time. I had drowned the woman in the tub, had held her under as she fought for her life. Stefano had been all but paralyzed by his fall onto the rocks in the Don River. She had bucked and slashed and clawed and thrashed until all the air went out of her.

Try getting around that.

I couldn't. There was nowhere to go with it. So I decided I was through trying to gather evidence against Birk, through trying to prove my point. Everyone in any position of authority—Hollinger, my brother, Avi Stern, Birk himself— kept saying it couldn't be done anyway. So enough already. Now it was time to do whatever had to be done to bring him down, make him pay for the corpses he had piled up. If anyone else was going to die on his account, it might as well be him. And Curry if he chose to ride along.

I drained the bathtub and closed the curtain on the corpse inside, then mopped the floor using my feet to push towels around. The wet towels went into the tub as well. Then I called the *Tribune* newsroom.

"Dude," Jericho Hale said. "You stood me the fuck up. Had to buy my own damn Macallan at twelve bucks a shot."

"I ran into trouble," I said.

"What kind of trouble would keep you from me?"

"Pirates."

"Right here in Chicago?"

I told Hale what had happened, leaving out the part in Daley Plaza and any mention of Gabriel Cross.

"Jesus," he said.

"Do I still get the info you had for me?" I asked.

"Remember I told you Tom Barnett was a head breaker back in the day? So I talked to one of the guys on our police desk—not the newbie you saw, Alvaro, but an old-timer, a real crime dog—and got some of the lowlights of his career."

"And?"

"The worst jam he ever got into was maybe a dozen years ago, when he first made detective. He and his partner pulled in a guy who matched the description of a rape suspect, wanted for a real vile assault on a fourteen-year-old girl. Guy practically ripped her insides out. So Barnett and his partner questioned the suspect—with extreme prejudice, shall we say. Shoved a damn broomstick up his ass and broke it off. Only problem was, he wasn't the guy. Not only was he not the guy, he was a church-going, God-fearing, Jesus-loving straight-A student whose father represented the Seventh Congressional District of Illinois. Barnett probably would have been kicked off the force, but his partner admitted he instigated it, not Barnett, that Barnett only did what he was told, being the junior partner. So only his partner got kicked off the force. Barnett just got suspended for two weeks without pay."

"I get the feeling I'm supposed to ask you who his partner was."

"'Cause you're one smart cookie."

"And if that's what I'm supposed to ask, then I know the answer."

"Let's hear it."

"Francis Curry."

"Give the man a silver dollar. You got those up in Canada?"

"We have loonies."

"So do we. And some of them, unfortunately, carry a badge."

"What about the third man?" I asked. "Any unsolved killings match up from that time?"

"A couple," he said. "Ronald Atkins, white male, thirty-six, five-eleven. Found bobbing along in the river, not far from the Ohio Street bridge. No suspects, no arrests. The other was Chuck Belkin, forty years old, six-foot-one, found shot to death in the Humboldt Park area. No arrests, but a theory that he was buying or selling drugs and stepped on some Latin King toes."

"That's him," I said.

"What makes you so—"

"Birk said something to me about dumping me on gang turf, make it look like I'd wandered into the wrong neighbourhood. What's Belkin's background?"

"He was unemployed at the time of his demise."

"Any police or security work in his past?"

"No."

"Carpet cleaning?"

"Dude, we didn't have his CV on hand. All our guy had on him was he was an army veteran, served in Desert Storm."

Ex-military. After my first meeting at Birk's office, Francis Curry had told me he was "ex a lot of things."

I was betting military was one of them.

—

Jenn called at ten o'clock. I'd never been so glad to hear her voice.

"Is Ryan with you?"

"Oh, yeah."

"What's that mean?"

"We left at five and we're making good time. Still in Michigan but close to the Indiana state line."

"You can't say what you want to say?"

"Nope."

"He's not your average bear."

"No," she said. "Not at all."

"You talking about me?" I heard Ryan say. "Hey, all I did was put my hand on your leg when we were crossing the border."

"It wasn't my leg," Jenn said. "It was my thigh. My upper thigh."

"I was trying to be convincing," he said. "You know what the border is like now. We're a couple on holiday, I figure we're supposed to be lovey-dovey."

"A little too lovey there, dovey."

"Put him on the phone," I said.

There was a pause and then Ryan came on. "Do yourself a favour," I told him. "Don't touch her tits. Last guy who did that is still trying to find his balls."

"And hello to you too."

"Thanks for coming."

"You know me," he said. "I still like a party."

"Did you bring your, uh, camera case?"

"Of course. I mean, I assume that's why we couldn't fly."

"You assume correctly."

"Hey, you okay?" Ryan said. "You sound a little dopey."

"I had some codeine for breakfast."

"What happened?"

"I'm a little banged up."

"How banged up?"

"I'm turning all the colours of the rainbow."

"This Birk again?"

"Yeah."

"Don't worry," he said. "We'll tune him up good."

"That's why I invited you."

I stood a long while at the window looking out at the city, grey now and overcast, the wind up, the waves churning and foaming on the shore of the lake. People on the street below were holding onto their hats, clutching their coats around themselves. At twelve o'clock, I took two more codeine and leafed through the sports section. I don't know when I fell asleep but it was two when I woke up, thirsty and hungry enough to order a club sandwich. When it came, I ate half of it. Could only look at the other half. Wanted to soak my aching muscles in another hot bath but had no desire to share the tub with a dead assassin. Lay back on the bed. Clenched and unclenched my hands, felt the raw skin pull against the gauze wraps. Got up and paced, bad knee and all, until there was a knock on the door.

"Yes?"

"It's us," Jenn said.

I removed the chair and undid all the locks, opened the door and there they finally were. Jenn looked at my hands, the welt on my arm, and threw her arms around me and held me. I felt like crying into her shirt the way Marilyn Cantor had. "Look at you," she said. "You're a mess."

"And you're only seeing the outside."

Ryan said, "Hey," and set his camera case down and got out his cigarettes. "Please tell me this is a smoking floor. Your partner here wouldn't let me smoke in my own fucking car. Hell, she barely let me speak."

Jenn rolled her eyes. "Only because so much of what you say is in Neanderthal," she said.

"Don't start that again," Ryan growled. "Christ, I say one little thing and she's all over me."

"One little thing?"

"All I said was that if I wasn't married—"

"Like that makes a difference," Jenn said.

"—that I would love to help you switching teams."

"Like that would do it."

"It was a compliment," Ryan insisted.

"From another century!"

"A way of saying you're a looker. Plenty of dy—sorry, plenty of *gay* women, I could give a shit, with their crewcuts and legs like Bulgarian wrestlers. But you're fucking beautiful, man."

"How can anyone resist him?" Jenn said. "How'd you get your wife to marry you? You club her and drag her to your cave by the hair?"

"There you go again with the caveman shit. I'm plenty modern, okay? I help my wife with our kid, with dishes, with laundry—"

"You help *her* with it, meaning it's still her responsibility."

"Twelve hours of this," he said to me. "She's lucky the guns were in the trunk."

"See? Threats of violence," Jenn said. "You don't agree with a woman, just shoot her."

"Finally," he grinned. "Something we can agree on." Then to me: "This the can here? I got to take a leak. I been holding it in since fucking Skokie."

"You might not want to go in there," I said.

"I'll hold my breath."

"It's not that. I had, uh, company this morning."

Ryan went into the bathroom. I heard the shower curtain swish along its rail, plastic rings clacking together. "Holy shit!" he said.

Jenn searched my face for a clue as to what was in there. I

shrugged. "You might as well look," I said. "So you know where things are going."

She walked slowly into the bathroom. Said, "Holy shit," too, and came out looking pale. Ryan, on the other hand, went straight to the phone book provided by the hotel and flipped through the Yellow Pages section.

"What are you looking for?" I asked.

"Sporting goods," he said.

CHAPTER 44

"If he comes back with a chainsaw," Jenn said, "I'm out of here."

"The only thing you can predict about Dante Ryan is that he's unpredictable. Listen, I'm sorry if the drive down was a pain."

"Don't be," she said. "It was a hoot."

"You're kidding."

"Apart from the smoking, the leg-groping and the team-switching bullshit, he's a lot more fun than PC guys who trip over themselves trying to be more sensitive than thou around a gay woman. But don't tell him that."

"My lips are sealed."

"While he's gone," Jenn said, "did you want to get yourself X-rayed?"

"No. What's done is done. I have some codeine. And a lot of ill will toward Simon Birk. That ought to get me through the day."

"Let's see your hands."

We sat opposite each other on the edges of the double beds and she slowly unwrapped the gauze.

"Uck," she said.

"Spoken like a true professional."

My palms were angry and raw, as if they'd been flayed. My

left hand shook when I tried to extend the fingers that had been hit by a bolt. Jenn picked up the phone and punched in a number, waited, then said, "Hi, babe."

As a nurse practitioner, Sierra Lyons had more advanced training and credentials than Nola Johnson. Jenn told her about me, listened, asked a few questions, listened some more, made a kissy noise into the phone and hung up.

"What did she say?"

"That you should get X-rays."

"What else?"

Jenn reached into her purse. "And take these as needed." She took out a sample pack of OxyContin. Made Tylenol 3s look like pikers. The clouds parted, rays of sunshine streamed through, a chorus of angels sang. And I hadn't even taken one yet.

"Sierra said to leave your hands unwrapped for now. Let the air get to them."

"Remind me to take you both to dinner when we get home."

"X-rays might be cheaper," she said. She popped out two pills for me and got me some water. "Before you get kooky, you want to tell me your war plan?"

"You're assuming I have one."

"My bad."

"What I have right now is more a vision than a plan."

"Go on."

"The vision is Simon Birk on his knees, begging to tell us everything. What happened to Glenn and Sterling. What happened to Maya Cantor. What happened to his wife."

"Does the vision tell you how we get him there?"

"No. But if past experience is worth anything, Ryan will have something to do with it."

We both had to laugh when he got back. He carried a goalie stick in one hand; the other was pulling a massive nylon bag on a wheeled frame, the kind goalies use to lug their oversized equipment. He wore a Chicago Blackhawks sweater with the name Kane and the number 88 on the back and sleeves. A Hawks cap covered his dark hair.

"Anyone sees me with this," he said, "they'll tell the cops Patrick Kane did it."

"And he seemed like such a nice kid," I said.

"How long has she been in the tub?" he asked.

"Eight, nine hours by now."

"Shit. She's going to be close to maximum stiffness," he said. "You might want to turn on the TV."

He went into the bathroom with the hockey bag. Was in there for close to half an hour, grunting and groaning like a man with dysentery. If only that had been the case: what was really going on in there was more painful to think about. Jenn kept thumbing up the volume on the remote. We could still hear the sounds of Ryan's exertion. At one point we heard a bone break. We both jumped off the beds. More volume on the TV, until someone pounded on the wall in the next room.

Then Ryan called, "A little help here?"

I held out my hands, glistening with ointment, for Jenn to see. She gulped and turned pale, even by her Estonian standards, and walked to the bathroom as if a hangman awaited her.

I lowered the volume. The pounding in the next room stopped. Then I heard both of them grunting. A zipper being closed in fits and starts. And finally Ryan's voice saying, "Got it."

The water ran, then Jenn came out drying her face with a towel. Ryan followed her, pulling the bag, singing, "Mama, don't let your babies grow up to be goalies."

I told him he was a sick individual. He didn't argue the point. He just sighed and said, "I'm here less than an hour and already I got a body to dispose of. Fucking stereotyped or what?"

Jenn packed all of my things into my suitcase for me then left the room with Ryan's gun case. Five minutes later, Ryan left, carrying the hockey sticks and pulling the equipment bag behind him, whistling the old theme song to *Hockey Night in Canada*. I waited another five minutes then went down to the lobby to check out. No way we were staying in the Hilton another night, not after the attack of the homicidal housekeeper.

"Was everything all right?" the concierge asked.

"Fine," I said.

"Would you like to fill out an evaluation card?" he asked. "It will help us tailor our services to better suit your needs in the future."

"My experience was unforgettable," I said. "Let's just leave it at that."

Ryan dropped us at a Holiday Inn Express just north of the Loop and went off to lose the woman's corpse. "Lucky for me they got a lake and a river and a whole lot of buildings going up. I should be back in a couple of hours."

I booked two rooms. When we were settled in, all gear stowed, I called Avi Stern's office on my cellphone. He answered yes to my first three questions: he was free this evening; he owned a mini-recorder, which he used to dictate letters for transcription; and he wanted to see justice done in the matter of Simon Birk.

The only negative response came when I asked if he owned a gun or had any experience in handling one.

"What are you getting me into?" he moaned.

I told him we'd keep him posted as the plan unfolded, and that we'd do our best to keep him from being arrested, shot or disbarred.

If he found comfort in that, he kept it to himself.

I called Nola Johnson, thanked her for the help she'd provided the night before, and asked for Gabriel Cross's home number. His wife answered and said he was still at work. I gave her my name and asked her to pass along a message if he called in: to leave when his shift was over and not hang around on any beams tonight.

"He still does that, eh?"

"Yes."

"You'd think he spends enough time up there as it is."

"I guess."

"Wish he'd take me up there sometime," she said. "I never get out of the city."

Unable to grip a pencil, I traced an outline of the Birkshire Millennium Skyline site for Jenn with my finger. I had her mark the entrance and the trailer that would house any security at night. I showed her the side of the building where the hoist went up, what the unfinished floor at the top was like. I provided notes about the lighting, the wind, the footing.

Ryan came back about two hours later. The shins of his pants were dusty. He went straight into the bathroom and spent five minutes washing up.

When he got out he said, "Anyone going to ask me where I dumped her? No? Good. Saves me the trouble of telling you it's none of your business."

He opened his metal case and showed us the guns he had brought, including his personal favourite, a Glock 20, and the Beretta we'd confiscated from the thug in our office.

"If we have to shoot anyone, I suggest we use the Beretta. If the ownership can be traced to anyone, it'll be to the scumbag who lost it. Anyone lets an unarmed guy take away his gun deserves whatever he gets."

We went over the plan a few times, then ordered in food. No one drank any alcohol. I abstained from any further medication.

After that, it was just a matter of waiting for darkness to fall.

CHAPTER 45

Avi Stern arrived in a tan trench coat and a grey loden hat. "Who's he supposed to be?" Ryan muttered. "Sherlock fucking Clouseau?"

I made the introductions. Avi's hand was clammy with sweat when I shook it. His brow and upper lip looked shiny too.

"You okay?" I asked him.

"I'm trying not to think about it," he said. "I mean, I never went into the army like you did. My idea of excitement is going somewhere new for lunch."

"You'll be fine," I said. "Got your recorder?"

He pulled a small chrome item from his coat pocket.

"Fresh batteries?"

"Oh," he said.

"Never mind. We'll stop on the way. How much time on the cassette?"

"What cassette? This one's digital. Sixty-six hours of memory."

"If we can keep Birk talking that long," I said, "we'll definitely have what we need."

"Why am I even here? Why don't one of you just take the recorder?"

"You're an officer of the court. You're going to observe

and record everything that is said and you can swear that it's authentic."

"Nothing he says will be admissible if it's made under duress."

"Duress? Who said anything about duress?"

"You've got guns," Avi said. "You've got him," indicating Ryan.

"How do you know I'm the duress inducer?" Ryan said. "You haven't seen Jenn here in action."

"All I'm saying is, I can record Birk like you asked, and as an officer of the court, I can swear it's him on the tape. But he could confess till the memory card's full. It won't matter if there's a gun on him."

"Let's see what we get out of him," I said. "Then we'll worry about getting it into court."

We took Ryan's car. Avi didn't want his anywhere near the place and I didn't blame him. On the way to the Millennium Skyline, we stopped at a convenience store and got fresh batteries for Avi's recorder. We also got him a bottle of water. "I don't think my throat has been this dry since we climbed Masada," he said.

We parked on Randolph, a short walk or fast run from the site. We divvied up the guns: a Glock for Ryan, the Beretta for me, a Baby Eagle with a polymer frame for Jenn.

"It's lightweight," Ryan said when he gave it to her. "Not that I mean anything sexist by that."

"You better not," she said. "You're already in my bad books for the thigh grab."

"Has more to do with your shooting experience, or lack of it. It's twenty-seven ounces but shoots like a much bigger gun."

"No matter what you talk about, Ryan, it still sounds like dick talk to me."

I swear I thought I saw him blush. "How come you can talk to me like that," he asked, "but anything I say to you I get shit for?"

"It's a woman's world, Ryan," she said. "We're just letting you live in it."

"One fucking generation," he complained. "That's all it took. Like the Cold War—boom, suddenly it's over and everyone's asking what the fuck happened. Wasn't thirty, forty years ago, a man knew his place and a woman knew hers. The old-timers didn't hear about it every time they put their hand on a woman's leg, unless it was someone else's woman."

"Kids," I said. "We have a criminal trespass to plan here."

"I'm a dead man," Avi said miserably.

We got out of the car and formed a tight huddle alongside the hoarding, moving along to the entrance where the trailer was. "Whatever we do from here," Ryan said, "we do it fast and quiet. Decisive. You're not sure what to do, look to me. Don't pull your gun unless you have to. It'll cut down the chances of shooting one of us. There's already a round in the chamber, so you won't have to rack the slide. Just keep the safeties on till I say otherwise. We good?"

I looked at Jenn. She looked back. We nodded at Ryan.

"Just remember what we're here for. We want to nail this fucker and anyone who's with him *and* we want to sleep in our own beds tonight."

"Please God," Avi said.

"Jenn," Ryan said. "You're up."

She leaned over, grabbed his sleeve and kissed him on the cheek, then walked toward the site entrance.

"What the hell she do that for?" he said. "She trying to throw me off my game?"

"She likes you," I said.

"Yeah? Suppose I'd done that to her?"

"You'd be counting your molars."

"Man, what a fucked-up world this is. Am I right?"

"No argument here," Avi said.

—

Jenn knows she's gay. I know she's gay. Even Ryan had grudg-
ingly accepted this "tragic fucking waste," as he put it.

The poor schlub in the trailer did not know this. It proved
to be his undoing. Jenn ran up to the gate and waved frantically
at him. Her breasts—or the Magnificent Ambersons, as she
sometimes calls them—were pressed up against the fencing in a
way that made them all the more fetching. The guard leaned
out of a window and looked at her—them—his brain shutting
down as his blood flow reversed itself to nourish his other head.

Jenn was doing her best horror-movie heroine shtick—
looking frantically behind her, rattling the fence and calling
for help.

The guard came out of the trailer. He was a portly sixty-
year-old with a day's growth of beard and a belly that hid most
of his belt. The perfect guy to have around to make sure no one
stole a brick or some tools. But in his mind's eye, I'd have bet,
he was a strapping young swain who was going to rescue this
maiden from whatever trouble she was in, then nuzzle the
Ambersons as the curtain fell. He came to the gate and said,
"Trouble, Miss?"

"I think someone's following me," Jenn said, her eyes wide,
her lips wet and parted. I almost jumped in to help her myself.

"He's old," she said—not wanting to scare off the guard,
who was hardly a paragon of studliness—"but he's still giving
me the creeps."

He breathed in deeply, trying to move his bulk from his
gut to his chest, trying to look like a hero and coming off more
like a pigeon. "Want me to call the cops?"

She looked him straight in the eye. "Do you think we
need to? Maybe if he just saw you . . . or maybe if I could wait
inside with you until he goes away."

"I'm not supposed to—"

"Please," she said. "It's cold out here." The evidence of
that was mighty clear. The guard stared at her nipples like he

was trying to memorize them. "I won't touch anything I'm not supposed to," Jenn said. "I promise."

"Well," he said, looking back at the deserted site, then at the Ambersons, then quickly up to Jenn's wide blue eyes. "Maybe just for a minute."

He had a heavy ring of keys hooked to his belt with a retractable chain. He pulled them away and unlocked a heavy padlock. As soon as he rolled the gate open, Ryan moved in and stuck his Glock in the guard's ear. He handed the guard a pair of swim goggles whose lenses had been covered over with hockey tape.

"Slip these on," he said.

The guard's weight sagged back to his belt. "A set-up," he sighed. "I should have known."

Ryan said, "You think?"

Avi and Jenn went to wait by the elevator and keep watch for any cars turning into the site. We took the guard, whose name tag said he was Henry, into the trailer. I locked the door and closed the blinds over the only window. Ryan took Henry's elbow and steered him behind a service counter that had been built at one end. He told Henry to kneel and put his hands behind his back. Henry looked like he was going to die of a heart attack before making it to the ground.

"If I was going to shoot you," Ryan said, "would I bother tying your hands?" He pushed his foot lightly into Henry's knees and they gave way, and he sank rather gently to the floor. Ryan got skate laces out of his backpack and bound Henry's wrists.

"We're going to make a phone call now," Ryan said.

Since he had already heard Ryan's voice, I kept quiet.

"Who do you call in an emergency?" Ryan asked.

"Mr. Curry. Francis Curry."

"From which phone?"

"Mine. On the table there."

"You're going to call that number and tell Mr. Curry a strange black woman in a hotel uniform showed up at the site and demanded a meeting with Simon Birk, immediately, or she's going to the police and tell them about this morning."

"A strange black woman. You don't want me to say African-American? That's what they tell me I'm supposed to use."

"Just tell him she wants to see Simon Birk. Alone. And she wants double her fee, in cash. Got that?"

"Double. In cash."

"If he asks what she looks like, you say tall with lots of freckles." Those were the main details I'd remembered and given Ryan.

"Tall, freckles."

"And a hotel uniform," Ryan said. "Like a chambermaid, don't forget that."

"Okay."

"If he asks to talk to her, you say she took the hoist up to the top of the building. You tried to stop her but she pulled a knife on you. Got that?"

"Okay."

"Say it," Ryan ordered.

"A woman came to the gate—"

"What woman?"

"Tall, with freckles."

"And?"

"And a knife."

"Okay, Henry," Ryan said evenly. "You got those goggles on, which is good for your overall prospects. But if you didn't have them on and you could see the look I'm giving you now? This is a look, Henry, that has brought a hundred deadbeats, snitches, tough guys, bikers and other unfortunate souls to their knees. So believe me when I tell you that if you say anything other than what I told you, anything cute, your blood will spill and your life will end right here."

"I don't want that," Henry said.

"Course you don't. So make it short and keep it sweet."

Henry turned in a fine performance as Night Security Guard #1. With Ryan standing over him, listening in on the cocked receiver, he stuck to Ryan's script. Didn't deviate or elaborate or say anything that sounded coded. Kept most of the fright out of his voice.

"Yessir," he finally said. "Forced her way past me and went right to the top, it looks like." Listened, nodded, said "Uh-huh" twice. Then, "Really?"

Ryan gave me a thumbs-up.

"If you say so," Henry said. "If you're sure, Mr. Curry. You know I wouldn't on anyone else's . . . Okay, good night then."

Ryan ended the call and turned the phone off. He said, "Mr. Curry told Henry to go home, take the rest of the night off, still get paid the full shift."

Ryan told Henry to lie on his side. He tied the man's ankles together with a skate lace then stretched a strong elastic, the kind used to hold hockey shin pads on, around Henry's shins. He knotted a third hockey lace between the bound wrists and ankles. Henry wasn't uncomfortable but nor could he move an inch.

Ryan opened a side pocket of the backpack and took out a pair of conical earplugs and slipped them into Henry's ears. "Don't worry," he said. "They've never been used." Then he looked around the trailer and found a set of headphone-sized hearing protectors and slipped them over Henry's ears.

"He wouldn't hear an explosion," Ryan said.

Ryan unclipped the keys from Henry's belt and flipped them to me. He produced a roll of duct tape and wrapped two lengths around Henry's mouth. Henry was now out of sight, out of mind, out of human contact.

"Check this out," I said. On a table next to Henry's half-done *Sun-Times* puzzle and Thermos were two walkie-talkies set in chargers. The green lights were steady: two fully charged units.

I handed one to Ryan, who pressed the talk button and said, "Breaker, breaker." It came through loud and clear on my unit.

"You try," he said.

"Leg breaker, leg breaker. Over."

"Very funny. Over. Get the fuck out. Over."

He unscrewed the bulbs that lit the trailer and closed and locked the door behind him, settling into the shadows to wait for Curry and Birk. I walked to the elevator, wondering where Ryan had dumped the woman's body. In the Chicago River, in a hockey bag weighted with stones or bowling balls from the Sports Authority? Down in the caisson of an unfinished building, a ton of concrete and rebar for her headstone?

I tried to resist the images coming to mind; there might be other bodies to dispose of before the night was through.

CHAPTER 46

The top of the Birkshire Millennium Skyline was not my favourite place in Chicago. Then again, neither was Millennium Park, Daley Plaza, Avi's den or my bathroom at the Hilton, so the competition wasn't that stiff.

It was colder and windier than it had been the previous night. The first of November in Chicago: batten down the hatches. Jenn had her hands thrust deep in the pockets of a navy peacoat. Avi looked like he was sweating and shivering at the same time. I had a sudden flashback of him at Har Milah: always sweaty, even at four in the morning when we started work to get in our hours before the hot sun came up. Beads forming on his forehead, running down around his eyes, his shirt darkening as sweat ran down his chest and back, his hands damp whenever we shook, even if he'd already wiped them on the back of his pants. I hoped his palms didn't get so clammy now that he dropped his recorder like a bar of soap. Like us, it wouldn't survive a fall from this height.

"You know what you're going to do?" Jenn asked me.

"I have an idea."

"That's it?"

The walkie-talkie crackled and Ryan's voice said, "They're here." So I didn't have to answer.

We looked down and saw headlights sweeping the street far below us, pulling to the curb outside the gate. I got out my field glasses and saw Birk get out of the passenger side. He looked at the dark trailer then nodded at Curry, who got out of the car and locked it with a fob. So it was just the two of them. Birk waited for Curry to roll the gate open—always leaving the heavy lifting to someone else—and close it behind them. They were walking toward the elevator when Ryan slipped out of the darkness and trained his Glock on them. Ryan spoke, then Curry and Birk both took off their jackets and let them fall to the ground. Curry took his gun out of its holster and handed it to Ryan butt first. Ryan gestured with the gun and Curry pulled up his pant legs one at a time. Nothing there. Ryan said something and Curry leaned against the trailer as though he were about to be frisked. Then the gun moved to Birk and he too pulled up his pant legs, showing pale legs above black socks.

When Ryan was satisfied, he pointed toward the elevator with his gun hand. Birk bent down to pick up his jacket but Ryan levelled the gun at him and shook his head. Birk gestured in complaint; Ryan's foot lashed out and caught him in the chest, sending him sprawling into the dirt. Curry held out his hand and helped Birk to his feet and then the three of them headed to the elevator, two in shirt sleeves, only one gesturing in complaint.

Ryan's voice came over the walkie-talkie: "How'd this turd ever make a billion? Over."

"Bring him up and we'll ask."

When the hoist arrived at ground level, Ryan made them get in first. He pointed downward with the gun, making them sit, then got in and started the car on its long, slow ascent. Watching the descending counterweight reminded me of my forced climb down. My hands clenched involuntarily, and painfully, at the memory, but I reminded myself that Birk had a lot more to answer for than that.

"Where do you want me?" Avi asked.

"What's the range on your recorder?"

"Normally very good. It has a zoom mike for meetings. But with this wind . . ."

"I don't want them to see you yet. Just stay in the shadow of the centre block for now."

"Here okay?" He was moving to his right when he stepped on a sheet of plywood that had been placed over a gap in the flooring. It sagged under his weight. "Whoa!" he cried, jumping back onto the firmer corrugated surface. "Did you see that? That almost broke under me."

"Relax, Avi," I said. "I'm sure workmen step on it all the time. It just gives a little."

"I don't—"

"Just pick a spot and stay still, okay? You'll be fine. You ready?"

"Yeah, yeah. I'm ready."

The elevator doors opened and Ryan backed out. Birk and Curry were both sitting on the floor of the car, hands behind their heads. Ryan pointed the gun at them and said, "Up."

They got up.

"Out," he said, pointing behind him with a little bow, palm up, as though welcoming them to Giulio's.

CHAPTER 47

Simon Birk stared long and hard at me, then at Jenn and back at me. Curry gave me the merest glance. If he was surprised that I was still alive, he didn't show it. He took in Jenn's presence, then turned his attention back to Dante Ryan, the man he needed to watch, eyes on his gun hand, looking for an opening, a move to make.

Birk said, "Where's Charlaine?"

"She won't be joining us," I said.

"I told you she was unsuitable," Birk said to Curry, like she was a maid who had put away foggy stemware.

"Do it yourself next time," Curry said.

"And you are Ms. Raudsepp, am I right?" Birk said. He held out his hand. She never moved or took her eyes off his. He slowly dropped the hand that had shaken a hundred thousand other hands, a hand that had rarely if ever been rejected.

Jenn said, "You're even shorter than you look on TV."

I handed Jenn one of the walkie-talkies and the keys to the trailer. "Go back to ground level," I said. "Keep an eye on Henry and call us if anyone shows up."

Ryan said, "Tell Henry if he makes trouble, I'll come down and hold his nose till he dies."

She got into the elevator and pulled the door shut and the car began to slide down.

Curry said, "Where's the third man?"

"What third man?" I said. There was no way he could see Avi from where he was.

"Your friend the lawyer. The one who looks like he's about to piss himself."

"You know the fellow," Birk cut in. "The one you had dinner with Thursday." Letting me know he knew more than he was supposed to. "Why don't you come out, Mr. Stern? For a lawyer, I have to say, you're not giving Geller very good advice."

Avi stepped forward, his eyes down, carefully avoiding the plywood patching he'd stepped on before.

Birk said, "Now we know everyone but your gunman."

"You really want to know me?" Ryan said.

"This is no party," I said to Birk.

"What then?" He was rubbing his arms to stay warm in the harsh wind.

"We're going to hear your confession."

"Really? And what am I confessing to?"

"Murder, attempted murder and fraud."

"Or what? You'll behead me while screaming in Arabic?"

"You had three people killed that I know of. You tried to kill me three times, you and your people, and you fucking well watched while someone beat your wife into a coma, just so you could steal your own artwork and cash in on the insurance."

"Pure fantasy," he replied. "All of it. That's all anyone will say."

I turned to Curry. His odd waxy face was expressionless in the dim light. "If he goes down," I said, "you're going down even harder. Are you willing to do all the time for his crimes?"

"You're a civilian," he said. "You have zero authority here. I don't have to say a word to you."

Ryan stepped forward and raked Curry across the face

with the barrel of his Glock. Blood spurted from a gash in Curry's cheek as he stumbled backward against the elevator doors, his features twisted into a snarl. A line of blood snaked down the hollow under the cut cheek. With his hairless dome and protruding ears, he looked like a vampire after a messy feast. "You may not have to say anything," Ryan said softly. "But you might *want* to."

Curry told Ryan to fuck off. I wondered if he had a death wish, or was simply hoping to catch Ryan off guard and make a play for his gun. Ryan looked like he was going to open the other cheek when Avi turned off the recorder and called, "Jonah, whoa. You can't do it this way. What value is a statement if you beat it out of him?"

"Listen to your mouthpiece," Birk said.

"He's here to listen," I said, "not advise. But he's right. There's another way to do this."

"Like what?" Ryan asked.

"Play a game."

"What kind of game?"

"Simon knows. Don't you?"

Birk was hugging himself tighter against the cold. "I don't—"

"Pirates," I said.

Birk said, "No."

"Why not? You invented it. You made the rules."

"Geller, you can't—"

"Turn around," I said.

He didn't move. I grabbed Birk by the shoulders. Marched him to the edge of the metal floor, where it met the same twenty-foot-long, twelve-inch-wide beam he'd made me walk the night before.

"You should have worn runners," I said, looking down at his highly polished loafers. "I don't know what kind of grip you're going to get with those."

"You're crazy," he said. "I'm not—"

"I'm giving you the same choice you gave me. Walk or get shot."

"If you kill me," he said, "you'll have every cop in the city after you."

"Led by Tom Barnett," I said. "He couldn't solve your robbery, what makes you think he'll catch your killer?"

"I'm big in this town! You have no idea how big. I bring billions into the economy. I have friends who are judges, U.S. attorneys. You can't treat me like some common criminal."

"I'm not. I'm treating you like—what was it you called me?—a pissant. A shit stain on the sidewalk? That's what I'm treating you like."

"Francis!" Birk said.

"Yeah?" Curry drawled.

"Fucking do something."

Curry looked at Ryan, who had a gun trained on him. "I'd say my options are limited."

I looked around the site and picked up a fallen bolt, hefted it in my hand. "Look on the bright side," I said to Birk. "The farther out you walk, the harder it's going to be for me to hit you with this."

"You wouldn't."

I held up my hand so he could see the welt between my knuckles. "That's one hit," I said. I pushed up the sleeve of my leather jacket to bare my forearm. "That's another. It hurts too much to get my jacket off so I won't show you the one on my shoulder. That was a hummer. How many do you think you can take before you lose your grip and fall?"

"We can come to some kind of agreement," Birk gasped. He was shivering. Whether from cold or fear, I didn't care. It looked good on him. "I know we can. I negotiate every day."

"There's nothing to negotiate."

"I can compensate you—"

"I'm not the one who needs compensation."

"Then these supposed victims of yours. Their families."

"Which victims?"

"The ones you mentioned. The ones you think I killed."

"The ones you ordered killed."

"No!"

"Walk," I said.

"Please!"

"One foot, then the other."

I cocked my throwing arm. He inched out onto the beam.

"My advice?" I said. "Don't look down."

"Jesus Christ, you're making a mistake."

"Keep going."

"I can pay you, Geller. Millions! Tens of millions."

"It wouldn't be enough. Everything you have wouldn't be enough."

"You can't do this."

"I'm already doing it," I said.

"Francis did it!" he said. "All of it."

"Shut your mouth," Curry said.

"Let's hear it," I said to Birk. I looked at Avi. He turned his recorder on and pointed it at Birk. "Loud and clear."

Birk started in off the beam but I stopped him. "Not yet," I said. "Let's hear it all first."

"All right! Rob Cantor called me," Birk said. "He told me his engineer was making noise about the land. About having to have it all cleaned again. I told him we couldn't. The hole was already dug. The caissons were already sunk. Starting over would have ruined everything."

"Ruined you, you mean."

"It's a precarious business we're in. And I was over-stretched, I admit it. Too many buildings going up and too many things going wrong. Acts of God, acts of war, sabotage, unions—one disaster after another. I couldn't handle one more, so I told Francis to take care of it. I never told him to kill the man. I just thought he'd . . ."

"He'd what?"

"Make it go away somehow. Bribe him. Threaten him. Then Francis went to Toronto and came back and all he told me was it was fixed. I swear I didn't know Glenn was dead until it was already done."

"And Will Sterling?"

"Who?"

"The student who discovered the Aroclor on the property."

"Same thing," Birk panted. "It was Francis who shot him."

"On your orders."

"Not explicitly," he insisted. "I didn't say kill the boy. I didn't say shoot him. I just said we had a problem, that's all."

"And you had no idea how Francis eliminates problems."

"None!"

Curry laughed harshly and spat out the words "You lying piece of shit." His white shirt was spattered with blood but unlike Birk, he showed no sign of being cold. Maybe he was just colder inside. "He knew everything. Every step of the way."

"No," Birk said. "I was blind to it. Wilfully, perhaps, but I never knew the details, I swear."

"What about Maya Cantor?" I asked.

"What about her? She killed herself."

"No," I said. "She didn't. And anyone who says she did is pissing on her grave."

"I swear I had nothing to do with that. Maybe Francis did, ask him, but not me."

"She called your office the day she died."

"If she did, I never spoke to her. No one gets through to me if I don't know them. Even people I know don't get through."

"Someone picked that girl up and threw her off her balcony."

"Why?"

Why. Why had someone killed Maya? The simplest of

questions. And not one I'd expected him to ask. He seemed genuinely in the dark about it.

"She was helping Will Sterling. Looking for evidence that her father was covering up the Aroclor."

"Then ask her father. Ask Francis."

Curry said, "Don't look at me. I wasn't in Toronto when she died."

"It doesn't mean you didn't contract it out."

"A double negative," he smirked. "That shit won't get you far."

"Should I hit him some more?" Ryan asked. "It gives his face character."

"Save it for now. What about the robbery?" I asked Birk.

"What about it?"

"Take five steps out."

"I can't!"

"Do it!"

"Why?"

I yelled, "Because I said so," and flung the bolt at him. He ducked and lost his footing and almost fell off the beam. He grabbed it with both hands and stayed in a squatting position. "Five steps," I said. "Or the next one drills you in the head."

He shuffled back five steps on his hands and knees. Avi was looking at me like I was crazy. Luckily for me, he was a lawyer, not a shrink, so I didn't have to pay it much mind.

"The robbery," I said.

"What about it?"

I looked around for a bolt. Ryan found one first. As soon as he picked it up, Birk said quickly, "All right! The robbery!"

"It was a fraud, from beginning to end."

"Yes," he whispered.

"Louder."

"Yes!"

"You planned it."

"Yes."

"You, not Francis."

"Yes."

"You circumvented your own security system and let Francis in?"

"Yes."

"And Chuck Belkin too."

Birk's eyes widened, as if he'd just seen a ghost. I glanced at Curry. He had taken note too. Birk said, "How do you know about Belkin?"

"For the record," I said, pitching my voice toward Avi and his recorder, "Chuck Belkin was found shot to death a few weeks after the robbery."

"So many people get shot in Chicago," Curry said. "It's hard to keep track of them all."

I ignored him. "So you let Francis and Belkin in the house and they took out all the artwork you subsequently reported stolen?"

"Yes," Birk said.

"Then what? You sold it privately?"

"Yes," he admitted. "Not for full value, of course. But there are always people who will buy art even if they can't display it publicly. They want to own it for the sake of owning it."

"Then you defrauded Great Midwestern Life for the full value."

"Yes." He glanced over at Avi, at the recorder glinting in the moonlight. "No one is going to admit this as evidence, you know. Surely your lawyer friend told you that."

"He tried," I said. "I didn't listen."

"You should have."

"You want to go back another five steps?"

"No!"

"Then forget the law and keep talking. Tell me about the beating. That was planned too?"

"Yes. They were supposed to rough us up, to make the robbery more convincing," Birk said. "They got carried away. Especially Belkin. He wouldn't stop hitting Joyce."

"Why?"

"I don't know. He went a little crazy."

"And you couldn't stop him?"

"No."

"And Francis couldn't?"

"No! I don't—I was already unconscious."

Until then, I believed, he'd been telling the truth. But all my instincts now told me he was lying. It was as if a surge of emotion had welled up inside him, and he was using every ounce of his will to suppress it. But the pitch of his voice had changed, and his body had tensed. In the dim light cast by nearby buildings, I could see his eyes flutter slowly before they blinked.

I held out my hand and asked Ryan for the bolt.

"What are you doing?" Birk shouted.

"You lied," I said.

"No," Birk cried, cowering as he gripped the beam with his hands and his knees. "Why would I—"

"You're lying!"

"Francis did it!" Birk said. "He beat her."

"Bullshit!" Curry said.

"I only said it was Belkin because he's already dead, but it was Francis."

"Why would he do that? Unless you ordered him to."

"No! I loved my wife." Birk was clutching the beam he was on like it was a bucking bull he was about to ride.

"Yeah," Curry laughed. "True love. You can see it on the tape."

"What tape?" I asked.

"The one of him beating her head in."

CHAPTER 48

The way Curry told it, Birk had wanted his wife dead from the outset. He didn't love her. He hated the way she spent his money on paintings that made no sense to him, sculptures that looked like scrap. Vases and rugs he could have bought for a tenth of the price. Like many rich men, he was tight with a dollar. He might spend thousands on a Rolex, millions on a private jet, but he begrudged the expenses Joyce piled up.

"Even this home she's in now is peanuts compared to what she used to spend, right, Simon?" Curry sneered.

"He's making it up," Birk insisted. "He's trying to save his own neck."

"You had your chance," I told him. "Let Curry talk."

Curry told us Birk had come up with the idea after seeing a news report on a fraudulent home invasion in Connecticut. He approached Curry with the plan, went over all the security systems with him, lined up buyers for the artwork in Switzerland, Japan and Russia.

"The inside camera, the one in the foyer, was supposed to be disconnected," Curry said. "But I needed insurance, in case Simon tried to pin it on me. I knew he wouldn't hold up if the police brought any heat on him. So I kept it rolling, and it's a fucking beauty. Nice crisp images of Simon taking a tire iron to his beloved wife. And you know what else? Belkin was supposed to do it. I was going to break a couple of Simon's bones and Chuck was going to do his wife. The story would be she resisted, kicked him in the nuts or something, and he lost it on her. But Simon insisted on doing it himself. Didn't you, *boss?* He took the tire iron and looked her right in the eye. Then *whack, whack, whack.* Six, seven times in the head. She only saw the first one coming, but what an image to take to your grave. Your own husband doing you in, in the home you made together."

"How did she survive?"

"We thought she was dead. Christ, you could see through her skull right to her brain. And we were running out of time. We had to get Simon cleaned up—he was covered in blood—and we still had to get all the shit out to the van. We were all surprised she made it. The wonders of modern medicine. Personally, I think she would have been better off dead, because she's got no life now. But in her own way, she contributed. As long as I have that recording—and I have plenty of copies—I have a job for life. Simon can't fire me, kill me or say anything to the cops."

"Why worry about that?" I asked. "You have Tom Barnett on your side."

"I wasn't sure Tommy would go along with it. He was a pretty good cop once. Even that thing—the one that got me kicked off the force—he didn't have much to do with that. Lucky for us he needed money to help his kid get off dope. What they charge for rehab programs, he wasn't going to make as a cop."

"You getting all this?" I said to Avi.

"Yes." He looked deathly pale. I guess corporate law didn't prepare you for sordid tales like this one.

I paged Jenn on the walkie-talkie: "Everything cool down there?"

"We're good," she said. "One car stopped here a minute ago but it moved on."

"Okay. We'll be down in five."

I told Birk he could come in off the beam now. He crawled forward until he reached the metal deck.

"What now?" he asked.

"Francis is going to tell us where that tape is. Then we're going to retrieve it. Then we're going to have you charged with the attempted murder of your wife, plus whatever other counts a U.S. attorney can come up with. Even Barnett won't be able to save you this time."

"How do you know that tape even exists? That it's not something Francis made up to put the blame on me?"

"Because he's still alive and working for you. Without it, I don't think that would be the case. Right, Francis?"

Curry nodded.

I called Avi over and asked him for the recorder. I rewound it briefly and hit play. Heard Curry's voice: " . . . money to help his kid get off dope. What they charge for rehab programs, he wasn't going to make as a cop."

I pressed stop and handed it back to Avi.

"I heard you like to box," I said to Birk, squaring up with him, my hands clenched.

"You're thirty years younger than me."

"Your wife was younger," I said. "And I don't have a tire iron. In fact, I have one pretty useless hand and the other hurts to make a fist."

He kept his hands down at his sides. "Go ahead," he said. "Hit me. Hit me all you want. The worse I look, the more people will believe this so-called confession is bullshit."

I wanted to crush his nose, make him taste his own blood. Break his jaw so he'd have to take meals through a straw for a month. Give him a taste of what his wife had endured when the tire iron had descended on her. But I let my hands drop. "Fuck it," I said. "Let's take them down. Avi, let me have that recorder till we can make copies."

Avi said no. I looked at him, wondering why he'd say that, then stopped wondering. He had an automatic pistol pointed at Dante Ryan. "Lower your gun," he told Ryan. "Or I'll shoot you and Jonah both."

"Avi?" I said.

"Do it now," he said.

Ryan set his weapon gently on the ground. Curry went to pick it up but Avi told him to stay where he was. He stooped to pick up the gun himself, then slipped it into his trench coat pocket. "I'm going to keep it for the time being," he said. "If it's the gun you used on those other people, like Jonah says, it'll make for good insurance."

"What insurance?" Birk said. "We have a deal."

"I know what a deal means to you," Avi said. "The gun and the tape are worth a lot more than you're paying me."

Suddenly it was all clear: how Birk had been aware of my every move since I had arrived in Chicago. It was Avi Stern who had sold me out.

"Your gun, Jonah. Set it down and slide it over to me."

I did as he asked. I watched him pick it up, smiling at me with his even white teeth, wondering what Birk could have offered him to betray me. But there was no way he would have known the connection. Which meant Avi had approached him. Which meant it wasn't the money. He was living well enough legitimately and would certainly have all the money he needed by mid-life. It had to have been something else. Then I recalled the image of him in his den, crying as we watched the Broza concert at Masada. And I had my answer.

Dalia.

CHAPTER 49

He had loved her from the moment he met her at Har Milah. An awkward sweaty kid from Chicago with thick glasses and a mulish laugh, he was immediately struck by her grace, her beauty, her bright blue eyes and mass of black curls. He'd been too shy to approach her as a lover and had settled for being a pal, but each day spent near her, with her, persuaded him he was inching closer to his dream. One more day, he'd tell himself, one more night of singing and laughing and dreaming together, and she'd be his.

"Then you showed up," Avi said, pointing my own gun at me. "Jonah Geller, fit and funny, not an ounce of fat on you, not a wrong move. You didn't sweat just getting out of bed. You were even from her hometown. And from then on, I had to watch the two of you together, holding hands, stealing kisses, sneaking out to the greenhouse. Stealing her from me by the hour."

"This is all fascinating," Simon Birk said. "Maybe you should save it for your memoirs."

Avi swivelled, put the gun on Birk.

"Or not," Birk said.

"Hanging out with the two of you, going to the concert, into Kiryat Shmona, a happy little trio, right? Except I was dying inside. I remember David Broza singing 'Yihyeh Tov' at

Masada, and we all had our arms around each other. I finally had my arm around Dalia, and she had hers around me, and it didn't matter how much I was sweating because we were all soaked through from dancing all night. It would have been perfect, but you were there on her other side. I looked over and she had her hand in the back pocket of your jeans. Fucking feeling your ass. Not me, not mine, no, just her hand on my waist. Barely touching it, like she was my sister. I hated you, Jonah. I wanted to pitch you off the side of the goddamn mountain, the way the zealots threw themselves off at the end of the siege."

"But she died, Avi. You were there when she died. You saw what—"

"Maybe she wouldn't have!" he yelled. "Maybe we would have left Har Milah and come back to Chicago and I could have been married to her instead of Adele."

"Don't do this," I said. I took a step toward him but he stepped back and told me to stay where I was.

"So I get Adele instead. She lives from headache to headache. Music's too loud? A headache. One of the kids cries? A headache. A glass of wine, the lights too bright, the lights too dim—a headache. And God forbid Avi wants a little action. Major headache time."

"You going to shoot me, Avi?"

"No. But someone will."

Curry said, "The line starts here."

"He'll kill you too," I said to Avi. "Curry will kill all of us."

"I don't think so," he said. "Not with my insurance policy." He patted his coat pocket.

"Why don't you give me one of the guns?" Curry said. "Doesn't have to be mine. Keep that if it makes you feel better."

"I don't think so," Avi said.

"The girl down there, she has a gun too."

"I'll deal with her when we get down there. I think she'll give up her gun before she lets Jonah get shot."

"Have it your way," Curry said. "You ready?"

"Yes."

"You, Simon?"

Birk said yes.

We all walked over to the side of the building where the hoist waited.

"There's just one more thing to do before we go down," Curry said.

"What?" I asked.

He didn't answer. He just grabbed Simon Birk by the shirt collar and belt and threw him screaming off the side of the building.

CHAPTER 50

"What the fuck!" Avi yelled. He didn't know who to point the gun at now. He finally settled on Curry.

"Everyone needs insurance," Curry said. His hairless, bulbous head looked pale and rubbery as an unpeeled garlic clove. "You have yours, right in your pocket," he said. "Birk was mine for a long time."

"Then why did you—"

"You saw how he cracked. He would have thrown us all to his lawyers. He became a liability the minute he let Geller turn him." He gave me a look that was mean as a snake's, a furious cobra that would take on a mongoose to get me.

"I told you before, Geller, I'm ex a lot of things. I had to scramble plenty of years after I left the force, believe me. Low-paying security jobs, personal protection gigs, but nothing I could seriously live on, until the day Simon Birk beat his wife into a coma on camera and I got a job for life! An easy two hundred a year," he said. "And I mean easy, feet-up easy, an occasional walk around his buildings, a few drive-by checks, a very good lunch most days, *plus* every expense I could dream up. But," he said to Avi, "he would have sold me out faster than you sold out your friend Geller. Now you take my advice, Stern. You come to a dance like this, you stick with the one that brung ya. You stick with me if you want to resume a normal family life after tonight. You quit waving that piece around and let me do what needs to be done."

"Avi," I said. "I understand how you felt about Dalia—"

"How I feel, *haveri*. How I feel."

"But it's not just me now. You think you had a right to sell me out, fine! But you're going to have to kill four of us now. You have enough revenge in your heart for that?"

He stood there silent as a dead man. I searched for light in his frosty blue eyes but saw none. "Four," I said. "There's me, Avi. You were okay with that, I was the guy who took your girl. But now there's also Ryan and Jenn. You didn't know about them till today, you couldn't have predicted it, but here they are. The three of us plus you have to throw in Henry."

His lips pursed and his eyes narrowed as he said, "Henry?"

"The old rent-a-cop down there. You're not a killer, Avi. Give me the gun."

"I think I'll just stick to the plan for now," he said.

"I'm your only chance to get out of this with anything," I said.

"You'll get more from me," Curry said.

Ryan said, "If I got anything to say about this—"

"Jonah!" Jenn's voice came crackling in over the walkie-talkie hooked to my belt. "Jonah, come in! I thought I saw somebody fall."

I reached for the walkie-talkie. Avi levelled the gun. "If I don't answer," I said, "she'll know something's up."

"Don't do anything stupid," he said. "Tell her there was an accident and we're coming right down."

He watched me as I unhooked the walkie-talkie from my belt.

"Jenn," I said. "It was an accident. Birk fell over the side. I repeat, an accident. Over."

"What should I do?"

"Stay in the trailer," I said. "We're coming down."

I looked at Avi as if to say, Okay?

"Turn it off," he hissed.

"Over and out," I said. I held up the unit and made a show of turning it off, then flipped it to him underhand. Only I flipped it a little to his left where he'd have to step over and catch it. He did and there was a loud cracking sound as all of his weight came down on a sheet of plywood bridging two sections of corrugated metal, the same one that had bent under him before. This time it broke in half, and his right leg plunged through it. As he fell, his hand hit the deck and the gun clattered away. Curry went for it without hesitating. I went too, launching myself off a bruised knee, trying to drop him with my shoulder. But I hit him with my bad side, my shoulder barely holding together, and he bodied me aside, ahead in the race for the gun. He was closing his hand on it when Dante Ryan said, "Don't."

His pant leg was pulled up to reveal an ankle holster and he had a Baby Eagle in his hand: the same model he had given Jenn. I remembered from our earliest meetings that he rarely travelled without at least two guns, along with his favourite stiletto.

Curry took a long look at Ryan and didn't like what he saw. He let the gun lie, sighed and shook his head.

Avi let out a low moan. "I think my leg is broken," he said.

"Give me a minute," Ryan snarled. "I'll break the other one too."

Ryan told Curry to get Avi out of the hole he was in. "And don't throw him over," he said. "There's got to be a limit to how many people you can toss off a building."

Tears were running down Avi's face. His right leg was bleeding through his pants. I picked up the Beretta from the floor and pointed it at him.

"I'll take the recorder," I said.

He took it from his pocket with a shaking hand and gave it to me. I wiped it on my jacket front and stowed it in my pocket. "You still sweat like a pig," I said. Then I picked up the walkie-talkie and turned it on. "Jenn?" I said. "Sorry, we were turned off for a minute. We're all okay."

There was no answer. Just a hiss and crackle.

"Jenn? Come in, Jenn."

Still no answer. Then the hiss and crackle died. Either her batteries had suddenly died or her unit had been shut off. I looked at Ryan. "Nowhere to go but down."

Once again, we divided up guns. Ryan put Curry's Beretta in his shoulder holster for safekeeping. It was a mess as far as prints went, because all of us had handled it, but Hollinger could at least test it against her Toronto homicides, settle once and for all on the idea that Curry was her killer.

Ryan gave me back my Beretta, the 92FS, and reholstered the Baby Eagle. We all got into the elevator and pulled the gate down. I kept a gun on Avi; Ryan kept his Glock on Curry. The hoist slid down the track, gusts of wind blowing through the sides, rattling the Plexiglas sheets in their frames.

CHAPTER 51

Simon Birk had landed on his back on the rutted earth, not far from a line of portable washrooms and a dumpster filled with odd lengths of wood and rebar. A pool of blood was fanning out around his head but the rest of him—his top half anyway—looked fine, good enough for an open-casket funeral. Most of the damage would be on the underside and internal: pulped organs beneath the intact skin.

"And there you have it," Curry said. "Simon Birk's final groundbreaking."

We made Curry walk ahead of us toward the trailer, supporting Avi with an arm around his waist, Avi moaning and limping, all the adventurousness knocked out of him. Then Curry said, "Fuck it," squatted and got his shoulder under Avi and stood, grunting, hefting him like a fireman would. A lot stronger than his slim frame suggested, handling Avi's weight and staying sure-footed among the deep ruts created by earthmovers' treads.

When we got to the trailer, he let Avi fall heavily to the ground. Avi cried out and Curry told him to quit moaning. "It's one fucking leg," he said. "It's not like you were shot."

I opened the trailer door and peered in. I could see Henry's thin white shins peeking out where his pants parted from his socks. He hadn't moved.

No sign of Jenn.

Just a walkie-talkie on the ground, its indicator light off.

"In back of you," a man's voice said.

We turned and saw Tom Barnett standing about fifteen feet in back of us, leaning against the cab of a backhoe. He held Jenn in front of himself. His powerful right arm was around her throat, with her Baby Eagle resting in his hand, its muzzle resting casually against her head. His own piece was pointed at us: yet another Beretta, the place lousy with them.

"You know the routine," he said. "Put the guns down. Both of you, now! Drop them easy and kick them this way."

I put the Beretta down, kicked it across the ground toward him. It would have made it all the way but it tripped up on a rut three-quarters of the way there and stopped. Ryan threw his Glock to roughly the same spot.

"They have any more guns, Francis?" Barnett rumbled softly.

"The dark guy, Ryan, he has my Beretta in a shoulder holster. And an Eagle in an ankle holster."

Barnett told Ryan to unbutton his jacket and open it. Saw the butt of the gun. Told Ryan to take it out slow with two fingers and lay it on the ground. Made him lift his pant leg and ditch the Eagle. "Now step back."

Ryan stepped back.

Curry stooped to pick up the guns.

Barnett said, "Uh-uh."

"But that's—"

"I said, uh-uh."

Curry said, "Tommy—"

"Step back. Both of you. I want all the guns first. Then we'll talk. You, Geller. You don't look as tough as your friend. Take the guns and toss them over here. Carefully. I been on this job too long to say 'or the girl gets it.' But that's the general drift."

When he had all the guns in his possession—and Curry's killing gun stowed in his own holster—Barnett shoved Jenn toward the trailer and covered us with his service piece and her Baby Eagle. Avi moaned on the ground, gripping his injured leg; if he was looking for sympathy from any of us, he'd wait till he dried up like a bird carcass.

I said to Barnett, "If anyone saw or heard Birk fall, you've got little to no time. You need to make a decision and there's only one that's going to save your neck *and* let you walk out of here a hero."

He looked at me with interest—too much for Curry's liking. Curry said, "Who you going to listen to, Tommy, this gaper here or your old partner?"

"The facts on the ground, old partner, are a little different than what you told me they'd be. I was supposed to put the arm on some broad named Charlaine. I not only find a fucking crowd scene when I get here, but everyone's armed to the teeth, even Angel Face here, plus that seems to be Simon Birk mashed into the fucking ground there, Francis, with no pulse. So I say to you, old partner, what the fuck did you just get me into?"

"Do things my way," I said, "and you'll keep your badge. Hell, you'll probably get promoted. You listen to Curry, there's going to be a bloodbath. A body count you won't be able to take."

Barnett said, "How do you know what I can take?"

"My way, you can close half a dozen major crimes. His way, you have to cover up ten murders."

"You're delusional."

"Count them, Detective. You'd have to kill everyone here," I said. "Five of us."

"I count four."

"There's a security guard tied up in the trailer. He's tied, gagged, deaf and blind, but Curry would have to kill him too because he spoke to him on the phone tonight. That's five.

Birk makes six. Then there's Chuck Belkin—you remember Chuck, shot to death after Birk's robbery. Add three homicides in Toronto that a very good sergeant is handling, that's your ten killings, all open and active, any one of which could connect with another one, then boom, you've sunk everything you've worked for. You know there's only one way out for you. If you're not seeing it, it's not because you're not smart enough."

Curry said, "Let me help you, Tom."

"You know what you have to do," I said to Barnett. "The only question is, Can you do it?"

"You're so damn sure," he said. He knew exactly what I meant, and that I was right because there was only one way out of this for him—to kill Francis Curry on the spot.

"It's the only story you can sell," I said.

"What are you talking about?" Curry said. "What story?"

"Ever see *The Maltese Falcon?*" I asked.

Curry said, "Sure." Frowning. "Everyone's seen that one."

"Remember they need a fall guy at the end, someone to give to the cops for the murders. They settle on Wilmer, the little guy in the coat with the two big guns. You can see his eyes getting wider and wider as he realizes Sydney Greenstreet is going to sell him out. We need the same ending, Curry. We need a fall guy. If it's you, Barnett gets the guy who killed Simon Birk and at least three others."

"Where does your story start?" Barnett asked.

"Birk brought Avi Stern—that's him moaning there—up to the top of the building to show him what the view would be like. Curry was blackmailing Birk over the phony home invasion, Birk threatened to cut him off, he followed Birk and attacked him up there. Pushed him over. Stern tried to stop him and was injured. Curry was fleeing the scene when you arrived and when confronted by him, you shot him dead."

"I just happen on a scene my ex-partner's involved in?"

"Doesn't have to be. You were following him. You always suspected the Birk home invasion was an inside job. You had no proof but, dedicated cop that you are, you couldn't let it go. Now you can finally close the case that haunted you. Birk admitted it all in front of a lawyer."

"Yeah, listen to it on tape," Curry laughed. "You can hear Geller winging bolts at Birk while he screams his fucking lungs out."

"Remember the broomstick Curry broke off in some guy's ass?" I said. "The one that got him kicked off the force? This is another stick of his, Barnett. You want to be the one left holding it?"

He was looking at the guns in his hands, the Baby Eagle barely visible. "So you're saying Francis gets shot fleeing the scene."

"The alternative is shooting five in cold blood."

"Nicely argued, Geller. Nicely done. If this was Toronto, someone would probably give you a gold star. But me and Francis," he said, "we go back too far. He broke me in, didn't you, Francis. Taught me what it was to be a cop in this city. Then he helped me learn about people like Birk." He took out Curry's Beretta and handed it to him. "Francis," he said, "your weapon."

Curry gave me a smile as cold and lethal as black ice. Eased the safety off the gun.

Barnett said, "Police, drop the gun."

Curry looked up.

"I said, drop the gun!" Then he fired three shots from his service pistol into Curry's chest, fast as firecrackers, sending him staggering back, his arms going like pinwheels. He fell onto his back, his head smacking hard against the cold ground, but that didn't matter—he was already dead. The pistol lay close to his hand. Barnett kept us covered, got his body between us and the gun.

"Talk fast," he said to me. "What does the security guard know?"

"He saw Jenn. Briefly. Could be coaxed into giving a very generic description. He heard Ryan's voice and talked to Curry on the phone. Curry told him to go home. Which works with the idea Curry was planning something."

"All right. Get into the trailer," he said. "All of you."

"We should get out of here. Someone's going to report the shots you just fired."

"I said, into the trailer. Now."

"You're halfway out of this, Barnett, don't turn back."

"I can't just let you walk out of here."

"Barnett—"

"What do I know about you people? How do I know who can keep his mouth shut? That one's a lawyer, for Chrissakes."

"We have no interest in pursuing you," I said. "As far as we're concerned, you're Chicago's problem. Not ours."

"And him?" Meaning Avi.

"He's in enough shit as it is." I squatted next to him and pulled his face up by the hair. "Aren't you, Avi? You'd like to get out of this with your life intact. Right? However much you hate me, you're not going to bring your family and practice down in flames too, are you?"

"No," he muttered.

"Okay, Barnett? Let us get out of here, now, and leave you to tell what happened. One teller, one story. Far less room for screwing up."

"No one's going anywhere."

"You could kill us all?"

"I'm a Chicago police detective," he said. "Tell me what I can't do."

"I'll tell you," said a voice above him.

Barnett looked up into the night sky.

Something metal fell and struck him in the face. A lunch

box. He dropped without a word. He lay dazed, bleeding from a cut above his right eye, while Ryan stripped him of his guns, including a .25-calibre belly gun tucked in an ankle holster of his own.

There was a rustling sound on the roof of the trailer above where Barnett had been standing. Then quiet, then a thud as Gabriel Cross dropped to the ground, wiping his hands of some dirt.

"I told you not to come here tonight," I said.

"I know," he said. "But I'm working on not listening to white men so much."

We hammered it out quick and dirty outside the trailer. With Ryan's gun nuzzling his ear, Barnett had little choice but to nod and accept our terms. Jenn and Ryan would start the drive back that night and I would fly out on the first morning plane, to stay consistent with our means of entry; three tourists going home after enjoying ever too briefly the wonders of Chicago, the Great Lakes' finest city. Avi would go back to a life that seemed entirely predictable on one level—the good Jewish lawyer, the father of three lovely kids—and beneath it his seething hatred of me, this grudge he'd nursed all these years, this idea that if I had never come to Har Milah, he'd be happily married to a lush beauty, instead of living in clenched misery with a wife as dry as a crumbling leaf. That was his life. Let him go back to it. Neither he nor Barnett could ever implicate the other without destroying himself.

Barnett would finally solve the Birks' robbery. He would close the cases on Simon Birk, Chuck Belkin and Charlaine Teal, the woman who played the role of evil chambermaid, whose death he'd also ascribe to Curry. He'd even rescue Henry, the loyal night watchman.

Gabriel Cross, of course, had vanished before Barnett regained his senses. As far as the official story went, he was never even there. Just like the rest of us. As if that night had never happened.

If only.

Back at the hotel, Ryan and Jenn loaded their few things into the car, got directions to the northbound I-94 and sped off.

I booked a flight on my laptop, leaving O'Hare at 6:35 the following morning, then fell back on the bed and worked on slowing my breathing, getting it right with the rhythm of my heart and body, instead of the Riverdance thing it was doing.

Advocating a man's death the way I had, so cold and logical about it—yes, I did it to keep the rest of us alive, one life to trade for five. And it was probably a conclusion Barnett would have come to on his own. Curry had sealed his own fate the minute he threw Birk to his death. But there I'd been, like Iago whispering in Othello's ear, a low baritone urging murder to keep the peace.

Not exactly the kind of world repairs I had set out to make.

I didn't think I'd want to be back atop a tall building for a long time. No more CN Tower climbs for charity. No going out on observation decks. Being so high atop a building with another man—someone you deeply feared or mistrusted—gave you an unsettling sense of power: you could end his life with the slightest shove. Birk had clearly felt it, ordering me out on the beam, chucking bolts at me as I clung to a girder below him. And I felt it when I forced him to walk out there. When I threw a bolt at him, making him drop to his beam and cling to it like a frightened child.

I lay there in a T-shirt and shorts. The king bed was more than big enough but I knew I wasn't going to sleep for a while, so I appreciated that the ceiling was in good overall repair: no flaking paint, no cracks, no spiderwebs. A chandelier free of dust. The chambermaid had done a good job. Got into the corners. Got the place fresh. Hadn't slipped in with a knife so far. This hotel was all right with me. I wasn't so all right with me.

Maybe that would pass once I had done the last thing I needed to do to close Marilyn Cantor's case.

CHAPTER 52

I walked along the side of Rob Cantor's house in the light of a pale moon that barely showed the chink in the brick where Perry had tried to take my head off with a shovel. Like I'd ever let myself get beaten by a guy named Perry. Bad enough a Simon and a Francis had almost killed me. But not a Perry. Or an Arthur or a Skippy or a Todd.

It had been an unusual day, to say the least. I went straight home from the airport, made myself eggs and sat in front of CNN, watching the news surrounding Simon Birk's stunning demise. There was footage of a covered body beside the unfinished Millennium Skyline tower, surrounded by grim-looking men. There were interviews with police and safety officials, with the network's business analysts, the *Tribune*'s architecture critic, Donald Trump and Birk's other competitors. "You couldn't really call us colleagues," Trump said. "Simon saw everyone as competition."

There was even a sidebar story on Tom Barnett, the Chicago detective who never gave up on the home invasion, who always believed Joyce Mulhearn Birk deserved to be heard, even if she herself could not speak, and who finally had been forced to shoot down his former partner. The circumstances were under investigation by the Chicago Police

Review Authority, but he was being spoken of in reverent tones.

Once the news of Birk's death got out, my phone started ringing. My mother called, relieved to hear I was back; I was relieved she couldn't see me, banged up as I was.

My brother called. I let his call go to the machine.

Hollinger called. I let her call go too. What could I say to her that wasn't offputting or outright incriminating?

At eleven, Jenn called to say she and Ryan were on the 401 approaching the Don Valley. Ryan had done all the driving, she said, pumped up on coffee and adrenaline. I told her they should come by for breakfast, see Tom Barnett on the news.

Rob Cantor called while I was waiting for them. "Jesus Christ," he exploded. "What the hell happened there? Did you see him? Did you talk to him? Did he tell you anything about—"

"Rob," I said. "I'm going to have to tell you this in person." *Not over the phone, you idiot.*

"Oh, Jesus. Of course. Look, I'm going into an emergency meeting of our board in about three minutes. It's going to be nuts, I can tell you, because not one of us has a clue what this means. Can you come by the house later?"

"How later?"

"The latest we'll go is seven because the chair and at least two other members have to catch the last flight to New York. Make it eight to be safe."

Ryan dropped Jenn off at eleven-thirty. I offered him more coffee but he waved it off. "Time for me to transform back into a mild-mannered restaurateur. Drive down to the market, hope I'm not too late to get good enough veal for osso buco. And then grab a few hours sleep." He hugged me and told me to come by Giulio's later if I was hungry. Then he turned to Jenn, held out his arms. She clasped his right hand and pumped it awkwardly. Just as his frown started to tighten, she sparked into laughter, grabbed him and held him close.

"He behave himself in the car?" I asked Jenn.

"You kidding? He's not such a tough guy after all. We spent most of the drive back talking about cooking. And cooking shows."

He said, "Don't start."

"Dante Ryan watches cooking shows?"

Ryan said to me, "The look I'm about to give you . . ."

"Not only does he watch cooking shows," Jenn said, "he even watches the horseshit reality shows where the chefs throw tantrums on cue."

"*Once*, I told you," Ryan said. "I watched it once. Most of the time it's—"

"Biba," Jenn beamed. "He watches Biba. She cooks like his Italian nana."

"That's real cooking, is all I'm saying."

She patted his cheek. "Thanks for the ride, tough guy."

I told Jenn what we needed to do before I went to the Cantor house. She agreed. We made the necessary phone call. The other party agreed—eventually—to provide what we asked for. Being entirely uninjured, Jenn agreed to fetch the item we had just procured.

Everyone so agreeable.

I took a hot bath while Jenn was gone. I could almost make fists. I tried to relax, breathe my way into a better state, but I couldn't even keep my eyes closed. Too hyper, trying to think of everything I knew, of anything I might have missed.

When Jenn got back, we turned off the news—CNN had nothing new to add to its reports on Birk, now packaged under the banner "A Tycoon Falls"—and played the tape she had retrieved. Played it and played it. Rewinding, fast-forwarding, pausing. Advancing frame-by-frame. Watching people's heads, shoulders, backs, parcels. Their feet coming and going. The passage of hours. Moments in time.

—

I could hear Nina's workout track going, booming bass and pounding drums getting into my chest like a defibrillator as I knocked on the French doors. And kept knocking, a good ten times over thirty seconds until the sound went down by half and she came to the door.

She made no pretense of being glad to see me through the glass pane but she did let me in. She wore a dark purple workout suit over a black sports bra. "The shit-kicking detective," she said. "I thought you were in Chicago."

"I'm back."

"I can see why. Is all hell breaking loose there or what? Rob is so freaked out about this. I mean, even I've been watching the news. Is it all true? Some lunatic pushed Simon Birk off his own building?"

"Yes."

Her arms were crossed tightly across her chest, the forearm muscles well defined. "Why?"

"Presumably because he was a lunatic."

"I mean, why now? Why Rob? He finally has it all in his grasp, he's got a partner who knows absolutely everyone, every door is open, he's stepping out in the spotlight, and boom, someone throws Simon Birk off a roof and that's it? Because the way Rob's talking, the whole deal is falling apart."

"He's home?"

"No, he called from the car a few minutes ago to say he was stuck on Bayview where they're digging up Moore. He'll be fifteen, twenty minutes."

"Is there somewhere I can wait?"

She looked me up and down. "Wipe your feet," she said. "Come on back to the gym."

I wiped as directed and followed her through the den, past the entertainment unit that took up all of one wall, its centrepiece a mounted plasma TV at least sixty inches wide, with speakers placed around the room to provide full sound. Hundreds of CDs, hundreds of DVDs. If Rob had set them up, they'd be alphabetical; if Nina, by the workout they provided. I noted with relief that among the many video and stereo components was a working VCR.

In the fitness room, Nina took a white towel off a pile of them and wiped a puddle of her sweat off the base of a stair-climber, then rubbed away dark wet stains on the grips. She tossed the towel into a laundry bin, then took another from the pile to rub her arms and legs, used a third to mop her face and neck. She squatted in front of a mini-fridge next to a stack of free weights that went in pairs from five to twenty-five pounds. She took a bottle of spring water. Offered me one. I decided to match her drink for drink.

She took a long drink of her water, half the bottle in three or four fierce gulps, wiped her mouth and said, "So do you know what really happened there? More than was on the news?"

"I know a lot of what happened."

"Can you tell me without Rob here? Or is it, like, privileged or something?"

"First of all, he's not my client. Marilyn is. And even if he were, you're his wife. So I think we're on safe ground."

I wanted Nina talking about it. Wanted to see what she would ask me.

She sat on a gym mat and stretched out her legs, not able to do full splits but coming close, dampness visible in all the expected places. She leaned out over each leg, exhaling slowly. "What are you going to tell Rob about Maya?" she said on an outward breath. Perspiration visible at her dyed hairline, above her lips, between her breasts. "Did they kill her?"

I said, "Birk was desperate to finish his building in Chicago. He was late, he had hit every possible obstacle, he was jammed up, and this man Francis Curry, the one who killed him, he had made a career out of removing obstacles from

Simon Birk's path. He would do anything to keep Birk going because it kept him going too."

"So he killed Maya?"

"He would have, if Birk had told him to. If he'd thought of it himself. He killed at least three others I know of, two of them right here. He admitted it. He also stood by while Birk beat his wife into a coma. Helped him commit massive fraud. He admitted all that. So did Birk."

"That's awful."

"He came close to getting away with it."

She turned away from me, stretched herself out over the far leg. "How?"

"Tape. He had tape of Birk beating his wife, taken off a security camera. I learned a fair bit about these systems while I was down there. And the thing that stands out, Nina, out of everything I saw, is how much power you have over someone once you catch them doing something bad on tape."

I figured it was as good a time as any to take the tape I had brought out of my jacket pocket and lay it on the counter above the mini-fridge, with the label facing the wall.

Nina didn't ask what it was.

"Like I told you," I said, "Birk and Curry did some terrible things. Admitted them . . . well, not exactly freely but out loud, on tape and in front of a lawyer. But neither of them owned up to Maya. No reason not to—in for a penny, in for a pound—but neither one did."

"So she did kill herself. Is that what you came to tell Rob?"

"No. I wouldn't tell him that. No one still believes that."

"Well, I do. Everyone did, till you came around."

"Someone threw her off the balcony, Nina. Someone hoisted her over and gave her a good start off her balcony. Maybe they stunned her first. Choked her out. I thought maybe Rob had, because he had the most to lose if Harbourview went bad."

"That's crazy," she said. "He would never."

"But somebody did. Someone else who wanted that build-ing to keep going up and up. And I came back from Chicago convinced no one there had anything to do with it. I thought about her brother Andrew," I said. "He's definitely strong enough to have done it and he's devoted to his dad and that building. It was a big part of his future."

"He never says very much," Nina said. "At least not to me. Although I'm pretty sure he'd fuck me if he got the chance. I've caught him checking me out."

"There was only one way to know who went into Maya's building that night and came out minutes after the fall. And that was to look at the tape."

She looked at the cassette on the shelf, then at me, smirking, "There's no camera in Maya's building. It's like a student dump."

I swivelled the tape around so she could see the typed label. "It's not from Maya's building," I said. "It's from the College View Apartments next door, from the night that Maya was pushed to her death. The security firm keeps digital recordings for thirty days and they let us copy the footage from that night. And we're going to watch it when Rob gets home."

Nina looked at me, her face impassive. "Sure," she said. "Let's watch your tape. We can set it up in the den. I can even nuke some popcorn."

"Were you there that night?"

"The night she died?"

"Did you go to her building?"

"Watch the tape," she said. "You can see for yourself."

I took the tape and my bottle of water into the den.

"Don't sit in the recliner," she said. "That's Rob's when he gets home. And put a coaster under the water, 'kay?"

I sat, keeping the cassette beside me. I didn't want to play it. Truth was it showed fuck all. I had thought it would show

Nina going in. I had feared it might show Andrew Cantor. But the camera didn't pan far enough to show the full entrance to Maya's building: you could see anyone who exited the building and turned to their left, or south. You could see the backs of people going in that way. You couldn't see anyone who would have exited to the north or come in that way.

Neither Nina nor Andrew nor anyone else I knew had been captured on the tape. If they had been at the building they had come from the north.

Nina was strong enough to have thrown Maya over. I saw how much weight she'd bench-pressed with Perry. I had looked at her rangy muscled body, saw the sweat she could generate. But I had screened the video three times and there wasn't a frame conclusive enough to force her hand if we did sit and watch it with Rob.

I was sitting on the couch with my water bottle neatly beside me on a coaster as directed. A good guest, someone you'd invite back. For my trouble, Nina came up behind me and slammed something hard and heavy into the back of my head, bang on the occipital bulge. I pitched forward and banged my bad shoulder hard on the edge of the coffee table in front of me. My vision went blurry and I felt nauseous. When I tried to push up on my hands, the floor fell further away. I was concussed and good, like Eric Lindros after a Scott Stevens open-ice hit, looking for the right bench to collapse onto.

I turned my head and saw Nina with a weight in her hand, a fifteen-pounder by the look of it, one end shiny with blood.

Seeing it, taking in the red end of it, made me realize the back of my head was bleeding and that I'd better try very hard not to pass out.

"She was going to fuck it all up," I said thickly.

"That she was," Nina said, coming around the couch, her hand flexing around the bar of the weight.

I made it to my feet, wobbling like a bandy-legged vaude-
ville drunk. I grabbed a framed picture of Rob and Nina off a
shelf and threw it at her. Didn't hit her. Didn't come close or slow
her down. She advanced. I rambled backward. Mumbled, "What
happened here that night? What'd you catch her doing?"

"Going through Rob's briefcase. I don't know what she
was looking for but she was looking."

She didn't know much of anything, Nina. Only what she
wanted. It haunted the room like cold breath in a morgue.

"She was serious about stopping him," Nina said. "About
sticking to her principles even if it meant bringing her own
father down. So stupid for someone supposedly smart. If she
knew a tenth of what she thought she knew, she'd be alive
today. But she was twenty-two years old and didn't know a
fucking thing. Do you have any idea what I already knew at
twenty-two? What I already was?"

She hurdled the corner of the coffee table and tried to
bring the weight down on my head. I lunged away and kept
my feet somehow and lurched left to keep the coffee table
between us. But she was faster than me. She got a leg behind
mine and shoved my chest and I fell onto my back. She tried
again to crush my head but I rolled away. She leaped astride
me, holding the weight easily with one hand while trying
to push my hands away with the other, to get a clear shot at
my head.

So fucking weak I was. Such a dazed head. A sure skull
fracture. I couldn't buck her off. My limbs flapped like useless
fledgling wings. Only the length of my arms was keeping the
weight from pulping my skull. Couldn't scratch or bite her.
Couldn't reach a weapon. I could feel a throb now in the back
of my head, wetness on the back of the neck. Getting harder to
focus, seeing four hands above me, two weights to fight off,
four cold eyes staring down.

Then a roaring sound: a voice calling Nina vile names,

asking how she could do it—the voice raging with hurt and hatred, surging with violence.

It wasn't me. I wanted to say those things to her. Wanted to ask how she could have done it. But it was a different voice. A man but not me. Then he stormed into view past me, moving so much faster than I could imagine moving—Rob Cantor, lifting Nina off me and slamming her into the entertainment centre. The weight dropped from her hand. Shelves rattled and compact discs poured out of the shelves around her. She put her arms up in front of her face, some stance she'd learned from Perry or some other trainer, but Rob was much taller and outweighed her by at least sixty pounds and had the full strength of rage. He simply punched through her hands and landed a solid blow to her nose, then banged her hard on each bicep, breaking down her defence. Slammed a fist in her gut. Then he hit her in the face again, holding nothing back. I could make out his words— "How could you?"—as he landed each blow.

I remember her slumped and weeping against the trashed entertainment unit, blood pouring out of her nose and a vertical gash in her upper lip.

I remember Rob turning to me with his fist still cocked, as if asking me if I thought she'd had enough.

I think I remember saying, "One more couldn't hurt."

EPILOGUE

I still get headaches. I get them when I stand too fast, when I stand too long, sometimes just when I stand. Working out is out of the question—has been for two weeks. Some of the headaches are sick ones and I lie on my bed or the couch like a stricken woman in a Tennessee Williams play, waiting for someone to mop my brow with a cool linen handkerchief and say, "There, there."

No one has done that so far, though Jenn has visited every day and her partner, Sierra, has come with her at least half the time. She's dedicated to her craft and, in typical Sierra fashion, has been swamping herself with information on post-concussion syndrome so she can distill it into a cogent, caring analysis and approach, all of which has gone for fucking naught. I feel gnarled and depressed. It doesn't help that we're losing light by the day, that what little we have is flat and cold as nickel.

Other people have come and gone to help out, to keep me company, to steer me through some of the touchier legal matters that followed me home from Chicago like flies around my fruit. Luckily I am on medication for pain, so little that I say can be held against me.

It had been hard enough to keep all my stories straight

before sustaining a Grade 3 concussion, but I think in the end it went something like this.

Working in close cooperation with Detective Thomas Barnett of the Bureau of Investigative Services, Chicago Police Department, Katherine Hollinger determined that both Martin Glenn and Will Sterling had been killed by Francis Curry, whose confession had been heard by Barnett and Chicago lawyer Avi Stern before Curry was shot to death in a desperate bid to escape. That was two cases closed for her, which put me on her good side.

Stern, an innocent speculator who happened to be viewing an apartment with Birk when Curry snapped, sustained a gruesome leg injury during the attack but was said to be healing nicely.

Nina Cantor confessed to killing her stepdaughter, Maya, but insisted a fight broke out spontaneously and there was no intent, and an overworked Crown will likely agree to a charge of manslaughter, which means she won't serve serious time. Probably three years of an eight-year sentence, being a first offender. She could be out by the time she's thirty-six, still time to wander into another gym and stretch out in front of some guy who'd welcome the thought of her straddling him—provided she wasn't trying to crush his skull.

It also means I'm three for three with Hollinger. Whether or not she likes being helped, her Super loves it when cases close in bunches. She called the other day to say she'd come and see me on her way home from work, then had to call again later saying she'd be pulling an all-nighter at a dead-end crescent west of the Allen Expressway, a brazen drive-by that left one teen dead and three more wounded, all because their basketball bounced off a passing car after a particularly piss-poor shot.

Hollinger said she'd try again soon.

My mother told me she heard through my brother that Rob Cantor was considering selling his interest in the

Harbourview project to a local consortium that included Gordon Avrith.

My brother hasn't called. Or has he?

My mother wants me to see a specialist. "He's the best in the city," she said. "He went to McGill with your cousin Steven— remember Auntie Gertie's son? Finished first in his class. I pulled a lot of strings to get you an appointment. Luckily for you, his wife takes an interest in the Cuban Jewish community and I chaired a fundraising drive last year to send Passover food."

No, my brother didn't call, I'm sure of it now, which means he isn't talking to me. Or maybe it's me that's not talking to him. Either way, neither of us is talking to the other. I would be very surprised if I got any more referrals from him.

Ryan sent in food the first week, and last week he came to see me. We watched a football game—Jets and the Patriots, I think. He had to keep reminding me of the down, the yardage, the score. He showed me some new pictures of his son, Carlo, taken at a fall softball tournament. He'd once told me, back when he was in the killing game, that he never carried a picture of his wife or kid, afraid that someone might follow that trail back to where they lived. Now he can watch his son play; he can take and carry pictures and show them with the pleasure and pride of a dad.

I have to make these headaches go away and get back to work. Marilyn paid us for a full week, and Rob kicked in another week's pay to see me through this slow phase. But it won't last forever. Scary Mary will call and be Scary Mary nice, and Jenn and I will cringe and pass each other the phone. Maybe Jenn will land some new work, log a few hours while I heal. Maybe a simple family matter.

How dangerous can they be?

ACKNOWLEDGEMENTS

Special thanks to my agent, Helen Heller, and to Anne Collins and Marion Garner at Random House Canada, as well as freelance copy editor Barbara Czarnecki, for their help in making *High Chicago* a better read.

Thanks to Michael Clarke, David Green and Jeff Oberman for their advice on matters related to construction and development; Terri Rogers and John Steele, Ontario Ministry of the Environment; reporter Dan P. Blake, of the *Chicago Tribune*; author James L. Merriner, whose book *High Steel* was the most entertaining and informative of all the texts I read on skyscraper construction; the folks at the Chicago Department of Buildings and cityfeedback website for their patient responses to my questions. Any errors or inventions regarding these aspects of the book are mine alone, as are certain liberties taken with geography.

Thanks to Norm Bacal, Rene Balcer, Amit Bitnun, Paul Chodirker, Jeff Cohen, Eddie Sokoloff, Jeffrey Harper, Maureen Jennings, Carl Liberman, Marion Misters, Enn (no relation to Jenn) Raudsepp, Shlomo Schwartzberg, J.D. Singh, Sherry Smith, Beth Sulman, Mutsumi Takahashi, Karl Thomson, Catherine Whiteside and Scott Wise for their support in various guises.

And thanks again to my parents for their love, understanding and promotional efforts on my behalf.

HOWARD SHRIER was born and raised in Montreal, where he earned an Honours Degree in journalism and creative writing at Concordia University. He began his career as a crime reporter for the *Montreal Star* and for the past thirty years has worked in a wide variety of media, including journalism, theatre and television, sketch comedy and improv, and high-level corporate and government communications. He now lives in Toronto with his wife and sons and is working on his third novel. For more information, please visit his website at www.howardshrier.com.

A NOTE ABOUT THE TYPE

High Chicago has been set in Janson, a misnamed typeface designed in or about 1690 by Nicholas Kis, a Hungarian in Amsterdam. In 1919 the original matrices became the property of the Stempel Foundry in Frankfurt, Germany. Janson is an old-style book face of excellent clarity and sharpness, featuring concave and splayed serifs, and a marked contrast between thick and thin strokes.

BOOK DESIGN BY JENNIFER LUM